Gods
of the
Greataway

Gods
of the
Greataway

VOLUME II OF
THE SONG OF EARTH

Michael Coney

HOUGHTON MIFFLIN COMPANY
BOSTON

For Kevin Coney
with love

CONTENTS

III. The Outer Think

come to terms with the cannon and make
friends with the Besieger.

Shake hands with the dragon and smile at the snake,
And jest with the Madmen Three.
But beware of the Mute with his shovel and rake,
He'll quarry the soul out of thee.

—Song of the Locomotive

But beware the Hawker of wonderful things

He'll bargain the soul out of your
bosom.

Shadows are the Ripples of the Void

Prologue: Starquin the Almighty

●●

Millennia ago Starquin visited the Solar System. Because he is huge—some say bigger than the Solar System itself—he could not set foot on Earth personally. Yet events here were beginning to interest him, and he wanted to observe more closely.

So he sent down extensions of himself, creatures fashioned after Earth's dominant life-form. In one of Earth's languages they became known as *Dedos,* or Fingers of Starquin. Disguised, they mingled with Mankind.

We know this now, here at the end of Earth's time. The information is all held in Earth's great computer, the Rainbow. The Rainbow will endure so long as Earth exists, watching, listening, recording and thinking. I am an extension of the Rainbow, just as the Dedos are extensions of Starquin. My name is Alan-Blue-Cloud.

It is quite possible you cannot see me but are aware of me only as a voice speaking to you from a desolate hillside, telling you tales from the Song of Earth. I can see *you,* the motley remains of the human race, however. You sit there with your clubs and you chew at your roots, entranced and half-disbelieving as I sing the Song—and in your faces are signs of the work of your great geneticist, Mordecai N. Whirst. Catlike eyes here, broad muzzles there, all the genes of Earth's life, expertly blended, each having its purpose. Strong people, adaptable people, people who have survived.

The story I will tell is about people who were not so strong. It is perhaps the most famous in the whole Song of Earth, and it tells of three simple human beings involved in a quest who unwittingly became involved in much greater events concerning the almighty Starquin himself. It is a story of heroism and love, and it ends in triumph—and it will remind the humans among you of the greatness that was once yours.

HERE BEGINS THAT PART OF
THE SONG OF EARTH KNOWN TO MEN AS
THE LOST ISLANDS OF POLYSITIA

*where the Triad enlists help
and sails eastward
to lands beyond the Rainbow's ken*

It was one fifth time he felt fear at what one common might be and R

THE RETURN OF MANUEL

• •

leaves curled
eyes were open
mouth agape
prepared her or who work
so either drin.

*T*he quiet boy was back.

Ellie saw him first, on a dull, windy day when the guanaco clouds swept in from the sea, promising rain with every gust. He stood at the rim of the tide, his cloak of pacarana skins flapping, ignoring the waves that rushed past him.

"Manuel! Hi, Manuel!"

She clambered down the bank to the beach, ran barefoot across the sand and arrived at his side, breathless. "Manuel," she said again. "You're back."

At last he looked at her. "Hello, Ellie." His eyes were different. There was a remnant of a vision in there, so that he didn't see her with all his mind. And he looked taller, his barrel-chested figure towering over her. Suddenly she was a little frightened of him, and her half-formed plan didn't seem such a good idea.

She tried it nevertheless. "While you were away, we had some high tides. Your shack was damaged." She indicated the tumbledown structure under the brow of the low cliff.

"I'll soon put that right."

"Perhaps you should stay in the village for a while, Manuel. We have room in our house, if you like."

"I'll manage, thanks." He'd turned away again and was gazing at the horizon so intently that she looked, too; but could see nothing.

"It's that girl, isn't it," she said unhappily.

"What girl?"

"I saw her around here—you can't fool me. A skinny girl with next to no clothes on. And sometimes with *your* clothes on. She looked as though she'd expire at the sight of a snake cloud. She stayed with you for days. And then you both went away. Where have you been, Manuel? I . . . I've missed you." Her head spun a little. She didn't know if it was because of the oxygen that the wind was bringing from the sea or the nearness of Manuel.

Manuel said, mostly to himself, "Belinda's out there somewhere. But how can she be? There are no islands—the Rainbow said so."

"The rainbow? What rainbow?"

"It's a big computer. You wouldn't understand."

"Come and stay with me, Manuel. Please."

He looked at her properly now and smiled. "Maybe. I'll walk you back to the village, anyway. I have to go up to the church. I need a few answers."

"You won't get them from Dad Ose." Ellie laughed breathlessly, happy now that he had half promised.

"I'll get them from God," said Manuel, and Ellie's smile died.

The village was preparing for the forthcoming Horse Day celebrations. Fat Chine, the village chief, strutted to and fro, supervising the seamstresses who worked on the bodies of the symbolic combatants—the Horse and the Snake. Nearby, the head of the Snake was being painted in bright and threatening colors, having been formed of clay and baked in a pit. The head of the Horse required little attention. The Horse was the hero of the celebration and the same head was used from year to year. The Snake was the villain and always lost the battle and was destroyed.

Subconsciously, each villager cherished the hope that one year the latest version of the Snake would prove to be of such a terrible aspect that it would put the Horse to flight and provide the spice of variety to the festivities, but this hadn't happened yet. Dad Ose, the priest, hoped it never would. He had quite enough difficulty persuading the villagers of the superiority of Good over Evil without their wretched little pagan ceremony adding to the confusion.

Meanwhile Insel, the most devout of the villagers, to the extent of being totally cloud-struck, lay on his back praying to the heavens for good weather.

Horse clouds keep blowing from out of the sea,
Make easy breathing for you and for me.

Manuel waved to the villagers as he plodded up the hill to the church, and they waved back, if half-heartedly. They were a little afraid of him. He had curious powers and strange friends—and an unwholesome lack of respect for their leader, Chine. For such a young man he was enviably self-possessed. Tongues were clicked in disapproval as Ellie left his side with obvious reluctance and approached the village huts.

"You'll come to a bad end, my girl," shrilled old Jinny. "The Snake will come for you one day, mark my words!"

"I can outrun you to the Life Caves any day, old woman."

"Not if you're dreaming on the beach like a lovesick llama, making eyes at that young goat!"

Meanwhile, the young goat himself, mind full of wonders, was nearing the ancient sandstone church. The priest huddled against the lee wall, sheltered from the wind, gazing at the mountains and practicing his daily Inner Think.

The fabric of my body is replenishing itself, he told himself, absently fingering an ancient religious symbol in the form of a faceted piece of rock, which hung around his neck. *Each cell is regenerating even as I think, and I shall therefore never, never die. The Clock that tells my body to age is stilled, stilled.*

If the villagers had known of Dad Ose's daily practice, they would have pointed the finger of ridicule. So he had kept his secret, imagining it to be a matter of exceptional spiritual control over the baser bodily processes, and certainly not a thing the villagers would have understood.

In fact, the explanation of Dad Ose's longevity—he was now 496 years old—would have alarmed the priest himself. There were tiny alien parasites within his chromosomes, known to an earlier age as Macrobes, and they didn't want to die. Since the priest was determinedly celibate, it was unlikely that he would ever sire descendants for the Macrobes to attach themselves to. So it was in the aliens' best interests to keep Dad Ose alive —forever, if necessary.

"Dad Ose!"

The priest sighed, recognizing the voice. Manuel was back from his wanderings and had come to pester and embarrass him again. Mentally releasing each body cell from his care, he stood, dusted off his robe and turned to greet the young man.

"So you've come back. Did you find your girl, Manuel?"

"No, I didn't. I met a lot of people and . . . things, but I didn't find Belinda. I know she's out there somewhere, but I must have been looking in the wrong place."

"So what are you going to do now? Continue your search?" asked the priest hopefully.

"Yes, but first I must talk with God. Do you mind if I use your church for a moment?"

On a previous occasion when Manuel had made such a request, Dad Ose had become involved in a futile argument. Now he had learned his lesson. "Certainly, Manuel," he said, as though it was the most natural thing in the world.

"Thank you." Manuel passed through into the dim interior and Dad Ose followed, smiling to himself. He knew what was going to happen next. Manuel—that naive young fool—walked confidently to the vestry door and addressed the Almighty as though he were a friendly neighbor.

"Are you there, God?"

And Dad Ose's smile broadened as the reply came: "I am here, Manuel. How can I help you?" It was a quiet voice, little more than a whisper, but Dad Ose was close enough to hear it. On the previous occasion he had *not* been close enough, and had, to his shame, panicked when it appeared that Manuel was listening to a ghostly voice that he, the priest, in his own church, could not hear.

"I did everything you said, God," said Manuel, "but I didn't find Belinda. Once I thought I had, but it turned out she was just a figment of my imagination. I went to a place called Dream Earth, where if you wish for something, it happens. And, well . . . I wished, without realizing it. And there she was, just as I remembered her. Then she was gone. Will I ever see her again?" His voice became urgent. "I have to know!"

"You will see Belinda again," came the whisper.

"When?"

"In the Ifalong, when the Triad is reunited."

"The Triad? That's what you call me and Zozula and the Girl, isn't it?"

"In the Ifalong, which is all the happentracks of what you call the future, the minstrels will sing of you, Manuel. The Triad will become famous throughout all the human peoples, right down to the Dying Years. They will sing of the Artist and the Oldster and the Girl-with-no-Name, who will be heroes in their spoken-and-sung history—the Song of Earth. You will defeat the Bale Wolves and remove the Hate Bombs, thus ending the Ten Thousand Years' Incarceration of Starquin, the Almighty Five-in-One."

"Well, fine. But when will I see Belinda?"

"Very soon, after the Triad is reunited."

"Are you telling me I have to join up with those two again? The Girl . . . well, she's fine. But Zozula is a pompous old ass."

"On many happentracks the Triad will not be reunited. The Girl will remain a neotenite for the rest of her life, Zozula will die in the service of the Dome—and you, Manuel, will never see Belinda again."

"Happentracks are all the possible ways things might happen?"

"That is true. They are infinite, diverging and multiplying from any given instant."

"So you're threatening me. If I don't join up with those two, I won't see Belinda."

"I don't threaten, Manuel. I foretell the Ifalong. It's your choice which happentrack you follow. And since there are an infinite number of Manuels, you will follow an infinite number of happentracks. I have pointed out the most advantageous."

"Advantageous for who?"

"For the almighty Starquin. You are simply my tool, Manuel. You will find the situation has certain benefits."

"Well, thanks," said Manuel, annoyed, turning away abruptly and almost colliding with Dad Ose. Together they walked outside.

"Well?" asked the priest.

"I must do some more searching. It's very complicated, Dad. You wouldn't understand."

The priest was nursing a secret smile. "I wouldn't understand? Me, foolish old Dad Ose? Well, Manuel my son, let me tell you one thing I do understand. *You have not been listening to the word of God.* You have made an arrogant and stupid assumption. Tell me this: Do you really think God would bother with you, a young beachcomber from Pu'este? God has more pressing problems, I assure you."

"Maybe he hasn't. After all, you heard him, too. I know you were listening."

"What I heard, Manuel," said the priest, slowly and distinctly, "was an old woman standing outside my church and talking to you through the cracks in the wall. Not God. Not an almighty voice from above. Just an old woman who has nothing better to do. No." He held up his hand as Manuel was about to contradict him. "I know this for a fact. The last time you spoke to God—as you call it—I saw her walking away. I was going to apprehend her, when I was interrupted."

"By Wise Ana?"

"She is not wise, she is just a storekeeper. But yes, she happened along, and the old woman got away. How did you know?"

Manuel just nodded absently, his expression thoughtful.

"Listen, my son, if you don't believe what I'm saying, I'll bring you proof. You and I will talk to this old witch together!"

"I'd rather not, Dad."

"Well, by God, I'll bring her to you!" Furious, the priest stalked off on skinny legs, his robe flapping in the wind. Ever since the last occasion, he'd been looking forward to confronting the old crone who had the gall to impersonate God. He could hardly blame Manuel—the boy was at an impressionable age—but this was just the kind of nonsense that gave religion a bad name and converted people to cloud worship. Rounding the corner rapidly, he gave a shout of triumph.

"I knew it! I knew it!"

An elderly woman stood there. She was dressed in a long black cloak with a cowl that fell across her face, so that he could not see her eyes. She stood unnaturally still, and if Dad Ose had been a little more observant and a little less triumphant, he would have noticed that her cloak hung in motionless folds, unaffected by the wind that sang among the stones of the church.

And he might have been more careful.

"I've got you this time," he exulted. "Now you can do some explaining, old woman. What do you mean by filling the minds of my people with your nonsense? What kind of sacrilege is this, impersonating God? Who are you, anyway?"

"My name is Shenshi." The voice was dead and expressionless. "Remember that. The rest, you may be happy to forget."

"I'll be the judge of that." Dad Ose was still panting from his sprint. "Now talk. Why do you pretend to speak the word of God?"

"Because I am God."

"You? God?" Amazed by her temerity, the priest struggled for words.

"In a manner of speaking."

She's crazy, thought Dad Ose. *A poor crazy old woman. She doesn't know what she's saying. One must have compassion.* He searched within himself for the appropriate emotion, and the Macrobes helped him.

"I feel sorry for you, Shenshi," he said eventually.

"You really don't have to."

"Let me give you the advice of one who has lived for almost five hundred years and seen much."

"I've lived for almost one hundred and fifty thousand years."

"God is an old, old man riding a horse cloud. He is normally good and kind, but if anyone ever takes his name in vain, by God he smashes them. So I advise you to be careful whose name you take, Shenshi. God is everywhere, listening." He tapped the stonework. "Walls have ears."

"You profess to many religions, Dad Ose. Have you ever heard of the Blessed Shu-Sho?"

Dad Ose had. According to the Sacred Tapes, the Blessed Shu-Sho had come into prominence in the 80th millennium, performing miracles and sparkling a religious revival. And now he came to think of it, giving Mankind the Rock symbol, one of which hung around his neck at this very moment. "I've heard of her," he said, smiling.

"She was my mother."

"What!" This was too much. Compassion can only be taken so far. The old woman deserved to be thrashed for such heresy. Dad Ose found himself stepping forward, his intentions not entirely clear, but certainly with a view to laying a rough hand on this disgraceful old hag.

And something obstructed him.

Almost blind with temper, he bumped into a solid object that deflected his hand, then brought him to a sudden stop. It seemed to be some kind of a column covered with thick, coarse hair.

A drop of moisture fell on Dad Ose's head. He brushed it off, puzzled. It was warm and slightly viscid. Shenshi appeared to be standing in some kind of a large cage, surrounded by these dark columns—eight of them. Dad Ose shook his head, suddenly feeling dizzy. What was happening? Where had the columns come from?

He looked up.

The columns canted over and joined around the edges of a hairy canopy about seven meters off the ground and almost as high as the church roof. Fluid dripped from one side of it. And now Dad Ose realized that the fluid fell vertically through the wind and that Shenshi's robe was still, whereas his own flapped erratically around his legs—and at last he felt a twinge of alarm.

Then the canopy moved, and he could see the joints and the segments. And his mind snapped into focus, and he realized that Shenshi stood directly beneath a monstrous spider. The fluid was dripping from the creature's jaws as it began to stoop toward him.

Bawling with horror, he flung himself to the ground. He drew his

knees up to his body and covered his head with his arms and felt another
drop of moisture fall onto the back of his hand. It began to eat at his
flesh, corrosively.

He heard Shenshi say, "I'm sorry you had to meet Arachne."

"Make it go away!"

"She's gone. She only comes when she's needed. She's not needed now,
I think. I've sent her back to her home happentrack. Stand up, Dad Ose,
and forget about it."

Dad Ose stood and forgot.

He rejoined Manuel at the church entrance. The young man was gazing
north, where the giant shape of the Dome rose from the plain, dominat-
ing the valley, tall as the distant mountains and crowned with clouds.
Man-made and ancient, it was an unquestioned feature of the landscape.
Manuel was the only inhabitant of Pu'este who had ever been inside it,
and now it looked as though he might have to enter it again, because
Zozula and the Girl lived in there, and God's word was law . . .

"Well?" asked Manuel.

"There was nobody there," admitted the priest.

"I knew there wouldn't be. What have you done to your hand?"

Dad Ose glanced at the angry burn. "I spilled some hot wine on it
yesterday."

"I'll leave you now, Dad. Thanks for letting me use your church."

"I hope you find Belinda, Manuel. It's time you had a steady girl.
Maybe she'll cure this wanderlust of yours."

At that moment the clouds around the Dome swirled suddenly, and a
peculiar phenomenon occurred. Neither Manuel nor Dad Ose could actually say they *saw* a flash of bright light from near the apex of the Dome,
but they could both truthfully say that they *remembered* such a flash. It
was a fairly common occurrence, believed to be caused by the sneeze of
the fire god, Agni.

"Bless you, Agni," responded Dad Ose.

"No," said Manuel, who knew better. "That was the Celestial Steam
Locomotive."

"The what?"

"Never mind," said Manuel, knowing it would take too long to explain
and that Dad Ose wouldn't believe him anyway.

THE DREAMERS IN THE DOME

*T*he Domes were designed to last as long as Earth itself; they are still out there now—huge and silent, but not quite empty. Their populations have fluctuated over the ages—and changed, too. They were built around the middle of the 56th millennium, in response to a growing demand for passive entertainment, and some people, even back then, spent their life from the cradle to the grave in the Domes, being entertained.

If that seems a trivial purpose for such gigantic structures, remember this: During the Great Retreat caused by the Nine Thousand Years' Ice Age, the Domes provided safe havens for the remnants of the human race. And as the Earth grew older, the Domes gave shelter from another disaster: the dwindling of the atmosphere's oxygen, due to the extinction of most species of oceanic photosynthesizers.

So the purpose of the Domes had changed as Mankind itself had changed. Now only a handful of people—known as Wild Humans—were adapted to the thin air outside the Domes. The majority of humans lived inside them, sustained by solar power and the life-support systems built millennia ago.

But they—the Dome's inhabitants—had changed too.

A raccoon-nurse brought Zozula the news.

"Another of the neotenites has died. I'm so sorry, Zozula." She was crying. Like all Specialists in the Dome, she was devoted to the sleeping humans in her charge and took the occasional death as a reflection on her competence.

"It wasn't your fault. Were there any symptoms?"

"No. He just . . . died. It was completely unexpected."

"It's the fourteenth death in three days."

"I know. I know." The nurse made little washing movements with her hands.

"I'll call a special meeting of the Cuidadors," said Zozula. "And I'll check the normal mortality rate with the Rainbow. This may be nothing unusual; perhaps mortality goes in cycles."

"Our own lives are short," said the nurse, gratefully. "We don't know these things."

"I'm sure we'll find the answer," said Zozula with a confidence he did not feel.

The meeting of Cuidadors took place one day later in the Rainbow Room. The Cuidadors were True Humans, custodians of the Dome, sometimes called Keepers.

Sharp-tongued Juni was there, and Postune the engineer. Pallatha the agriculturalist sat next to Ebus the psychologist. Shrewd Helmet, the electrician, murmured to Selena the zobiologist and geneticist, who had come from the People Planet specially for the meeting.

Zozula called the meeting to order. "Fellow Cuidadors," he began formally, "I hardly need to remind you of our sworn duty, but recent events make it appropriate. We are here in this Dome—as were our ancestors—for the sole purpose of looking after ten thousand sleeping human beings, who cannot be awakened because their bodies have evolved into a form unsuitable for normal life Outside."

They didn't know what had gone wrong with the breeding program, so long ago. They inherited the pathetic creatures they called neotenites, and from time to time Selena replaced them when they got sick and it seemed they might die. But meanwhile their minds were immortal, living on in that part of the Rainbow called Dream Earth. Their duty was to work toward the day when they were able to set the breeding program right, produce True Human bodies for all those minds, and repeople the Earth.

"And recently we have suffered a severe setback. Fourteen neotenites have died so suddenly that we were not able to replace them before their minds, deprived of life support, were snuffed out, too."

Juni asked, "What's fourteen, when we have ten thousand here?"

"It's fourteen failures by us," Selena answered her. "And it could be the tip of the iceberg. What's happened these last three days could be the beginning of the end of the human race."

"There are many other Domes," said Ebus.

"I've contacted them," said Zozula. "The problem's widespread. The neotenites are dying."

"I suppose it couldn't be some ancient disease that has resurfaced?" said Pallatha.

"Not in all the Domes at once."

Suddenly Helmet said, "It's Dream Earth. That's the problem. They've lost all incentive in there. Wouldn't you, if you could have everything you wanted, forever?"

"Let's ask the Girl," said Ebus. He pressed a button on the table. "If anyone knows about Dream Earth, she does."

The Rainbow Room was vast; a kilometer long, half a kilometer wide, half a kilometer high. A distant figure sat at a console, watching a three-dimensional display. She stood and began to walk toward them, slowly, painfully. She was a neotenite—the only waking, walking neotenite on all of Earth. Her legs were plump, her body gross and her face round. She was a big baby, big as an adult, but with her physical characteristics arrested at the infantile stage. That was what had happened to the human race. The only True Humans left were the Cuidadors, and they could no longer breed true.

"In another generation, people like her will be in charge of the Dome," said Juni. "Can you imagine that?"

"If there are any people like her left," Zozula pointed out.

"If not, the Specialists will take over," Helmet said, glancing at Juni.

She reacted, as he'd known she would. "I'd destroy the Dome rather than see the human race come to that," she snapped.

A Specialist stood nearby and he must have heard, although he gave no sign of it. He was Brutus, a huge gorilla-man whose ancestors had been created in the Whirst Institute. He was a brilliant geneticist and Selena's assistant; he was also a man of infinite compassion. Suddenly he walked away from them, away across the Rainbow Room, took the arm of the Girl and helped her toward the table.

Juni flushed. "He's touching her."

"He has the decency," said Selena. "Did we?"

The Girl sat down, smiling at them uncertainly. She had no name, although in the Ifalong she, like Manuel, was destined for glory. Then she would find a name, and a world would be named after her.

"Girl," said Zozula gently, "you've heard we've lost some neotenites recently. Helmet suggests their minds have lost incentive because they have all they want in Dream Earth. What do you think?"

She replied, "I lived in Dream Earth for thousands of years before Eulalie died and you brought me out here to operate the special effects." Zozula's face became suddenly expressionless. Eulalie had been his much-loved wife of many centuries. "I never lost incentive. Life isn't so easy in there. Certainly you can have whatever you want by making a smallwish, as they call it. But a smallwish expends psy, and there's a limit to how much psy you can expend before you have to wait for it to regenerate. Most of the people in there are living quite normal lives between smallwishes. Dream Earth has become much more like real life, recently."

"Why do you say 'recently'?" asked Pallatha.

The Girl turned pink. "Oh, I . . . cleaned Dream Earth up, the last time I was in there. It was bursting at the seams. People had been using smallwishes to create other people. They'd create imaginary friends and enemies, and prostitutes and such, and other people would believe in these creations, and their psy would reinforce them. It got so that nobody knew who was real and who was imaginary. I put all that right."

"Tell them about Bigwishes, Girl," said Zozula.

"That was built into the original Dream Earth program. Over a period of about fifty years you can accumulate enough psy to make a Bigwish, which means you can change yourself into whomever you choose. You forget most of what happened in your previous life and start off with a whole new personality." She sighed, looking down at herself. "With it goes whatever Dream body you like. My last Dream Persona was a Marilyn, and they're very beautiful."

"You haven't noticed anything unusual in there, these last three days?" asked Pallatha.

"No."

Zozula said suddenly, "How about the Celestial Steam Locomotive?"

"I . . . I'd rather not talk about it." She shivered.

"Forget the Locomotive, Zo," said Juni. "It's an obsession of his," she explained to the others. "It's nothing, really. It's just a collection of smallwishes that looks like an ancient steam train."

"All right, all right," said Zozula. "So Dream Earth seems to be in order. What does that leave us with?"

There was a long silence.

*

It was like a huge morgue. There were shelves as far as the eye could see, stretching off into the distance. They were tiered one above the other and the floor was transparent, so you could look down and see another infinity of shelves, and look up and see the same.

And a body lay on each shelf, but the bodies were not dead. Tubes were embedded in them and coupled to fixed pipes, and at the junction of pipe and tube was a meter to show the rate of flow. From the heads ran wires, color-coded, leading the thoughts of the minds away into that corner of the Rainbow that people called Dream Earth.

Until recently, the Girl had occupied one of those shelves. Now, following Zozula, she lumbered along the transparent floor, looking up, looking down, feeling a sudden vertigo and thinking: *This was me. Oh, my God.*

Zozula, leading the way, felt not vertigo but oppression. *Suppose,* he thought, *all these neotenites awakened, all at once, and arose and attacked us, all of them, all these gross babies swarming over us, furious because we don't know how to give them proper True Human bodies . . .* But he kept his thoughts to himself, because he was a Cuidador and therefore must appear fearless and wise.

"This is the latest fatality," said the raccoon-nurse.

She was either a woman or a baby girl, according to the way you chose to regard her. She was a little over a meter and a half long. She was naked, unwrinkled and unmoving. A nurse was in the process of uncoupling her from an autopsy machine.

"There's nothing wrong with her," said the nurse. "Not physically. Her brain simply stopped working."

"You mean the mind died first, and then the body?" said Zozula.

"That's right, sir. The body died because the mind simply stopped giving signals to it. All the organs shut down."

"That's impossible," said Zozula. "A mind can't die."

"The autopsy machine showed the same cause for the other deaths. It's been happening ever since I've been working here," said the nurse. "But only occasionally; perhaps once every five years."

"There are only ten thousand neotenites here! Even at that rate, they could all be dead in—" Zozula struggled with the unusual concept of mental arithmetic "—a few thousand years!"

The Girl said, "You'll be dead too, Zozula."

"At least *I've* enjoyed a good life."

"It's not so bad in Dream Earth."

"It's not real!"

"It *seems* real."

"Girl, I have a duty to these people. I will not go down in history as the Cuidador who allowed them to die. When you've lived among us a little longer, you will begin to realize the demands of our high calling, and I hope a little of our sense of duty will rub off on you." Zozula had mounted his high horse. "Now we have a catastrophe on our hands. The solution must lie in Dream Earth, where their minds are. We must talk to Caradoc."

"Now that's a good idea," said the Girl.

✳

They returned to the Rainbow Room and the Girl seated herself at the console. Her fingers played over the tactile surfaces—clumsily, because she had not yet learned all the skills of her predecessor, the late Cuidador Eulalie. But the mists began to form, and soon a huge image appeared in the center of the room.

He was a young man of princely bearing, dark and handsome, dressed in glittering chain mail and holding a sword. Beside him stood his princess, fair-skinned and beautiful. They were Caradoc and Eloise, dwellers in Dream Earth, and for various reasons they were the only such dwellers to be able to communicate with the real people in the Dome. Caradoc was unusual in other ways. He had a mind of staggering brilliance, and had only recently been placed in Dream Earth by Zozula, in an attempt to investigate the inner workings of the Rainbow.

Eloise didn't really exist. She was Caradoc's smallwish, somebody he had known on real Earth who had died, and whom he had re-created because he loved her. She didn't exist, but nevertheless she stood at his side, smiling, ready to talk with warmth and intelligence because that was the way Caradoc had known her in real life.

"Hello, Zozula. Hello, Girl," said Caradoc, sheathing his sword. "Can I help you?"

Zozula explained the problem of the dying neotenites.

Caradoc frowned. "Dream Earth is huge. After all, it includes the Dream Earths of all the other Domes. It would be very difficult to trace the deaths of a few minds among a million or so. And there are still probably five million humanoid smallwishes here, in spite of the Girl's work."

"Well, keep your eyes open, will you?" said Zozula. "This makes it even more vital that we solve the genetic problem and get the Dream People out of there and into proper bodies. And Selena hasn't had much success with her breeding program lately. She had to deprocess every one of the last crop of babies from the People Planet."

Suddenly, Caradoc said, "I may be able to help you there."

"How?"

"I've been able to access some of the Rainbow's memory banks. Did you know this computer has eyes and ears everywhere? It monitors nearly everything we do. And I was able to find out what Manuel was doing, a little while back."

The Girl had flushed at the mention of the young Wild Human's name. "Show us," she demanded.

Eloise looked at her. "Do you really want to see?"

"Of course. Why not?"

"I'll set it up for you right away," said Caradoc, and he and Eloise vanished, leaving the vaulting Rainbow Room empty.

Then the mists began to form again; when they cleared, the Rainbow Room was displaying a giant panorama. After a moment's disorientation they recognized the coastline and the Old South Pacific, seen from above. The scene narrowed, zooming in dizzily as though the viewers were falling from the sky. A washdog, trotting through the room on some cleaning errand, yelped and scuttled past, tail between its legs. The Girl blinked and shook her head.

Manuel's shack sat in the middle of the Rainbow Room. There was no sound, but clearly a storm was raging. Steep surf smashed at the beach, bringing thick mats of some kind of fibrous weed. Manuel was nowhere to be seen. Two vicunas stood unhappily beside the shack, their hair plastered to their plump bodies.

"Look!" Zozula pointed.

A figure could be seen beyond the breakers, sitting on a large raft of weed and gazing at the shore. The scene enlarged again until she was several times life-size, rocking in the Rainbow Room, staring before her with dread in her eyes.

"She's beautiful," said the Girl. "I suppose she must be Belinda."

Belinda's hair was fair, although darkened by the rain that drove it past her face. Her face was pale and oval, and her large blue eyes watched the breaking waves with apprehension. She wore a fine skin shirt that had torn away from one breast, and her body was unusually slim, showing none of the deep-chestedness of the Wild Humans. She looked like a mermaid from the old Earth legends as she sat there, but she was a real human with real legs.

"She's a True Human," whispered Zozula. "A True Human, living outside the Dome. I'll stake my life on it."

Then a breaking wave picked up Belinda's raft and tumbled it toward the beach. Belinda could be seen dragging herself to her feet. She was very weak, and a receding wave pulled at her, causing her to stumble to her knees. She began to crawl away from the water, and all around her were the buoyant mats of weed, some of them as thick as she was tall. One came surfing in and nudged her, and she fell again. Then she was clear of the waves, walking unsteadily up the beach. She knocked at the door of the shack.

In all of the Song of Earth, one of the most famous scenes is Manuel's meeting with Belinda. It has been painted, sung and spoken, and Manuel himself captured it on his Simulator, a device that puts thoughts into visible form. Manuel's mind-painting, titled *Belinda: The Storm-Girl,* was rediscovered six thousand years later and became part of a group of paintings called the Maloan Simulations and entered into the Rainbow, thus ensuring their immortality.

All those versions—the paintings, the songs, the poems, the mind-painting—they all tell the story from Manuel's point of view. They are visions of Belinda, the mysterious girl who came into Manuel's life one stormy night, lived with him for a while and then disappeared, never to be seen again—or so most legends tell.

But now the Rainbow Room showed Manuel himself. It showed a young man dressed in shabby furs dragging his cabin door open in a hurricane and seeing a vision outside. It showed his face. It showed anxious curiosity turning to pity, turning to adoration, in the few short seconds before Belinda stumbled inside and Manuel, his expression now slightly dazed, shut the door.

The Girl swallowed heavily, hoping that Zozula hadn't heard her gulp. *One day,* she couldn't help thinking, *Manuel will look at me like that. One day when I've changed out of this terrible body.* As a sometime resident of Dream Earth, the notion of changing her body came easily to her —which is why she never lost hope.

"Is there any more?" asked Zozula, apparently unmoved.

"A little," said Caradoc. "The Rainbow only watches land surfaces, it seems. The beach is on the fringe of reception. There are several breaks in the recording, and we aren't getting any sound."

Some days later—they guessed at the time lag because the weed had rotted—Belinda emerged from the cabin in the cold predawn light. She looked very weak, and her hand was pressed to her breasts. Now a bright stone rested between them, hung from a silver necklace. Clearly, Manuel had given this trinket to Belinda; the Girl sighed. Belinda stumbled toward the place where the beach ended and the cliff fell directly into the sea, and the water was deep and dark. The storm was finished now, the sky clear. Belinda reached the cliff and sat on a rock, watching the ocean. The water heaved sluggishly, as though exhausted from its efforts. After a while it seemed that there was a shape out there, heading for the shore.

Later Manuel walked into the morning sun. He looked around and his lips were moving, framing the name *Belinda,* casting it soundlessly around the beach. Unconcerned at first, he began now to move with increasing urgency; then running, searching, climbing the cliff and trotting to the top of a low inland hill, running back to the beach, going back inside the shack and quickly emerging, looking around, looking up, looking out to sea, all the while his lips moving: *Belinda! Belinda! Belinda!*

At last the Rainbow Room emptied of all clouds, of all images.

The Girl was crying. "Poor Manuel," she said.

Zozula said, "She came from the sea and she went back to the sea. I wonder how. I wonder where she went. We asked the Rainbow for a display of ancient charts, and there are no islands out there. None at all —none so close that Belinda could have come from them. One thing is certain: She's a True Human. If we could locate her tribe, we could breed bodies for every neotenite on Earth!"

Caradoc spoke. "You asked the Rainbow the wrong question," he said. "I think I've discovered the right one. Now watch this."

KAMAHA THE INDOLENT

*H*ere at the end of Time the minstrels are all dead, but their work lives on in the Rainbow. I, Alan-Blue-Cloud, am able to choose from the infinite resources of that great computer the most suitable legend, fact, thought or other device of communication to illustrate the story of the Triad.

Caradoc had discovered the secret of Polysitia—the floating islands that were created long before the coming of the Triad, in an attempt by Mankind to replenish the Earth's oxygen. Polysitia had a culture and legends all its own, but occasionally they interfaced with the culture and legends of the mainland. Such an example of converging legends is the story they tell of a grossly fat and indolent king named Kamaha. At the time of the story, Kamaha's island, which measured approximately five kilometers by ten, was called Tama-oas—but the name changed as often as the island's geographic location. Such was the custom of the times.

The Rainbow Room filled with a tossing ocean as the Rainbow told Zozula and the Girl the story of the lazy Polysitian chief.

Kamaha spent most of his days squatting on the resilient and heady grass of the island, popping triggershrimps between his slack lips and complaining about his lot. He was domineering and unpleasant toward men and women alike, and he dared not set foot near the shore, because the guidewhales, intelligent beasts, had taken a dislike to him and were in the habit of squirting water at him. So he grumbled his life away, earning the dislike of those around him, trapped in the prison of his environment.

One day of high east winds and cold spray that flew a kilometer inland, something primeval urged Kamaha to his feet. With the wind pressing hard at his back, he walked west, staggering slightly as the ground rose and fell. He passed a few of his subjects on the way, barely glancing at them as they worked at the grass, cutting out diseased sections and piling it for disposal, fertilizing other areas that showed promise. They noticed him, though, watching him go with astonished eyes, then discussing the phenomenon in their liquid tongue after he was gone.

Eventually Kamaha reached the coast, and here the ground swell was so strong that he had to fall to his knees and crawl. Finally, clinging to a coarse tussock, he paused and surveyed the scene.

The coastline tossed with the waves that hurried beneath the island and raced in solid ranks toward a distant shore. Mountains rose behind that shore, solid and massive, capped with silver, like no land Kamaha had seen before. He gazed at the sight, while deep longings awakened from somewhere inside him. This was the legendary Dry Land.

His subjects toiled along the water's edge, some bent low under loads of dying and diseased grass, which they tossed into the sea, others instructing the guidewhales with yelps and barks. The huge beasts rolled and scattered and reorganized, venting spray, working as a vast team with two main purposes: to keep the island from breaking up in the heavy seas, and to head it away from the distant land. They thrust their heads into the vegetation and, along a wide front, shoved with churning flukes. The people yelled encouragement.

Kamaha regarded the distant mountains. The island trembled to the thrusting of the whales.

Suddenly Kamaha rose to his feet. "No!" he shouted.

Little is known of the expedition ashore—the walk through the deserted town with its monolithic dwellings, while Kamaha's subjects watched from their island home, becalmed in a sweeping bay. It is known that Kamaha returned with artifacts, one of which, a small crystal, caused him to experience wonderful visions when he plugged it into his ear. It is certain that from that day Kamaha was a changed man: still fat and indolent—maybe more so—but no longer domineering, no longer unpleasant. He spent all day sitting in the sun and let his people do as they pleased. With the crystal in his ear, he experienced visions of beauty, of an Earth that men had forgotten and only the machines remembered.

His people, concerned by his blank expression but relieved by his personality change, left him alone. He had no desire to share his treasure, no urge to discuss the wonders he was experiencing. He retreated in on himself, allowed the crystal to take him where it would.

Matters would have remained that way until Kamaha died and his body, together with the crystal, had been committed to the ocean—if a strange occurrence had not taken place late one foggy evening.

Kamaha's island was by that time called Zo-ben-tzintl, having moved far north into a region of cold nights and sparkling icebergs. When strange sounds first whispered across the foggy sea, people thought they heard icebergs making love. Nothing was inanimate in or around Zo-ben-tzintl, neither the land, nor the sky or sea. Life was everywhere.

The sounds increased, a deep rumbling accompanied by a high clatter, punctuated by fierce puffings like the exhalations of the greatest whale in the ocean. The people stirred uneasily, drew their sealskin wraps closer and huddled beside their shelters, staring into the mists that surrounded them. Even Kamaha looked up when the sounds interrupted a vision of ancient Athens. Something showed in his face, and a nearby girl forgot her apprehension to regard him in surprise. He touched the crystal in his ear and looked around him as though awakening from a long sleep. The sounds were very loud now, and the island seemed to tremble.

The fog lifted. Out of the evening sky a huge thing bore down upon the people of Zo-ben-tzintl. It was enormous, a frightening monster, snorting fire and bellowing and whipping a long, glowing tail behind, so long they could not see the end of it. Afterward, when they dared speak of it, they called it the Fire Dragon of Northsea—and so it was absorbed into legend. Its din hurt their ears, and the sight of it struck some men mad, so that later they had to be committed to the ocean. As it passed they caught a glimpse of its entrails, exposed and flaring, and it seemed men were trapped there, consumed by the dragon, tiny figures working feverishly within the very flesh of the creature. Then the tail passed close overhead, bright and segmented and rattling. It took a long time, beating at the ears of the people with its din. That is what the people saw. A frightful dragon.

Kamaha saw something incomparably great and thrilling. The crystal had tuned his mind to the glories of the past and he saw the apparition for what it was—a steam locomotive of the late 525th century drawing a train of endless length, unsupported by rails, which was visible through some quirk of the Greataway, some rare conjunction of dimensions. Kamaha saw the Celestial Steam Locomotive on its eternal journey through space.

Magnificent and lordly, it rode its happentrack with a long moan from the whistle and a roaring beat from the exhaust, seeding the night sky with scarlet stars. That cold, long whistle raised the hairs on Kamaha's neck with a nostalgia for sights and sounds he had never known—and smells, too, as the sweet scent of oil-perfumed steam filled the night with its evocation. Polished steel scintillated as the driving wheels spun, the rods rose and fell, the valve gear oscillated.

Above one splasher, a brass plate bore the name of the Locomotive—and this name meant nothing to those who saw it, yet it meant everything.

And the Locomotive slammed past, the stack blasting cannonfire at the sky, the whistle crying for yesterday, the wheels whirling their burden into tomorrow. Kamaha saw into the cab, just a glimpse of brass gauges and handles and levers, all swamped in a fiery glow—and of two men, one staring ahead through the spectacle plate, the other bent low and shoveling, shoveling as though the Devil himself cracked a whip around those black-clad shoulders.

Then the carriages followed, windows glowing enigmatically, the occasional glimpse of a head, a raised fist, or some other quick movement against the inner lighting. Kamaha saw this and understood it. The wheels beat a rhythmic tattoo on phantom rail-joints, the couplings creaked and screamed as the Locomotive pulled its train into a long curve and climbed toward the moon. Upward and onward it went until the smoke stained the sky like a distant nebula, and the last carriage rushed past Kamaha in a twinkling of taillights, and the sounds died into low music from long ago.

The people stirred. They looked at one another and looked away, minds numbed by the menace of the dragon. They were scared witless. They looked toward Kamaha, their chief. They needed reassurance and leadership.

Kamaha lay back with his eyes closed, and there was a wetness on his face that had not come from sea spray. He uttered tiny sounds. As they watched, he plucked the crystal from his ear and held it in his hand for a moment. He opened his eyes and regarded it, and now they could see that his eyes were wet, too. They backed away, their fear increasing. Kamaha smiled and blinked, and this caused a freshet of water to trickle down his cheeks. The people moaned.

He tossed the crystal away. It fell into the grass. In two seasons it had worked its way through the fibrous layers to the underside of the island, which was now called Bo-chuzza, and one afternoon it fell free and slid into the depths of the ocean, coming to rest close by a joint in the Earth's mantle where molten matter oozed out and forced two continents ever farther apart.

And afterward the sound of the wind became a song for Kamaha, and the black-white backs of the guidewhales were things of wonder, and every night was a gateway to a new tomorrow. In time he grew slimmer, and he ruled his people wisely and well. Sometimes in the evenings he would glance at the stars, and the people would see again that odd moisture in his eyes—but then he would shrug, blink and grin, remember yesterday and yesteryear and the things that Man had done, and the things that Man had still to do.

✳

"They're True Humans," said Zozula slowly. "Living out there in the middle of the ocean, for all these years. And we never knew. They're going to be our salvation, Girl. They're going to be the parents of the new human race. Did you see how slim they were—just like us Cuidadors? Except that fat chief, of course."

"They're beautiful," said the Girl.

"You'd be happy with a body like a Polysitian woman?"

"Well, what do you think, Zozula?" said the Girl, smiling.

"More important, what would Manuel think?"

"Shut up," she muttered.

As they made their preparations to leave the Dome, her brief happiness faded, however, and she found her thoughts returning to the Celestial Steam Locomotive, with its passengers in their insane pursuit of unearthly delights, and the crazed driver and the sinister stoker. And worst of all, now that Dream Earth was firmly in her mind, that terrifying figure of the Blind Man, from whom she'd escaped but who still chased her through the night, his white stick taptapping its way through her dreams . . .

Then Zozula and she climbed onto shrugleggers, and the ground-floor airlock swung open. Their bipedal mounts carried them into the bright sunshine and fresh, keen air of Outside.

Soon she would be seeing Manuel again.

THE HOME OF ANA'S EYES

*S*he looked about forty physical years old, by natural reckoning. Her face was plump and smiling and friendly, her mouth large, her lips like petals, her teeth perfect. Her breasts were big and they moved as though they had intentions of their own, sliding behind her sapa blouse as she moved her arms in animated conversation. She wore a skirt also of sapa cloth—her specialty and chief trading advantage—which fell to mid calf, showing strong legs and ankles and suggesting more. Her voice was like low, soft music, and her body had the fragrance of the spices that lined the shelves of her store.

And her eyes . . .

Ana's eyes were almond and slanted like a Polysitian's, but the resemblance ended there. They were luminous, and no man had ever been able to state exactly what color they were, because every man saw what he wanted in them.

Many times a vision of Ana would jiggle in the mind of a village man as he drank before his hut, the day's work done. He would wipe his mouth with the back of his hand and, grinning furtively, would make his way down the road to the little store with the bright cloths hanging outside. His mind would be glowing with a vision of the mature and delectable Ana, and what he was going to do with her. He would stop outside the store, finger the cloths, and chip at the sandstone with his fingernail while he peered inside, wondering how best to declare his intentions. The evening sun would slant across the entrance, so he couldn't see much, but his imagination would fill in the shadows. And the wind, rustling among the grasses that hung above the cave entrance, would be the rustlings of her clothes. Then, blinking, he would enter.

Her loom would be working; that was for sure. The warp would be stretched across the frame—Ana did that herself, working quickly with strong fingers—and the two tiny animals, the sapas, would be scurrying to and fro, shuttling the weft. The sapas were one of the wonders of Ana's cave. The villagers had never seen *useful* (in the human sense) rodents before, and they couldn't understand how Ana had trained the little animals to carry out this intricate task. They themselves had tried, with cavies, and the cavies had simply sat and eaten the warp.

The sapas weren't trained, of course. It was in their nature to weave. They were a relic of a bygone age, when man had been in partnership in the stars with the kikihuahuas, who worked together with nature and the creatures around them. How Ana had come by the sapas is not recorded, but she had bred them carefully down the ages.

Then there would be the spices and the curios and the dried fruits and fish; shelf upon shelf of goods that Ana bartered with the villagers and anyone else who might be passing. Pu'este had no currency, and barter was the rule. Ana was so experienced—and so honest—that she was often called upon to arbitrate in village transactions.

At the very back of the cave was a dark, damp hole that was rumored to be a Life Cave, because Ana had never taken shelter with the other villagers when the snake clouds threatened.

So—Ana the Wise: a mysterious woman of boundless experience and knowledge and beauty, who lived alone in her cave beside the road and only occasionally ventured afield, who was desired by every man in Pu'este—and who had been possessed by none.

The villager would enter, blinking, seeing the outline of Ana and her dark hair and breasts, and soon his eyes would become accustomed to the gloom.

"Can I help you?" she would say, in that husky voice.

"I . . . I . . ."

"Come over here, and I'll do what I can."

A counter would separate them, a balk of hewn driftwood resting on two stumps. He would see Ana leaning on it, her elbows against the wood, her face cupped in her hands, her eyes looking up at him.

Her eyes . . .

They looked up at him like creatures apart, twins of incredible beauty who knew his every wish. Her face was simply a frame for those eyes; it provided them with a place to live and a window to look out of. He forgot her face and with it her body. He communicated with the eyes of Ana. He told them his longing, his needs.

They invited him into their home.

He dwelt there for an unknown time: Time had no meaning in the home of Ana's eyes. It was a warm place where everything happened, everything good. No man ever spoke of it, afterward. It was a secret place, and to tell about it would spoil the delight. It was a place where a tired man rested and where an angry man found peace and, if they but knew it, where a sick man was healed. Men entered the home of Ana's eyes with lust in their minds, and they came out gently happy. They could not say why they were happy, but the glow would stay with them all the way back to the village. And only when they were among their fellow men, among the nudges and grins and innuendo, would they grin and wink, too, and the sublime home would be forgotten, and they would convince themselves that they had got what they went for. As, in fact, they had.

Ana would blink, and the spell would be broken.

"Thank you," the villager would say, and prepare to leave.

Ana would give him a little bag of dried fruit or a pinch of some spice, as a reason for having come.

The Small Rainbow

••

*I*t was late afternoon when Dad Ose arrived outside Ana's store. She was beginning to gather in her wares, unpinning a row of children's dresses from a line strung between two ancient trees. Dad Ose would have found it difficult to explain why he had come to see her, but it had something to do with Manuel's having mentioned her name, and a lot to do with a curious mood of restlessness and uncertainty that had come over him. He sensed that big events were afoot. Something was happening that was much more important than the wretched Horse Day celebrations, and he wanted to be a part of it. So he had come to see Ana, who knew everything, and was understanding and beautiful. Did he need any other reason?

She looked at him, reaching up for a tiny dress.

He said quickly, hoping she hadn't seen him looking at her body, "Manuel's back."

"That's good. He's the only one who can keep the Quicklies in order." Ana smiled her wonderful smile, and Dad Ose tried to concentrate on what she was saying. "They've been bothersome recently. I think they're at war again. They leave the beach when they're unhappy, you know. They come up the road and take things from the store. I can't stop them. One minute a sapa cloth is hanging there, the next minute, poof! it's gone." And she smiled again, as though to say the Quicklies were no problem really, in the greater scheme of things.

"Always fighting," Dad Ose grumbled.

"No more than Humanity, really. Cultures and factions come and go so fast with the Quicklies. We only notice their bad times. Manuel will set them right."

"I hope so." Dad Ose's concern was dogmatic. It was wrong that creatures should fight, particularly humanoids. They should live together in harmony, one with God. It was also rather annoying that Manuel should have more influence over the Quicklies than he, a priest. It was that toy of Manuel's, that machine he called a Simulator. It seemed to fascinate the Quicklies and to calm them.

Later he and Ana walked together to the beach. The evening was drawing on, and she expected no more customers. The weather was fine and the stars were beginning to wink from behind a scattering of high horse clouds.

Manuel was sitting on the beach before the Simulator, which showed a swirling, incomplete mind-painting. He could not concentrate; at their approach he looked up and took off the helmet.

He said, "Do you know I've seen Quicklies cry? They cried at a mind-painting I once did, and I saw the tears. I *saw* the tears—do you know what that means, Dad Ose? It's the same thing as my crying for a year and never wiping the tears away."

"What are they doing now?"

"They had a big fight earlier. A battle." He picked up a curious object from the beach, a triangle of straight sticks, each about a hand's length, joined with thongs, with other thongs running crosswise like harp strings. It was insubstantial and tingled in his hand. "They left a lot of dead, and these things. I think they're weapons. The tide's covered most of it up, now."

"Can't you stop them? They've been bothering Ana." Dad Ose's voice was stern, as though it were Manuel's fault.

"It's nothing, really," said Ana. She was watching a nearby patch of sand that seemed to be glowing.

"I can't seem to get them interested in the Simulator anymore. And . . ." he hesitated. "And I'm not so interested myself, now. My painting . . . I know it's not very good." He wanted to explain. He would have liked to explain to Ana—but Dad Ose was there. He had evoked his original painting several times—*Belinda: the Storm Girl*—but it didn't seem to have the same meaning anymore. So he'd been fiddling with it, unsuccessfully. He felt like kicking in the front of the Simulator.

Ana said carefully, "Drop in at my place sometime, Manuel."

"There's something funny on the sand," said Dad Ose.

And a group of Quicklies jittered by. "Ya-heeee!" They darted to and fro, and Manuel felt a quick pluck at his clothing; but no one was there. Fast blurs flitted through the evening shadows and, for an instant, a small, inert figure lay nearby, dying fast before disappearing. The Quicklies were one of the coast's mysteries. Their lifespan was measured in days—and very few days, at that. In later millennia, the minstrels would speculate that the Quicklies were one of the results of the war with the Red Planet; but whether they were victims of the frightful Weapon, or a human experiment created to counteract it, was never clear. Some learned minds held that they were a perfectly normal, though primitive, tribe living on an adjacent happentrack with a different frame of duration, sometimes impinging on normal Earth time. Another group suggested they were the offspring of a terrifying race of creatures known as the Bale Wolves.

The village mothers used them as a threat:

> *Lazy boy, lazy boy, what a surprise!*
> *Little blind Quicklies are stealing your eyes!*

So ran a local ditty.

That evening they were busier than usual. Occasionally they stood before Manuel and he would catch a glimpse of an inquisitive chimplike face, eyes a blur of blinking; then they would be gone. A violent turmoil took place in the shallows and a few bodies rocked in the waves for a second before flickering out.

"They don't remember me," said Manuel. "They used to be more friendly than this." His voice was sad. His absence from Pu'este had cost him a lot.

"These are many generations removed from the ones you used to know," Ana reminded him. "And your influence has faded with time. I think . . . You used to be a kind of god to them—you know that? You taught them love, with your Simulator. They'd never known love before, and for a while it calmed them. They were docile for many days after you left. But then . . ." She shrugged, and her breasts rose under the sapa cloth. "Now, they're at war."

Indeed, the situation seemed to be worsening. Two opposing mobs had become evident, hordes of skittering shadows at either end of the beach. A major conflict was about to take place. Meanwhile, one Quickly was busy nearby on a lone project. He darted to and fro, occasionally sitting.

A shapeless, shifting mount of some unknown material rose in front of him, and he seemed to be working on it.

"Me, a god?" said Manuel wonderingly.

"Love . . ." muttered Dad Ose. He was shocked. Love was something that people didn't talk about. Love was an artificial extension of sex that had—so legend had it—been the downfall of the First Variety of Man. Ana was known to be outspoken, but this was going too far.

"Have you ever wondered just what the Quicklies are?" asked Ana.

"They're God's creatures," replied Dad Ose shortly.

"Human or animal?"

"Animal, of course."

"Maybe we'd understand the Quicklies better if we thought that point through," said Ana.

Manuel was watching the mound grow into a small tower. "I think it makes no difference," he said. The busy Quickly kept flitting across to him, looking at him, darting away. Now the two armies were quieter and a number of Quicklies were clearly visible, sitting down. Others came to view the tower for a brief instant before rejoining their factions. The waves had stilled. The little tower leaned to the north and glowed with pale light, becoming brighter as evening deepened. It was about a meter high, shaped like a child's crude sandcastle, but not made from sand. Rather, it was built from one of those unidentifiable substances that the Quicklies invented from time to time and then forgot. The Quickly was now building another tower close to the first. Another Quickly, viewing the construction, dropped suddenly dead. The armies waited.

Two huge misshapen figures were walking down the beach toward them, coming from the north.

The three people, who would soon be joined by two more, stood there in the darkening evening, each busy with his own thoughts. Manuel, the dreaming youth, thought of romance and, strangely, a face he'd never seen and a name he'd never heard. He'd dreamed about this face last night. At first it had been Belinda; then it was a different face, dark where Belinda was fair, with brown eyes where Belinda's were blue.

"Who are you?" he'd asked.

And she'd grinned, elfin, mischievous, and said, "Elizabeth."

The clarity of this vision had remained with him all day.

Dad Ose was struggling to understand love and the Quicklies, sick at his own ignorance. It wouldn't have mattered if nobody else had been able to understand the world around them; that was the will of God. But somehow he felt other people understood more than he. Even Manuel seemed to sense dimensions to existence that he, Dad Ose, would never know. And all that traveling recently, of which he would say nothing . . .

And Ana, now. Little better than a whore, so men said—yet she made him feel small; she seemed possessed of a wisdom far beyond his ken . . .

Ana's own thoughts during those moments are not known.

Three people, then, watching the Quicklies preparing for war while one lone Quickly built twin towers that glowed in the dark. Thinking there was nothing unusual in what they saw. The Quicklies were the Quicklies, and they often did strange things.

The little towers leaned toward each other. Each was slightly bowed, so that if they met—and it looked as though they soon might—they would form a curved arch. The base of each tower spread into a pedestal, but the towers themselves were of consistent diameter, and smooth. There was a tension in them. They seemed to be almost trying to meet, straining toward each other. The gap between them was less than half a meter. The glow was brighter now, and refracting. Colors showed, in hazy stripes—red, orange, yellow . . . Manuel thought: *Yes* . . .

The Quickly was building a miniature rainbow.

He was sitting beside it now, utterly motionless, so that every detail of his body showed as clearly as in death. In his short lifetime—he was aging visibly now—he had progressed from building manually, with sand and other materials, to building by mental power alone. And the towers had become transformed from a solid construction to a rainbow of beauty and light.

But it was not quite finished.

The rainbow hummed as the two ends crept toward each other, a musical hum like a chime of many chords, harmonizing in a way not found in man's music. The Quickly aged, sitting there in the glow of his own creation, a sad little chimpanzee with wise eyes. Others came to look and to bring him food. Many died, as though seeing the rainbow was the final justification of their existence.

The opposing armies waited. Soldiers died, recruits joined up.

"But . . . what *is* it?" asked Dad Ose.

Ana knew. She looked at him and smiled, the way a young mother smiles at her child. She looked at him and saw beyond the wrinkled skin and barrel chest. She saw him as the Quicklies saw him, and she knew he would never believe what they were doing. So she said nothing.

So rapt were the three that when the other two finally arrived they were barely acknowledged. The Girl and Zozula nodded at Manuel, Ana and Dad Ose, then they, too, turned their attention to the almost-rainbow. It was small, the thing they watched, just a bright arch a little over a meter high on a beach under the stars, but it absorbed all their senses and they spoke no more.

The Quickly was very old. His shoulders were bowed, his eyes closed, his tiny fists clenched. Companions sat with him now, almost as motionless as he, supporting him and willing him to continue.

The rainbow had little more than a centimeter to go, and little sparks flashed where the twin columns were beginning to join. It affected senses other than vision, and Manuel was aware of a feeling of hope, of growing joy, of many things. Dad Ose felt all this, too, and mistrusted it; it reminded him of nothing so much as a couple of times when he'd been incautious enough to examine Manuel's mind-paintings. Ana just watched, smiling. The Girl and Zozula sat still, understanding.

The Quickly trembled, and began to go out of focus. The rainbow flickered.

The Quickly fell forward, supported by his companions. They turned him and laid him gently on his back, where he died. The rainbow, still incomplete, winked out, leaving a lumpy mass of damp sand and weed. A low moan ran along the beach like the wind, an ululation of loss from a thousand Quicklies. And the two armies flew at each other, and clashed, and the beach was a whirling battleground.

Manuel turned away and, together with the others, climbed the bank out of harm's way. For the first time he became fully aware of the newcomers.

"Oh . . . hello, Zozula," he said. "Hello, Girl."

Zozula said, "You're lucky, Manuel. All we humans are. We have time —time to finish what we begin."

And Manuel looked at Ana. Dad Ose would always remember that, looking on it as one more hurt to remember through the years to come, never knowing how much history hinged on Manuel's looking at Ana.

She said, "Come with us, Manuel."

THE VOYAGE WITHOUT AN END

•••

*D*ad Ose had gone back to his church.

The Triad sat in Ana's cave and Ana leaned in her usual position, elbows and breasts resting on the counter. Manuel was tired, yet excited at the same time because of what Zozula had said to him. The Girl dozed, exhausted.

Zozula had said, "I think I know where Belinda is, Manuel. Caradoc is beginning to understand how to reach some of the old memories in the Rainbow, and it seems there are people out there at sea. But the islands they live on—they float. That's why we couldn't find them on the old charts. They move about with the currents. Caradoc showed us. We saw people with slim bodies—True Humans."

"Did you see Belinda?"

"No—we were viewing some kind of historical scene. But I'm sure she's there."

Manuel had been silent for a long time, thinking and hoping . . .

And now Ana had, in some subtle fashion, taken over. She had brought them back to her cave and they were discussing plans. Outside, the night was quiet and there were no travelers on the road, neither man nor animal. The wind gently stirred the sapa cloth hanging over the entrance, the tiny rodents shuttled endlessly to and fro in the corner, and Ana spoke of the sea.

"You have a boat, Manuel—I've often seen you fishing in it."

"I built it myself. It'll take me anywhere."

"Belinda came from the sea, so she probably went back there. We can follow her, but I don't think your boat is big enough for four of us. We must build another, and you can show us how."

Manuel said doubtfully, "I think the sea is empty. There's never been anything out there except me."

"You have no idea just how vast the sea is, Manuel. You could sail for days and never come to the end of it."

"No, you couldn't." Manuel was practical. "The wind always blows you back."

"Always?" And she leaned forward, her shoulders smooth, her dark hair falling across her face. Her eyes glowed in the lantern's light. "Always, Manuel?"

"Well . . . except at the time of the snake clouds. And nobody can sail then. Everybody goes to the Life Caves, or else they die. Even the guanacos go away." He asked the question that everyone had asked themselves from time to time. "Where do *you* go, Ana?"

She pointed to the back of the cave. "In there. I have plenty of lifeweed there."

It was a comfortable evening in Ana's cave, with the warm draperies, the fat cushions to sit on, the friendly glow of the lantern, the company of one another and, most particularly, of Ana. She fed them a hot stew, which bubbled before a fire of a type that Manuel had never seen before. The fireplace was cut into the sandstone and the chimney was a separate tunnel, so that the smoke didn't get into the cave. Manuel made a mental note to build a chimney like that for his shack, at the same time feeling a little foolish that he hadn't thought of it himself.

The stew was tasty and full of strange meats and herbs that Manuel found delicious, although Zozula, accustomed to the bland food of the Dome, thought it a little too spicy. He didn't say so, though. Like many men before him, he had fallen completely under Ana's spell. He couldn't take his eyes off her as she moved about the cave serving them food. When she bent low to hand them fruit, he could see the heaviness of her breasts; when she tended the fire, her body was outlined through the sapa cloth. Yet he didn't feel any lust. Men felt lust when they thought of Ana from a distance. When they were with her, they felt only wonder. Zozula felt an uncomplicated fascination for this practical, mature woman. The Girl, too, watched her with admiration.

Later Manuel fell asleep on his couch of soft cushions, to the low voices of Zozula and Ana discussing the future and the voyage. He fell asleep in safety, with the feeling that everything was being taken care of. He didn't really believe he would ever see Belinda again, but meanwhile he was warm and full and with friends. He slept comfortably against the soft plumpness of the Girl.

Zozula said, "The idea scares me, Ana. Going out there at the time of snake clouds? The villagers call it the Chokes, and I know why. I was caught out there once, years ago, and . . ." He fell silent, remembering an old woman who had saved him, and her daughter, who in some way reminded him now of Ana.

"It's only the idea that's frightening, Zo. We're all so used to running for shelter when the snake clouds come—it's drilled into people from childhood. All I'm really suggesting is that we take our Life Cave with us. We build a cabin on the boat, and we put plenty of lifeweed in it."

"You've been talking as though you're coming yourself." Zozula hesitated. "We're grateful for your ideas, Ana, but . . . This voyage is for Manuel, the Girl and me."

She came close and took his hand, and later he remembered having looked into her eyes for a long time.

And later, also, there seemed to be no question about it. Ana was coming with them.

✳

They built the boat under the skeptical eyes of the villagers, on the beach near Manuel's shack. In fact it was a raft rather than a boat, ten meters by six, with a cabin set centrally, big enough for four people to lie down beside their provisions and a big mound of lifeweed. During construction of the cabin Ana proposed a modification: The lifeweed would be better laid on tiered shelving. It gave off its essence better if it was spread out, and it was easier to keep it uniformly damp that way, too, for it died if it dried out.

Hasqual the wanderer, watching from the clifftop, called down, "A raft can't sail against the wind, Manuel. You need a keelboat—surely you know that?" He clambered down, anxious to help.

"We sail at the time of snake clouds," muttered Manuel, embarrassed at how ridiculous that sounded.

Hasqual didn't laugh. Instead, he investigated the raft, opened the cabin door, saw the shelving and put two and two together, then said, "That makes sense." And he set to and helped, tying vines around the logs with expert knots, making suggestions for rain-proofing the roof. "Dad Ose has been praying for you," he said at one point.

"That's good. I haven't had a chance to speak to God lately."

"You're going to need all the help you can get. I . . . Maybe I ought to come along, Manuel." There was a longing in his eyes as they drifted from the raft to the blue sea. The old wanderlust was getting to him again.

Manuel looked for the others, but they were farther up the beach, cutting vines. "There's not really room," he said. "Ana's coming as well, you know."

"Ana . . . ? Yes, that's a good thing. She's a clever woman. I . . . I wish you the best of luck, Manuel. I suppose you're hoping to find that girl, eh? The sea's a big place, you know. Don't be too disappointed, will you? And . . . Come back here, afterward. You may not realize this, but we need you in the village."

Two days later, Insel, lying on his back, cloud-struck and mumbling, forecast snake clouds.

❋

The sail filled, and Ana held the sheets while Manuel and Zozula splashed through the shallows, guiding the raft into deeper water. Then, with the thin air whistling in their lungs, they hauled themselves aboard.

"In the cabin, you two," said Ana. "Quickly!"

They shut the door after them and, breathing the rich essence of the lifeweed, soon recovered.

The wind had changed within a day of Insel's prediction, shifting around so that it blew directly from the distant mountains. The puffy, rain-laden horse clouds of the trade winds had disappeared, to be replaced by the sinister lofty trails of the snake clouds. The villagers had fled for the Life Caves, so nobody was at the clifftop to watch the great departure. Or so Manuel thought, sadly, as he emerged from the cabin and watched his home receding.

Then a lone figure waved. Manuel waved back and, feeling better, sat beside Ana.

So began what is called in the Song of Earth "the Voyage Without an End." Of course, the voyage did have an end, because it is recorded that Ana reappeared at Pu'este; and the further adventures of Manuel, the Girl and Zozula are well known. But of the voyage itself there is no factual record—only hearsay and legend—because the Rainbow does not monitor the happenings on the oceans of Earth. Did Manuel find his Belinda? On some happentracks he did, and the Girl mourned the loss of him.

The Girl Called Kelina

She was the prettiest girl in Polysitia, and she was brave and intelligent, too, but all this was of no use to her when the crisis came. In the end it was Starquin himself who saved her, the minstrels tell. They sing of Kelina to this day, of her escape from a fate that used to be described as worse than death, her adventures following the escape, and her final death—by the hand of Starquin, so they say . . .

Tall, slim and brown-skinned, she was a king's daughter, and people often thought she was proud, although in point of fact she was shy. Every day she would walk to the water with a skin of triggershrimp shells on her head—she may have been a king's daughter but he was a very small king, and nearly all Polysitians must work—and she would throw the soft shells to the guidewhales and the orcas, who would gather round the island's edge to feed on the debris. She rarely spoke, rarely looked at the poor jerkfishermen sitting on the edge of the island, rarely acknowledged the women tending the grass and working at the fishponds. She was torn between her desire to be friendly and her fear that it might be misinterpreted as condescension. So she walked alone, and there were many young men who longed to light the fires behind those beautiful, slanting Polysitian eyes.

None more so than Rider Or Kikiwa.

Kelina's father was King Awamia, ruler of all Uami, which was one hundred fifty square kilometers in extent, and Or Kikiwa was one of his Riders, and probably the least trusted one.

"I can't think why you ever Mounted that man," Queen Lehina said.

"He performed a Feat of Valor," King Awamia told her once again. "I had no option."

"I consider his Feat suspect. And on the basis of one suspect Feat, he now rides an orca and is granted lands. It's not right, Awamia. There are more deserving men."

"His lands are in poor state."

"Healthy enough for him to build a tower and treat his workers like dirt."

Polysitians have no written or computerized history. Everything of importance is remembered by minstrels and sung at the evening meals beside the sunset walls of the towers, when work is over. The most important songs—or possibly those containing the most vivid images—are those remembered. The story of Kelina was both vivid and important. Historians of a later era discovered it on a remote floating island, and made the essential connection between it and the Song of Earth.

Kikiwa's Feat is part of the story and, according to the latest versions, that Feat was certainly suspect. It seems that Kikiwa was once a trainer of orcas, little better than a worker but, through an accident of birth, a protégé of Or Halohea, a Rider of some renown. The island at that time had fifteen Riders, brave men clad in sealskin who rode the killer whales, driving away any predators who might seek to tear at the fabric of the island or worry the domestic fish that lived beneath the shoreline. In token of their station, Riders were granted land and assigned workers.

One day Kikiwa was exercising Or Halohea's whale while the Rider was at his tower, dealing with Riderly matters. Kikiwa sat upright behind the dorsal sail, grasping a rein of kelpite, holding his breath as the whale plunged and gazing arrogantly around whenever he surfaced. He wore the tough elephant sealskins of the Rider, a pretension that did not endear him to the jerkfishermen sitting on the shore. He uttered shouts of instruction to the whale, although he was, like many Polysitians, in empathy with the beast and probably could have directed him telepathically.

"I'd like to see him shouting underwater," one of the jerkfishermen remarked to his neighbor, sourly.

"He couldn't stay down long enough to try."

In point of fact, Kikiwa could hold his breath for over five minutes, as long as most Riders. Physically he was well qualified for advancement too, being tall and strong and a fine swimmer. Aware of the dashing figure he cut, he circled the orca around the bay, hoping Kelina might happen this way and pause to admire him.

The event that was to change the course of his life happened quite simply, by accident. A child, walking along the shore, caught her foot in a loop of grass and, thrown off balance by a sudden swell, tumbled into the sea. At first, nobody saw her. Like all Polysitians, she had been able to swim almost from birth, but a strong offshore wind and underisland current carried her away. Kikiwa heard her screams and headed the orca in her direction.

The huge black-and-white animal cut the water like a battleship, throwing an impressive bow wave. Kikiwa sat upright, holding the rein with one hand, the other arm extended theatrically for balance.

And then, suddenly, he and the orca were no longer the only large creatures in the bay. Another dorsal fin cut the water nearby. A sinuous shape was clearly visible underwater. With a yell of fear Kikiwa caused the orca to veer away, allowing the shark to move in on the little girl.

The violent swerve of the orca unseated Kikiwa, however, and he fell howling into the water. The orca, released from the immediate proximity of his fear-thoughts, swerved again, sighted the shark, and attacked. The water churned red. Kikiwa and the child drifted on. Then the whale returned, triumphant, and a shaking Kikiwa pulled himself on board, at least having the presence of mind to drag the little girl after him. He urged the orca shoreward and shortly was basking in the plaudits of the crowd. The next day, in a brief ceremony, King Awamia pronounced him Or Kikiwa, and it seemed to him that Kelina, at her father's side, regarded him in admiration.

When he tried to follow the matter up, however, he was rebuffed. "Yes, you are a Rider, Or Kikiwa," she said, "but there is more to a man than simple physical courage."

Or Kikiwa was no hero. Although his appearance was impressive and his riding ability adequate, he knew, deep down, that he was a coward dressed in Rider's skins. He tried too hard to compensate for this, dealing arrogantly with his people and snapping back at imagined insults. If he had been a difficult man before, he now became impossible. His workers left him. His exploits on the back of his orca became so foolhardy that the other Riders began to refuse to accompany him, for fear Or Kikiwa would lead them to purposeless death. "You are neglecting the Code," said Or Halohea at last, pointing up the ultimate folly of Or Kikiwa's behavior. "Squid and parrotfish are eating at your shores while you take on sharks as though they were dragons. And your land is so decayed it begins to threaten your neighbor's."

Indeed, Or Kikiwa was in danger of suffering the ultimate disgrace for a Rider: isolation. His neighbor, Or Honu, had made representations to King Awamia. He wanted Or Kikiwa's lands cut adrift before his own lands could be poisoned. "I invoke the Code," he said. "What I ask is for the good of the grass."

Possibly this is when that fated man's reason finally snapped. Or Kikiwa disappeared and was never seen again by the islanders. His domain lay deserted and rotting, his tower listed and sagged, in danger of falling through the ground that decayed beneath it. His orca was gone. It was said that he'd ridden off on it, seeking new lands and a fresh start.

And Kelina was gone too.

King Awamia was beside himself. He dispatched his ten best Riders to search the ocean, bending the Code in leaving only a handful of Riders to defend the island. In due course the search parties returned with tales of strange beasts and strange lands, but no word of Or Kikiwa or Kelina.

King Awamia decreed that Or Kikiwa's rotting land be severed from the island, and for six days the Riders urged their mounts to chew, and all the people tore at the fibrous blades and roots with their bare hands and chopped with sharpened turtleshell and cuttlefish. On the seventh day, the domain of Or Kikiwa drifted away on the trade winds, with no guidewhales to restrain it.

And, unknown to King Awamia, his daughter Kelina drifted with it. She lay where she'd lain for many days, in a chamber of Or Kikiwa's tower so tightly woven that it would have taken her weeks to pick herself free. She had food: a pool of triggershrimps and fish enough for a season. She had air, for the dense mesh of her prison was still porous enough to allow the trade winds through. Water she didn't need; like all Polysitians, an occasional immersion in the sea fulfilled all her body's requirements. Hope she didn't have—after two weeks she had only unraveled a fraction of her prison walls. She thought of diving into the pool and swimming under the island, but the tower was situated in the center of Or Kikiwa's domain, and she knew she would never be able to reach the shoreline before she drowned. So she lay there, day after day, quietly picking at the mesh of fibrous roots.

Or Kikiwa was elsewhere. He had visions of glory. He had dreams of an empire so vast that all people would be forced to acknowledge his greatness, even the powerful Black King Usali. He would bring Kelina back a domain of inestimable size, propelled by guidewhales of prodigious strength, peopled by workers of unusual skill and subservience.

A normal man, possessed of such a vision—if normal men do have such visions—would have set to and captured wild guidewhales and trained them, a process that would only have taken a few years. He would have then set his guidewhales to rounding up uninhabited rafts of grass. Grass soon knits together, and a sizable island could be collected in a lifetime.

But Or Kikiwa didn't have a lifetime. Kelina was waiting for him, so the empire must be built rapidly. He must conquer. Drunk with the madness of omnipotence, he shouted his desires at the sunrise as he urged the orca eastward. The low profile of a small islet appeared on the horizon.

He attacked at noon and was driven off by three contemptuous Riders waving whalebone clubs. He attempted to outflank them and gain the shore, and they let him do this and followed him inland, pinioning him and taking his orca-rib dagger from him. The ordinary people laughed at him. Women cast clumps of stinking, diseased grass at him, men slipped wriggling fish inside his sealskin. They dragged him before the king.

"Submit or be conquered!" Or Kikiwa shouted. By now he was totally mad.

"Throw him back," said the king. "He's not worth keeping."

If he was mad, his first experience nevertheless lent him cunning. When he approached the next island, he behaved with more circumspection. Asking for an audience with the king, he was received into the royal tower. In a sagging, swaying chamber he proposed a great alliance, linking his host's lands with those of his own, which, in his imagination, by now covered a fair percentage of the ocean. The king was puzzled.

"Alliance against what?"

Or Kikiwa explained that the alliance would involve a pooling of knowledge and resources and, in accordance with the Code, would result in betterment of the grass. With all the smaller islands eventually joined into one, the boundaries would be proportionally shorter and easier to defend against predators.

Now the king's advisor spoke. "That is Black King Usali's talk. The grass only grows at the shoreline. It is more in accordance with the Code to have a large number of smaller islands. Thus will the grass prosper. And in any case, the domestic fish thrive at the shoreline, too. There is a maximum size for an island, and we have reached it. Go and join Usali, Rider."

Insane, enraged, Or Kikiwa rode on, to receive progressively more hostile greetings as King Awamia's Riders spread the story of the kidnapping. Finally he rode homeward. His thoughts were twisted and malignant. He felt betrayed and scorned by the Polysitian race and, in particular, by Kelina, who had caused him to undertake this mission. If it had not been for Kelina and her arrogant airs and her notions of superiority, he would not have found himself in this predicament. He would have been, instead, a respected Rider on a prosperous island. She had brought him to his knees with her sly ways—and now she would pay for it.

He thought of her lying there helpless, and his thoughts were crazed and vengeful. She would pay. He shouted his intentions at the stars as he rode westward, and his intentions were inhuman. The orca swam stolidly, trying to blot out the insane thoughts that its gentle mind could not help but receive. Or Kikiwa raved on.

Legend tells that Starquin heard him.

Meanwhile, Kelina lay picking at the roots. She had reached a point where she could distinguish night from day through the thinning mesh, but she had a long way to go. Occasionally she let herself wonder about Or Kikiwa, and she wondered if he were dead. She guessed that his domain had been cut adrift. She expected to crawl out of her hole in a few days' time to find she was completely alone. She couldn't bring herself to feel vindictive toward Or Kikiwa; she knew the man was not normal. Soon she would be free and would send a dolphin to find an orca. Then she would locate her father and ride home. As the mesh thinned under her busy fingers, her spirits rose—but by that time Or Kikiwa, mad with vengeance and lust, was one day's ride away.

Then the sky began to streak with high hurricane clouds. Kelina felt the motion of the raft change. Long swells rolled underground. She sensed a change in the air and redoubled her efforts to escape. It is not a good thing for a tiny island to be caught in a hurricane without guidewhales. She had to return to the safety of her father's land, which was big enough to ride out anything the gods might send.

That night was one of the wildest in memory. The hurricane, changing direction for no good reason except divine intervention, fell upon a small area of Polysitia and scattered the islands far and wide. King Awamia's land was driven three hundred kilometers north, other islands were pulled into the Roaring Forties and raced eastward. Many broke up, and new kingdoms arose, and new domains. Many good people were lost in the howling winds, swept from their lands, never to be seen again.

A week later a trained orca, riderless, was seen patrolling a bay off a large continent where there are real mountains, real rivers. The orca was scarred from many floggings. The rider was never found. It is said that nobody cared, anyway. Or Kikiwa was never heard of again.

And Kelina? She became famous and found her place in the Song of

Earth so that both land-based minstrels and the minstrels of Polysitia sang of her, forevermore. Although the minstrels tell the same story, the language is different. In the land dialect, with its multiple consonants, so different from the liquid tongue of the floating islands, Kelina is called Belinda.

THE STORY OF THE BLIND
CRAFTSMAN

So the Song of Earth is not composed solely of the embellished observations of the Rainbow. There are other sources, such as the legends of Polysitia, which were fed into the Rainbow by scholars and historians when they came to light. The Rainbow was then able to examine these legends and search its memory banks for links with observed history.

The trio of Polysitian stories that make up the Legend of Kelina were finally linked with the epic tale of the Triad. The dating—so far as it could be established—was approximately correct. The events and the characters were unmistakable. The triumph of the historian who first pieced together the Rainbow's findings can only be guessed at.

On a remote shore of Malaloa, which is the biggest island of Polysitia, there lived a sun oven craftsman named Peli.

Over the years Peli had built up a reputation for good work, and his sun ovens were things of beauty and utility, able to cook the thickest seal steak to a turn, on a fine day. Peli was proud of his ability and, in his earlier years, not a little boastful. He could afford an orca of his own, on which he traveled to the coastal villages to set up his ovens, bringing back payment in the forms of meat, vegetables and artifacts. He grew rich by the local standards, and his woven dwelling was not far short of a Rider's tower in opulence.

Then his eyesight began to fail.

Possibly this was due to the nature of his work; certainly it seemed to be an occupational hazard with sun oven craftsmen. Sun ovens are built as follows: First, a large basket is woven, hemispherical and about five meters in diameter, carefully aligned with the direction of the sun's travel so that the sun will shine directly into the basket at cooking time.

Next, the inside of the basket is liberally daubed with a glue made from fish bones boiled in a whale-skull pot.

Finally—and this is where the real craftsmanship comes in—hemitrexes, which are the hard, reflective shells of certain mutated jellyfish, are set in glue. Now the builder must squat inside the basket, with the sun high, and adjust each hemitrex until the focused rays of the sun pass through the central point of the basket where the food will be hung. It is hot, blinding work, and the builder will usually pick a day of slight overcast and arrange for the villagers to keep his body well cooled with water. It is work that demands an accurate eye.

And Peli was going blind.

"Peli's ovens are not good these days," people would say. Usually the oven is situated in the middle of a village so that its use can be shared. It was noticed that meat cooked unevenly in them. Ovens need constant attention—realignment according to season and to correct for warping of the basket and the shifting positions of the island itself. After each adjustment by Peli, an oven seemed a little worse than before. But Peli was a proud man and would not admit his infirmity. People asked for his services less and sought out other craftsmen to maintain the sun ovens.

Peli began to spend much of his time sitting on the shore outside his dwelling, idly fingering the stock of hemitrexes that he could hardly see, his mind full of unhappy and bitter thoughts. And here he might have remained for the rest of his days, if a strange thing had not happened one evening as he sat staring into the setting sun.

A ripple appeared in the calm crimson of the sea. A faint melody carried across the waters, a sound like the most beautiful choir of women's voices, yet without words. The sounds soothed Peli's troubled thoughts and he felt peace and a quiet joy. It seemed suddenly that he'd led a good life; he'd been respected in his craft, and now he was taking a rest that he'd earned many times over.

And the outline of a girl sat there in the water.

He blinked, peering, thinking his eyes were playing their tricks again. The music stopped. The girl raised her hand.

Peli stood. She was close, now, riding the water to the very edge of the grass. She clutched at the shore, but the grass broke off in her hands. She uttered a funny little whimpering noise, and Peli realized she was in trouble. He bent down, took her hand, and swung her up beside him.

As he did, he caught a brief glimpse of a great swirling back that glowed indigo in the sun's last rays, rolling past and down, heaving the shore with the wash of its passing, so that he had to sit down quickly. Then it was gone, but the grass rippled for a long time afterward.

He turned to the girl. She sat beside him, looking out to sea while her hands ran over the grass, feeling it, allowing its tough coarseness to enter her senses and awaken memories. Tears ran down her face, but her eyes were blank.

He asked her, "What's your name?" but she didn't reply.

She only spoke once from that day until the day, not so long afterward, when she died.

✳

She wore tattered sealskin clothing, so he knew she was of the islands. The only other clue to her identity was a pendant that hung on a silver chain around her neck. And this was a great wonder to him because he'd never seen silver before—or any other metal, for that matter—neither had he seen a stone like the one at the end of the chain. It flashed like a star when the sun caught it in a certain way, so brightly that even Peli blinked.

She stayed with him. She slept in a room that he built for her, on the sunny side of his dwelling because she reminded him of the sun, with her pale face and golden hair and the sparkling thing she wore around her neck.

He showed her the ways of the sun oven, and some of the light came back into her eyes as she played with the hemitrexes, arranging them at sunset so that the shoreline blazed with winking red stars and the inside of the dwelling glowed pink. Soon he took her with him when he visited his few remaining customers.

It was quite by chance that he discovered a wonderful thing.

He was sitting inside a sun oven, sweating while the lights danced in his brain and fogged his eyes, so that adjustment of the hemitrexes was well-nigh impossible. A few villagers watched. The youths were eyeing the girl but were unwilling to make approaches because of the remoteness in her manner and her silence. She leaned over the edge of the basket, dribbling water onto his head from a sealskin gourd.

Something flashed. He blinked. The flash was so bright that it cut through the fog. He looked up, wiping the sweat from his eyes. A couple of youths stood there, watching the girl's breasts as she bent forward. Peli shook his head, trying to clear the mists from his eyes.

Again the flash. It came from the girl's breasts. No, not the breasts—it came from the pendant that hung low as she leaned over the rim of the basket. It had caught the light of a focused hemitrex . . .

From that moment to Peli's great invention was a short step. He experimented at his dwelling, away from curious eyes, assisted by the girl. She helped him build a basket. Over the basket they erected a driftwood tripod and hung a thong from it. On the end of the thong they tied the pendant, so that the bright stone was suspended at the focal point of the basket. Then they plastered the inside of the basket with glue, and they stuck the hemitrexes in there, roughly, with no careful regard for alignment. Then they climbed out of the basket.

Now Peli took a long stick and, reaching into the basket, adjusted a hemitrex until the stone flashed as the light was focused on it. Then he moved the tripod a fraction, and focused another hemitrex. And so on—the whole task could now be carried out from outside the oven. In time he devised refinements: an attachment on the tripod so that the stone traveled on a regular path, a more open weave to the basket so that the hemitrexes could be focused with the fingers through the mesh instead of with the clumsy stick.

He was a craftsman again, and it was all due to the girl. He recognized this, and worked on her room until it was as luxurious as his own and did everything he could to keep her happy. He knew that if she left him he would feel bound to return the pendant to her, and his days as a craftsman would truly be over. Maybe she understood this too, because she stayed. But she never spoke.

One day the Riders came. The girl saw the commotion from a distance, a confusion of disturbed water down the coast that resolved itself into a group of Riders and their attendants, traveling fast. She ran to Peli and he hurried from his shack, peering north. Riders, all together and heading this way. No good would come of it.

Then they were close, thirty in all, with a number of spare orcas in tow. One drove alongside the shore and climbed onto the grass. Peli recognized Or Kala, who owned lands hereabouts, including the land on which Peli's dwelling sat. He greeted the Rider respectfully.

"I'm sorry, Peli. I have to commandeer your orca," Or Kala said.

"What? But the orca is mine! How else can I travel to my work?"

"You'll have to walk, I'm afraid." The Rider was sympathetic but firm. "It's war, and we need all the orcas we can round up." His eyes dwelt on the girl several times, in puzzled fashion. Obviously he couldn't quite see where she fitted in.

"War? With whom?"

"We ride against King Awamia of Uami. It seems he's acting in contravention of the Code, and we must annex his island."

"I've heard of King Awamia. I always understood he was a devout man."

Or Kala began to get annoyed. A reasoned discussion with his subject was permissible, but this craftsman was contradicting him. "It is for the good of the grass that Uami be joined to Malaloa—linking of islands has always been our policy; it makes for better management and reduces drift —only last season Awamia lost a section of his land in a storm. Small islands are always vulnerable. Recently Uami drifted near, and in accordance with our policy, we told Awamia that the gods obviously wished a merger. Not only did he refuse, but he enlisted the help of four evil giants to increase the distance between our lands. We have no option but to fight!"

So saying, Or Kala rode off, taking Peli's orca with him.

That night Peli prayed, repeating the Vow and reaffirming his devotion, in puzzlement and some fear . . .

> *I love the grass, and my purpose in life is to*
>   *protect it.*
> *The grass sustains me in the mighty ocean, and*
>   *without it I would drown.*
> *The grass provides food and drink, and without it I*
>   *would starve.*
> *The grass fills my lungs with the essence of life,*
>   *and without it I would die.*
> *In return for this bounty, I vow to keep and protect*
>   *the grass for all of my days, and will lay down*
>   *my life when, in so doing, I preserve the grass*
>   *from evil. Ah-hey.*

He went to sleep eventually, and he dreamed of the four giants, who were truly monstrous and ate islands for breakfast.

✳

Two days later rumors reached him from a nearby village. It seemed the four giants of Uami were not huge at all. Indeed, they were almost human—and clever too, because they had arrived on an island small and fast-moving, yet stronger for its size than any known, and they had fashioned this island themselves. Then they had instructed King Awamia in the building of vast flat towers with no rooms, which in some mysterious way farmed the wind and sped the island of Uami away from Malaloa.

Then, the very next day, disaster struck Peli.

Or Kala arrived with a handful of armed Riders. He stepped ashore. "Peli, where is the girl?"

"In her dwelling."

"Bring her here."

Peli, full of forebodings, fetched the girl. She had been brushing her hair with a sea urchin and it shone like the sun. Her eyes were the color of the ocean, and Peli, peering dimly in his blindness, realized she was very beautiful. He said unhappily, "She can't talk."

Or Kala regarded the girl carefully. "Where does she come from?"

"The sea . . ." he waved a hand.

"How long has she been with you?"

"Many days, now . . . A long time." The fear was within him.

"Peli . . . I know who this girl is. There is no doubt in my mind—she is the lost daughter of King Awamia. Her name is Kelina. Here, Kelina!" He spoke sharply at the girl, but she gave no sign of recognizing the name. "No matter. It is she. She must come with me. She will be a very useful bargaining point in our next talk with King Awamia."

So they took the girl who may have been the lost daughter of King Awamia, and they mounted her on an orca behind Or Kala, and they rode away, fast, throwing high bow waves.

Peli watched them go and they soon became a blur in his eyes, whether from tears or blindness he couldn't tell. He blinked, but he couldn't see them any more, and after a while he turned and stumbled back to his dwelling.

He is never mentioned again in the legends of Polysitia.

SAGA OF THE GREAT BLUE

*I*n Polysitia the minstrels tell of the Great Blue, the huge whale that, over the centuries, has appeared in times of need. They say the whale is over two hundred meters long, and that he sings a song more beautiful than any minstrel's as he cruises the oceans of Earth. Stories of the Great Blue are uplifting stories—of islands saved from destruction during hurricanes, of children saved from drowning while at play, of fish herded to desolate shores during times of starvation. All the islands have stories that tell of the Great Blue, and students of later years have remarked often on the one common factor: that the Whale seemed to have the power of sensing human distress from afar. Where he came from nobody ever knew; but he came, and he helped people in need, and he went away.

Kelina was back. In his mysterious way—so the minstrels say—the Great Blue had found Kelina, where the emissaries of King Awamia had failed, and had delivered her to the island of Malaloa. Now, the Great Blue was good and acted only in the interests of man, and could not have known that Malaloa had recently declared war on King Awamia's island of Uami. War was unthinkable to the Great Blue.

So the soldiers of King Usalo of Malaloa took Kelina, and held her in a small coastal village that was the nearest point to Uami at that time. And they sent word to King Awamia, telling him that they held his daughter captive and that he must surrender his lands if he wanted to see her again.

Now, King Awamia had enlisted the help of four strangers in the war against Malaloa, and these strangers had shown him how to build huge sails to propel his island farther away from his foe. If they had but known it, this practice would eventually have wrecked the island upon the barren shores of Dry Land, but at the time King Awamia was interested only in flight. The strangers were evil, so the minstrels tell, and of peculiar shape. One of them had a chest as big as an orca but with normal legs, and another, a female, had breasts like two huge puffer fish. The third stranger was incredibly old and wrinkled, and the fourth was like a giant baby.

The soldiers of Malaloa stood at the shore, waiting for King Awamia's response, and in due course they saw a Rider approaching. He pulled up and stepped ashore, while his mount cruised away to join fifty other orcas, all ready to carry soldiers against King Awamia if his reply was not satisfactory.

The Rider's name was Or Kala and he bowed before the king. "I took the message," he said, "and King Awamia gave me audience. When I told him we had his daughter, he cried and embraced me. He had his servants prepare a vast meal, and we celebrated long into the night."

"Wait a moment." King Usalo frowned. "We are at war with these people, in the name of the Code. We don't celebrate with them. The girl Kelina is a hostage. Did Awamia understand that?"

"He couldn't think about war. All he could think of was his daughter. If we'd asked him to surrender the whole world, he'd have done it gladly. So far as he's concerned, the war's over."

"Oh." King Usalo was somewhat disappointed. "So what happens next? You gave him the full message—that his daughter would not be returned to him until the gap between our two islands was narrow enough for her to step across?" His voice was a little pompous. He was rather proud of this stipulation, which killed two fish, as it were, with one spear.

"I told him. It didn't bother him. He sent his Riders to round up the guidewhales, and he set his villagers to tearing down the sails that the strangers had built."

"The strangers . . . Are they as ugly as we hear?"

"Yes, although the older woman has a certain charm."

"How did they react when Awamia gave orders to destroy their invention?"

Now Or Kala looked puzzled, remembering. "Oddly enough, they didn't mind. In fact they were as happy as the king, particularly the young one shaped like a sunfish."

"You don't suspect a trick?"

"I don't see what tricks they could pull."

"Strangers often have unusual powers."

"Not these strangers. They are just ordinary people from a culture that differs from ours. I think they come from Dry Land."

"Oh, that explains it." Satisfied, the King went to check on Kelina. He could hardly believe his good fortune. Indeed, it was something of an anticlimax.

✳

Seven days later the towers of Uami could be seen on the horizon, and within another day the shoreline could be discerned. Slowly the islands moved closer, and soon the seabirds began to fly between them. Two days later again, figures could be made out on the Uami shore.

"Last night I had a foolish dream," said King Usalo. "I dreamed that Awamia had tricked us after all, and when our two lands touched, a huge army sprang onto Malaloa and captured us." He chuckled ruefully. "Just make sure we have adequate forces at the point of contact, Or Kala."

Ten meters separated the two islands now, and the Uami people could be clearly seen—probably not more than a hundred strong and most of them idle bystanders. On Malaloa, well back from the shoreline, there must have been a crowd of a thousand or more.

"You can bring Kelina out now," said King Usalo.

Minstrels tell of Kelina's last smile. They say it lighted up the land, it shone in the sea. They say that men who saw it dreamed of nothing else for the rest of their lives. They say that a sigh of wonderment came from the people on the Uami shore, and that there was nobody there who could but smile with her.

And she spoke. More, she cried out in happiness, the first sounds she had made for many days. And she held out her arms, stepping to the edge of the grass, and now the gap was almost closed, and in a few moments she would be able to jump across and be reunited with her people and her father . . .

But it was not King Awamia that she smiled at.

She did not hold out her arms to her father.

Neither was her cry of happiness directed at him.

There was a hush, as people realized. And then came an ugly, disbelieving murmur. King Awamia stepped back as though he had been hit.

Kelina was greeting the monstrous stranger—he of the orca chest and coarse black hair. It was the monster she smiled at, the monster she held her arms out to, the monster she called to so gladly.

And he shuffled forward like some grotesque crab, extending a limb across the gap to her.

A moan of outrage came from the people of Uami. Kelina the beautiful, the King's daughter, was spoiled.

And in the deeps, the Great Blue knew, and his rage knew no bounds. His mighty flukes thrust downward and his body leaped forward and upward, and he rose from the depths like a rocket.

Now Kelina's hand grasped for the monster.

The Great Blue hurtled from the water in a fountain of spray, rising through the narrow passage between the islands, hurling the shore back so that the people were flung from their feet. A flashing azure shape unbelievably huge, he filled the sky as he arched up, across, and down into the ocean again, a moment's vision of glistening majesty becoming a shallowing ripple on the surface.

Kelina was gone.

A jagged rent in the shore showed where she had stood.

The ugly stranger had been thrown onto his back, and the other strangers crawled to him across the tossing land. They helped him to his feet and they stood awhile, as the Riders and their orcas sought the sea in vain for some trace of Kelina. Then, at nightfall, the strangers walked away and were seen no more.

King Awamia and King Usalo, shocked by the Great Blue's rage, agreed on a compromise, and Uami became a part of Malaloa but retained its own shoreline, connected by a narrow bridge of grass. Kelina was never seen again, and it is thought that her broken body floated under one of the islands to feed the fish.

And the Great Blue? As the Song of Earth says, he was so shocked at the results of his moment's rage that he sank to the bottom of the ocean and remained there until he died, having vowed never again to interfere in human affairs, even with the best of intentions.

✳

The snake clouds had gone and the horse clouds rode the trade winds. The voyagers were returning, and now the cliffs of Pu'este rose above the waves.

"Cheer up, Manuel," said the Girl. "We're nearly home." She was concerned for the young man—and for herself. Manuel's melancholy had lasted for several days now, during which he'd hardly spoken. All right, thought the Girl—so Belinda had been pretty, if a little fragile. And all right, so he'd loved her. But life goes on, and this was where the Girl was concerned for herself: She didn't like her own reactions. She didn't like that sly voice within her that kept saying, *With Belinda out of the way, maybe Manuel will have more time for you, Girl . . .*

It was not a happy ship. Zozula, too, was sunk in gloom, although at least he spoke from time to time.

"They aren't True Humans," he kept saying. "They're no different from Wild Humans, basically. They just evolved a different way. And I'd been hoping for so much . . . God only knows what Juni will say."

They had spent several days with King Awamia, who had respected their technical knowledge and, until that last dreadful day, had made them very welcome. In the evenings they had sat around the base of his tower while young men sang songs of Polysitia and beautiful girls danced in the crimson light of the setting sun, highlighted by sun ovens. The songs told of the beginnings of Polysitia and of a terrible fate that waited for these gentle islanders on the shores of Dry Land.

During a pause for refreshments, Zozula asked for details of this unspecified doom.

"It is death for us to leave the life-rafts, friend Sossola," said King Awamia. "The islands breathe an essence without which we cannot live."

"Oxygen," said Zozula, an unhappy suspicion growing inside him.

They sang to him of the Redemption, when a canoe filled with their ancestors had been caught far from land in a flat calm and the people had begun to suffocate. Half of them had died before they came across a raft of unusual weed floating in the doldrums—and found they could breathe again. They climbed aboard the raft and there they found the skull of the Redeemer, together with the Knife and Gourd, which became their great religious symbols.

They sang of the Code: their people's duty to the grass, as the weed came to be called. Centuries went by, and the people of Earth were grateful to the Polysitians, who had helped to make the atmosphere breathable again—but the Polysitians by now were trapped on their own islands. So many generations had passed that they were now unable to breathe anything but the rich air given off by the grass.

They sang of the Greatest Voyage, when an archipelago of the islands left the Pacific and, at the request of the True Humans, made the perilous journey around Cape Horn and into the South Atlantic. They sang of battles, when the islands drifted too close to land and rough parties of Wild Humans attempted to board them, finding their slim, beautiful women irresistible.

They were a people apart, and they were not what Zozula was seeking.

"A waste of time," he said, as they stepped ashore on Pu'este beach. "And Manuel could have got us killed, too."

"He had no way of knowing they looked on Belinda as a princess," said the Girl hotly.

"It was unfortunate, Zozula," said Wise Ana. "Nothing more than that. We're home now, and it's all over." She looked at him with her wonderful eyes, and he began to feel a little happier and to look forward to seeing the Dome and his fellow Cuidadors again.

Ana walked, even though she didn't have to. That was the human in her. She walked inland, past the huge Dome with its adjacent Bowl, toward the mountains. She paused at the top of a rise and looked back to see three small figures in the distance, heading for the Dome. It seemed Manuel was accompanying the Girl and Zozula. This was probably all for the good. Ana's mother had often spoken of the importance of insuring that those three people, collectively known as the Triad, stayed together.

Ana's mother . . .

Ana suppressed a slight shiver at the thought of that black-cowled, enigmatic figure who spoke in riddles and demanded instant obedience. She walked on, climbing a dry watercourse between hillsides where vicunas nibbled at the sparse vegetation, tended by long-necked Specialists. Her mother knew she was coming—having probably taken a casual glance into the nearby Ifalong, thought Ana in mild exasperation. Consequently her pavilion was visible, a purple tent set in an alpine meadow. If anyone other than Ana had come thrusting through the trees, the pavilion would have been hidden on an adjacent happentrack.

Shenshi said, "Ana. You come."

"Not unexpectedly, Mother."

"And how are your human protégés—the Triad?" Shenshi led the way into the tent, where they sat on soft cushions. Opposite them stood the Rock, touching the fabric of the ceiling.

"It was terribly sad. Manuel found his girl, but she was killed by a whale just when it looked as though everything was going to be all right."

"If Belinda had lived, nothing would have been right," said Shenshi coldly. "The purpose of the voyage was to rid the boy of that foolishness, once and for all. He and the other two have been chosen, and they have important work ahead of them. Starquin's will be done."

"You know I can't stand it when you talk like that, Mother."

"It may please you to know that on many happentracks Belinda lived and was reunited with Manuel, and they were given estates and lived happily until she died in childbirth, or Manuel was eaten by a rogue orca, or was poisoned by bad fish. As you well know, happentracks are infinite. You are privileged to have witnessed one of those happentracks where Starquin's will was done."

"Was that blue whale an agent of Starquin?" asked Ana suspiciously.

"It's possible. Manuel's love for Belinda was very strong. Perhaps the whale was the only way it could be extinguished."

"I thought Starquin knew everything and never needed to use mere animals to carry out his will."

"Starquin is not omniscient. When you become a Dedo, you will understand the limitations. He is motivated by a strong sense of self-preservation, and by your present standards he is ruthless. He is *alive,* Ana—a mighty living being. He is therefore imperfect in many ways, as am I. And you . . . But your time will come, very soon."

Ana was suddenly interested. "What's that?"

"I shall soon be leaving you, my daughter."

"But . . ." A thrill of apprehension made Ana stammer. "B-but I thought you would live forever!"

"If I were going to live forever, I wouldn't have needed to give birth to you . . ." Shenshi's voice softened a little. "I remember when it came to me—oh, over one hundred and fifty millennia ago, during one of the ice ages. It was long before Starquin's Incarceration, of course. I happened to be scanning the Ifalong, and I saw my own death. It was no big thing; just a fading away, at that time very uncertain. But time passes, and now I know my death is very close. It's a pity it had to happen so soon, when such great events are building, and our recent Purpose is so shortly to be fulfilled."

"Mother!"

"I apologize. I forget there is so much you don't know. As I was saying, I foresaw my death, so I gave birth to you, to take my place."

"Who . . . who was my father?"

Shenshi sighed. "You think like a human, Ana. That must all cease. A

Dedo has no need of another human when she wishes to conceive a child. You will find out, when your time comes."

Ana's exasperation grew. "Would you mind telling me what you're talking about?"

Shenshi appeared to withdraw into herself. For a long time she sat motionless, seeming not to breathe, while the fabric of the pavilion rippled in the soft wind and somewhere an animal cried. Her cowl had fallen over her face and Ana was visited by an unnerving fantasy: that if she reached out and lifted the black cloth, she would see nothing inside it. Just for a moment she found herself thinking longingly of the village and the mothers there—and how they were liked or laughed at or respected by their children. How good to have a human mother.

But such emotions were not needed by her species. Ana had been lent those emotions by Shenshi, as a disguise. They would soon be taken back.

"It's time you knew," said Shenshi at last.

∗

Shenshi indicated the Rock. "Such Rocks are situated all over the Galaxy to serve as staging posts in Starquin's travels through the Greataway. Certain other races are permitted to use the Rocks, too, traveling by the psetic lines that stretch between them. Our Duty is to tend the Rocks and to speed Travelers on their way by use of our skills.

"I said that other races are permitted to use the Rocks. These races do not include human beings. Humans used to see Space as a four-dimensional thing. They traveled through it laboriously, in huge manufactured Spaceships, with a great expenditure of energy. It was tiresome and wasteful, but at least it kept humans busy, and out of the Greataway . . .

"Until one day in the year 92,613 Cyclic."

LAUNCH OF THE STAR KINGDOM

•••

*T*hey were the last days of the Great Age of Space, although nobody knew it at the time.

On that afternoon of hope and triumph, the LeBrun Starshell was crowded as never before. Spectators, well-wishers and tearful relatives jammed every available vantage point around the inside of the giant sphere, so that even the Spaceship yards themselves had their share of private citizens, who clung to scaffolding, stumbled over chains and hurt themselves on the angular accouterments of Space travel of the 926th century Cyclic.

They swayed, they cheered and they gazed upward. A thousand kilometers away, the inhabitants of Earth watched the scene, too, gathered around their 3V alcoves. They watched and they wondered.

In the center of the sphere hung the *Star Kingdom,* five kilometers long. Earth had never before seen such a ship.

In those days they loved nothing so much as opulence, extravagance, technological wizardry and sheer, overpowering, staggering size. The *Star Kingdom* had all of those. She was four times the size of any ship built to date. Her passengers, even now crowding her thirty thousand shatterproof ports to catch their last glimpse of the trappings of Earth, numbered one million. Each one had his own cabin, complete with deep-sleep cubicle, Vicaripeep hookup, autochef with optional ethnic bias, and direct link to A-Citizen-of-Your-Choice. To while away those periods that passengers might elect to spend awake, the *Star Kingdom* had one hundred bars stocked with every drink of the known Galaxy, fifty health spas, and a giant diorama portraying in every detail the pleasure isle of Barbuda.

Earth loved the ship. She was the symbol of the final conquest. She was big enough to be unaffected by gravity storms up to the maximum violence recorded. She carried not one but five Navigators, whose chromosomes had been enriched at birth by genes derived from pigeons—noted for high psy content. Three Captains ruled over all this: Captain Pounce, a muscular, tawny man with the slitted eyes of a mountain lion; Captain Albo-Dey, a woman of recent derivation and supreme intelligence, said to have certain alien genes in her make-up; and Captain Steady, noted for caution, the perseverance very necessary on long voyages, and an oddly reptilian blink. All of Earth knew their names and their faces. In the eleven years it had taken to build the ship, the officers—selected at the outset and publicized so much that their names had become synonymous with the glory of Space—had become legends. Probably one name, and one only, was more intimately associated in the public mind with technical brilliance and human mastery of High Space: the name of K. Isaac LeBrun, designer of the *Star Kingdom.*

LeBrun was no dilettante architect who drew pictures and left other men to fill in the details. From the initial laying of the spine of the *Star Kingdom* to the imminent launch, he had never left the Starshell, that man-made satellite of Earth where the ships docked and were maintained, and from which they set off on their voyages through Space. He supervised every moment of building, and personally hired—and fired—senior technicians in charge of the various aspects of construction. He had designed the giant engines, all eighteen of them slightly different to allow for differing needs and gravities. He had designed the control layouts, the recycling equipment, the very pattern on the fifteen million pieces of genuine chinaware. He had designed the Starshell itself. It was rumored, even, that he had designed Captain Albo-Dey.

Now he sat in his private suite in the great control tower that rose from the interior surface of the Starshell. He could see the people crowded and staring, pale faces upturned in a concave panorama as if seen through a wide-angle lens. In the center of everything, the *Star Kingdom* floated in zero gravity, dwarfing three freighters and the multitude of shuttles and tugs that swarmed around the inside of the Starshell like bees in a hive. Fifteen kilometers away, the constellation Leo glittered in the aperture of the Starshell through which the great ship would depart. That opening had been enlarged to accommodate the *Star Kingdom*, at a cost that did not bother Isaac LeBrun one iota.

He was a man of medium height and casual appearance, eighty-seven years old and athletic. (This was before the discovery of the Inner Think, which extended the human life immeasurably.) At this moment he was lounging against a pillar, watching his grandson play with a scale replica of the *Star Kingdom*, zooming it around the room with chubby arm held high, small feet dancing over the thick fur of the living carpet.

The child brought the toy to a neat, if impractical, landing on a table. "Waah . . ." he said, his voice fading in imitation of engines being shut down. He stood back from the model, measuring it with his eyes against the immensity of the prototype on the other side of the window. "Clever Gramps," he said happily. This toy was his favorite at present, having replaced the magniblox that lay in untidy heaps on the other side of the room, where the living carpet was ineffectively trying to clean them away.

Now a woman entered, tall, considerably younger than LeBrun, with a shock of silver hair and yellow eyes curiously dead. She glanced at him, then followed his gaze out the window. After a long pause she said, "So what's next, Isaac?"

It was uncanny how she could read his thoughts—despite her terrible accident. "Next? Give me today, will you, Taha? At least give me that."

"Today is yours, Isaac," Her voice was as dead as her eyes. "After all, you've bought it. You've bought it with the lives of twenty-three technicians who died during the third engine test last year."

"The inquiry found a manufacturing fault. The design was good."

"You've bought it with forty thousand passengers scattered through High Space when the Jason came apart. Forty thousand lives, Isaac. That's big money."

She wanted him to make excuses, to keep on making excuses while she blamed him for every death in the history of galactic transport. Ignoring her, he walked over to a console and touched a button. The screen showed a busy scene inside *Star Kingdom*'s bridge. All three Captains were there, and four of the Navigators. Captain Albo-Dey towered above them like a mountain, her face a network of tiny lines where the scalpels had transformed her into something acceptable for publicity purposes. LeBrun said into the voicebox, "What's happening? Is something wrong?"

"Nothing we can't handle." The big Captain turned away from the camera.

In a moment of irritation—after all, LeBrun was under considerable strain—he very nearly shouted: "You owe me some respect, Albo-Dey!"

Owe. Give. Build. Bought.

There is a tiny race of benevolent aliens known as kikihuahuas who travel all through High Space in living Spaceships, helping people for no reason other than their genes dictate it. One of them had once said to K. Isaac LeBrun, "We often call human beings the Benders. When we set out to build something like a house or a Spaceship or a beacon hydra, we sit down and guide it into shape, gently, from organic matter. Human beings tear and twist and melt and freeze metal, which is one of the most difficult substances to work in, second only to rock. They do it the hard way. They don't let things build themselves—they bend them instead.

"You, Isaac LeBrun—you are the greatest Bender of them all."

And Taha was saying, "You bought today with the souls of your Navigators—poor kids who enter your Space College full of life and fun and psy and who come out zombies, dedicated to furthering the glory of K. I. LeBrun."

The screen showed one of the Navigators at that moment, a pretty girl, smiling, brown-haired, slightly altered . . . And why not? "There was a time when service was compulsory for anyone with powers," snapped LeBrun.

"Did *I* have any choice?"

He said quietly, "You married my son. That was your choice." It hurt, still, the way his son had died—a passenger in a ship that Taha had been Navigating, which had come under severe gravitational stress when Taha's mind was captured by an insane Flunnulf, or Space Guide . . .

"At least David has no LeBrun blood in him."

She was trying hard to hurt him, really hard. David had stopped playing with the model *Star Kingdom* and was assembling his magniblox into a convoluted structure, maybe a Space station. He'd ignored his mother since her entrance; indeed, he seemed slightly uneasy with her presence.

Maybe he sensed what LeBrun suspected: that Taha, despite the best treatment money could buy, was permanently insane, half her mind burned away by contact with that Flunnulf . . . Imagine it, out there in High Space and responsible for fifty thousand souls, relying on your fitful psy powers to make contact with the next human Flunnulf in a network of them scattered among the stars on beacon hydras—and then to find, too late, that the next one in line is mad.

Taha saved the ship, at the cost of her own sanity. How she did it is another story, but her hair turned white, and she kept it that way to punish LeBrun.

LeBrun asked casually, "Whose child is David, then?"

"I don't really know. Does it matter? Some young fellow down Old Argentina way—a little place called Puerto Este."

"Did he have . . . psy?"

"Did he ever!" Her enthusiasm was like a knife.

"It doesn't show in David."

"I should hope not!" And now she snatched the child up, peering at LeBrun cunningly from behind the fair curls. "You won't get your hands on my son, Isaac!"

"I have plenty of Navigators—take a look at the college enrollments."

Realizing that he was being drawn into argument, he turned back to the screen. Captain Pounce was smiling back at him, all suppressed energy, sharp teeth and high cheekbones. "Everything under control now, Isaac." He checked a bank of dials, a fleeting glance with slitted pupils. "Just some kind of emanation that was troubling one of the Navigators. All these people, I guess . . ." He shrugged, a supple movement. "I sometimes wonder if the Starshell acts as a kind of lens, with the *Kingdom* at the focus . . . Two minutes to launch. Counting."

The image shifted, picking up the First Navigator lying back in his seat, helmet on, wired into the initial guidance system that would take the giant ship beyond the Solar System and into the unchartable whorls of High Space, where the Flunnulfs took over.

The massed spectators were waving, and the sound of cheering came faintly to LeBrun.

He glanced at Taha, who had put David down and who now, despite herself, was standing at the window, her expression intense. *You can't take this away from me,* he thought. The child picked up his model again. Had it really been four years since Jack had died? LeBrun had thrown himself into his work; the time had passed so quickly.

And now the ship was moving, and Taha's words came back to him like an echo above the cheers of the crowd and the bursting of rockets. *So what's next, Isaac . . . ?*

The ship was moving. The masterpiece, the ultimate triumph of human technology. It looked so huge out there, gliding slowly toward the disk of the exit. What next? A bigger one? Little bits of publicity statistics came to him.

Three times as long as the Amsterdam Building is high . . .

Broad enough to bridge the Great Sahara Canal . . .

Food enough for all eternity . . .

Suddenly, LeBrun shivered. The great ship slid on. She was so vulnerable against the majesty of the stars. She was going, away from him, out into the vastness of High Space, with its twists and warps and its stars hotter than a thousand reactors. He didn't want her to go. He wanted to abort the launch. A few more checks, a few more safeguards . . .

"Isaac, we have a problem."

And Captain Steady blinked at him from the screen with lizard composure. Behind him, somebody was struggling with the First Navigator, fumbling with the fastenings, ripping the helmet from his head, leaving the *Star Kingdom* rudderless, a great blind whale blundering toward the tiny exit into Space. The Secondary Navigator waited, twitching with urgency, for the seat to be vacated. They carried the First Navigator away. He was jerking in the throes of some kind of fit. Little bubbles of foam beaded his lips. The Second Navigator pulled the helmet on. "Okay now, Isaac," said Steady in his monotone.

The *Star Kingdom* glided on, the course correction imperceptible to the onlookers.

LeBrun let his breath go, hearing his own gasp, and remembered Taha. He didn't look at her. He waited for her comment on the incident.

She was silent.

LeBrun whirled round. David had built a big wall with his magniblox, with a hole in the middle. He held his model aloft. He was simulating the launch. He was a stranger—not a grandchild at all. He looked at LeBrun and smiled, as always, as though nothing had changed.

Taha was looking out of the window.

Her expression was fierce, a concentrated stare as though she were willing the ship—all ships—to disintegrate, to cease to exist, to never have been. Her lips were moving. *This for you, Jack . . .*

And on the screen, the Second Navigator jerked, as though in sudden pain.

"Stop that!" LeBrun threw himself at the woman, hurling her to the floor too fast for the tendrils of the living carpet, which had no time to rise and check her fall. She bounced and yelped. Her concentration was broken.

The Second Navigator, released, relaxed. The *Star Kingdom* moved into the circle of black Space, glowing in the light of a thousand spotlights and a million bursting starshells. Taha ran from the room. For an instant, LeBrun wished she'd taken the other door, the one into the vacuum . . .

But she was gone, and the moment was his again. Today was his—and as for tomorrow, so what? There would be more challenges, another ship. It was just a question of size. The next ship would be bigger and better, and the cheers would be louder. In his mind, that next ship began to take shape, even as the *Star Kingdom* eased its vastness through the circular exit, as accurately as a laser scalpel, and as cleanly. That next ship . . . Earth didn't have the resources. He would have to move the Starshell, set up camp in the rings of Saturn, nearer the raw materials. Camp? A city, he'd build. A city of workers, self-contained like a starship, living and giving birth and dying while they built the greatest ship of all time. A ship to move a billion people to new worlds, a ship to . . .

Isaac Lebrun—you are the greatest Bender of them all.

Smiling at his thoughts, he took his gaze from the departing masterpiece, needing another human being to share his dreams, and having one nearby: David, who was not his grandson, but who was the child of the mad Taha and some unknown Argentinian. That fact could not affect him today.

"David . . ."

David sat near the exit hatch—too near. Once a fool mechanic had opened the hatch from the other side, unthinking, and sucked the wiring diagrams for the *Star Kingdom* into Space.

And David smiled at him, proudly. David was simulating the launch of the *Star Kingdom,* all on his own, for the benefit of his clever Gramps.

Just like the real thing, the model starship was gliding through the center of the circular hole in the magniblox. Unsupported.

Bereft of the wires, strings, rails, or chubby hands. All by itself. Suspended in Space.

"Clever David," said David, child of mad Taha and some unknown Argentinian with powers, leaning back against the exit hatch.

It was, in fact, the very last day of the Great Age of Space, and one person knew it instantly. Dreams evaporated. Cheers sounded like jeers. The Space city, the rings of Saturn, the generations of workers, the LeBrun *Star Kingdom,* the LeBrun College for Navigators, this very LeBrun Starshell, seemed suddenly insubstantial, unrealized—obsolete. As did LeBrun.

And the little model hung in the air, sustained only by David's mind.

Nobody would need Benders in the future . . . possibly. The child, small, vulnerable, smiled proudly and wriggled, his back pressing against the exit hatch.

"David," said LeBrun after a long pause. "Come away from that hatch —it's dangerous. We must go and find your mother. I . . . want to talk to her . . ." He stooped, and gently gathered the child into his arms.

David, a little disappointed at the lack of reaction to his trick, wondered briefly why his grandfather looked so old, so scared.

✳

"They didn't look back," said Shenshi. "Humans never did, in those days. It was Onward and Outward, always. They isolated the gene that allowed that young boy to tap into the psetic lines and they called it "mynde," and they reduplicated it and improved it—they were good at that, given the first lucky mutation. Then they spilled into the Greataway.

"In due course they encountered an enemy, who had a weapon against which they could do little. This weapon was particularly terrible for creatures so short-lived as humans, because its effect was to age them well before their time. Many of Earth's colonies collapsed as quickly as they were founded. Mankind was driven back through light-year after light-year, dimension after dimension, until it was trapped in a tiny corner of the Greataway little more than sixty light-years across, with Earth at its center.

"Starquin was watching with interest. He knew what would happen. He was sitting in the Greataway and encompassing the Solar System and a couple of nearby stars, at the time. Mankind, at bay, turned to its own genes for help and created a monstrous trio of pseudohumans who became known as the Three Madmen of Munich. These creatures were sent into the Greataway and they placed what can only be called Hate Bombs at the Pockets in psetic lines.

"Greataway travel depends on mynde, and mynde is very largely made up of love. Nobody could get past the Hate Bombs. They sealed Earth off from their enemy. They also sealed Earth off from its remaining colonies.

"And they sealed Starquin in. He's up there now, trapped. He's been there for almost fifty thousand years, unable to wander free among the galaxies.

"Our Purpose is to release him."

Ana spoke tentatively, not wishing to sound skeptical about the great story her mother had told. "If Starquin can foretell the Ifalong, why did he allow himself to be trapped?"

"It's easier to foretell the Ifalong than to change it," replied her mother. "And you must remember, happentracks are infinite. On many happentracks Starquin was not trapped. But we, in the here and now, exist on a happentrack where he was. So we must work toward freeing him."

"How?"

Now Shenshi said the words she'd said so often before, but this time they made sense to Ana.

"Manuel, Zozula and the Girl form the Triad—as it will be known in ages to come. They will remove the Hate Bombs and free Starquin. The means are not clear, and perhaps they will do it in many different ways on many different happentracks. But in the Ifalong, when all the stories and songs and legends and facts have coalesced into something approaching truth, Mankind will tell of the Triad in its Song of Earth. The minstrels will sing a song that starts like this:

> *Come, hear about the Trinity of legendary fame,*
> *The Artist and the Oldster and the Girl-with-no-*
> *Name!*

"We must make it happen," said Shenshi.

HERE ENDS THAT PART OF
THE SONG OF EARTH KNOWN TO MEN AS
THE LOST ISLANDS OF POLYSITIA

OUR TALE CONTINUES WITH THE GROUP
OF STORIES AND LEGENDS KNOWN AS
MANKIND'S CRADLE

where a crystal of memory is lost and found,
a prisoner is released
and the Triad discovers the recipe
for True Humans

THE POET

There are no half measures in legends. They deal with absolutes—with men of chivalry, with monsters of fearsome aspect, with villains of unspeakable evil. The women in legends are beautiful. Often they are the most beautiful women in the world; occasionally, in all of Time, too.

The Song of Earth is a heady liquor, a mash of legends, facts and half-truths brewed in the minds of minstrels and distilled into their lyrics. Out of all this has emerged one perfect woman. She was brave and strong and clever. She was an ancient tiger-woman from the chromosome factory of Mordecai N. Whirst. She was the captain of a great starship named the Golden Whip, which sailed the tides of High Space less than a thousand years before little David LeBrun made nonsense of it all with his mynde.

Her name was Captain Spring, and she was the most beautiful woman who ever lived—so the minstrels say. She mothered a famous line, including Karina, who was supposed to be a felina; John, who gave his name to an Age of Man; and Jimbo, a poet. And there was Antonio, another poet.

As if all that was not enough, she accidentally brought to Earth alien parasites known as the Macrobes, which changed Mankind. She did this in the year 91,702 Cyclic. Over fifty thousand years later, a priest in Pu'este was using these same parasites for the purpose of prolonging his life. Dad Ose and the people of that period called this process the Inner Think.

It is sometimes said that the Macrobes spread through the human race like wildfire, but this is not so. In fact, the process was gradual and accompanied by setbacks, such as the infamous Pogrom of the Hosts, when many millions of Macrobe-carrying humans were wiped out by enemies jealous of their longevity.

The chief characteristic of the Macrobes was their intense desire to live. Because of this, they made sure their host lived, too. However, incidents such as the Pogrom caused them to revise their tactics. They evolved into a recessive gene and lay low for thousands of years.

"It was a paradox," said Shenshi. "Once the Pogrom was over and it became clear that the Macrobes still existed—and would always exist— Mankind began to accept them as beneficial. After all, they could extend the life of a man for several hundred years. What could be better?"

"So what was the paradox?" asked Ana.

"Humans lost all incentive. The drive and urgency went out of them. What was the hurry, when suddenly they had a lifespan of centuries to play with? They called it the Age of Regression, when people began to drift back into their Domes for entertainment. They lay down and plugged themselves into Dream Earth, and there they stayed."

"I remember that happening," said Ana. "It was quite a gradual thing. Then one day I realized there were two types of humans: the people in the Domes, and the Wild Humans outside."

Shenshi said, "The people in the Domes were the ones with Macrobes, of course. And now the Macrobes were trapped, because human reproduction had virtually ceased. The beginnings of neoteny had been observed in the Dome people, and the Cuidadors had set up an experimental station on another planet, well away from Earthly influences, where they were trying to breed humans with normal characteristics. They called it the People Planet, and it was founded in 107,357 Cyclic.

"The Cuidadors began to take an interest in the Wild Humans, seeking suitable breeding stock. And the Macrobes realized they must obtain a foothold on the People Planet and in the breeding program if they were to survive.

"And I scanned the Ifalong, and foresaw a happentrack on which Starquin was freed from his imprisonment. So I sent you into Puerto Este . . ."

"I remember that day," said Ana thoughtfully. "And the boy—Antonio, was it? He was a nice boy." She smiled reminiscently.

"The recessive gene had surfaced in him."

"You make it sound so clinical, Mother. Does there always have to be a reason for niceness?"

"Always," said Shenshi.

She was a foreign girl; he could tell that by her complexion. She was paler than the local girls, and her features more delicate. She had arrived some months ago and had set up a little shop in an old stone cottage near the beach. Her name was foreign, too—a curious name, at first lumpy on his tongue like clotted uida, but soon gaining a poetry and a meaning of its own.

He watched her each morning as she walked to the beach in the early sun, picking her way over the pebbles as though they were hot coals—she was not yet accustomed to going barefoot—then striding across the sand toward the water with her head high, never glancing his way as he lay beside a grass-tipped dune. Each day he moved a little closer to her accustomed route, but still she didn't look at him. Chin up, eyes ahead, she moved with a swing of rhythmic poetry in her strong thighs and her slender waist. After a week she was tanned, but it was a golden tan, and in the boy's eyes the local girls with their dark skins looked merely dirty beside her. They taunted him, too, suspecting his enchantment.

"You're too young for her, Antonio! You're only a child!"

Possibly she was two years older than he, but he was at that age—or maybe was that type of person—to dismiss this as irrelevant. She was a beautiful creature and he loved her, but he'd never spoken to her, and perhaps he never would. Unless that occasion arose which he often dreamed of, when he heard her screaming from the surf in danger of her life, and he swam out and saved her. Then she would thank him, clinging to him, and he would say with mature casualness, "It was nothing. You're shivering. Come along to my place and I'll make you a hot drink."

Antonio's place was a stone cottage like all the other stone cottages, thick-walled and cool in summer, warm in winter when he covered the windows and stacked the fire high. It contained a bed fashioned from driftwood, a chair and table of similar construction, a few metal pots left by the previous owner, some simple tools, a pile of vicuna skins (on which she would lie, her shivering abating, her eyes warm as she watched him heat a potion of milk, ground coffee beans and peyote) and Antonio's prized possession, a shelf of books. Many years ago Antonio, an introverted child, had taught himself to read from a cache of books he'd found in a buried village. Not many people in Puerto Este could boast of this accomplishment.

Or his other accomplishment, about which he had never told anyone . . .

The interior walls of the cottage were worn smooth with the occupancy of millennia. The cracks held little curios—bits of beach-worn glass, shells, unidentifiable artifacts from long ago. The surface of many larger stones bore carvings of stylized fish and whales, goats and guanacos. And one stone, near the fireplace, bore an etched symbol. Probably no one in the village except Antonio knew what it meant.

Under the symbol was a shelf, and on the shelf sat a pot of flowers. On a rock projecting from the wall below the flowers lay a piece of white bark, with characters inscribed on it with a charred stick. Antonio was writing a poem.

He'd never written a poem before, although he had a book of poems that he frequently read, feeling strange stirrings within him at their rhythms, sounds and emotions. So it seemed appropriate that he write the girl a poem. It was taking a long time, although it was a short poem. The bark was smudged from many erasures. In a few days it would be finished, even though Antonio felt there was an infinity of ways in which the choice and setting of words could be improved.

It had to be finished soon, because Antonio had seen Hernando, a much older boy, muscled and swarthy and strong, talking to the girl yesterday. So—in a couple of days he would give her the poem and she would melt in his arms, just as if he'd saved her life. He selected a charred stick from the fireplace and began to edit, to perfect.

He wondered why things should be so complicated, here in the simple surroundings of Puerto Este. In his books he'd read of other times when the world teemed with people, clustered in large cities in their millions, when even in the countryside every available hectare was cultivated. Strange social structures had held sway, and complex laws that were altered many times in a lifetime. How could a person keep up, in those far-off days? How could one handle differing currencies, differing languages, different customs as he rushed from one city to another? And the laws . . . How could one stay out of jail?

Things were so much simpler here and now. The mountains, the village, the sea. The sun and the sand. And the girl . . .

No, it was not simple. Man could still create complications within his own mind. Otherwise he would have walked right up to the girl and said,

"You are beautiful and I love you. Come and live with me in my cottage . . ." Now *that* was simple. That was real poetry.

Love can be pain. Antonio endured the pain because it was outweighed by the joy. And in a very short time, he had finished the poem as best he could. It was not perfect and it didn't rhyme, and in a way it contradicted itself by denying the need for its own existence. Yet its uncomplicated statement found its way into history.

> *But love should be a simple thing*
> *Of silence, with no need to justify.*
> *No honest reason to write down*
> *Neat unities of charcoal, bark and mind,*
> *Instead of simply trusting in*
> *Emotions you read better from my eyes.*

And the girl was tanned and straight, with hair the color of a fair sunset and she stepped delicately over the pebbles, although her feet were now becoming accustomed to the rough ground. Now she was on the sand, wearing two pieces of bright dyed leather, walking to the waves, toward the dune where Antonio lolled with seeming indifference. She didn't glance at him yet. She didn't glance at the little knot of spectators who leaned on a broken groyne nearby, either. These were Antonio's contemporaries, who suspected he was about to make a fool of himself and wanted to see it happen.

The girl's feet were small, and she left a straight trail of small footprints behind her. If that line of footprints were extended from the moving girl toward the water, they would pass directly over a low dune. To the right of this knoll lay a piece of bark, paper-thin, about the size of a man's chest. To the left of the knoll lounged Antonio, trying to hear the sound of the girl's approach above the pounding of his heart. The girl would turn right, he knew, choosing not to climb the knoll and choosing not to walk too close to where he lay. So she would see the poem, right in front of her. Antonio lay propped up on one elbow, hearing his heart and the murmur of surf. Suddenly, hearing a tiny click as two stones met, disturbed by the girl's passing.

A shadow fell across the dune. She was here. The shadow shifted. She was turning right, around the base of the dune. Antonio gulped as his throat misbehaved. His fingers traced an endless pattern in the sand. Love should be a simple thing.

"Pick it up! Pick it up! Pick it up!" The spectators at the groyne, wickedly knowing, set up a chant.

The girl had paused. Antonio risked a sideways glance from under his hair. She was looking at the bark at her feet. Now another figure appeared, walking diagonally across the beach. A slow geometry of disaster.

The girl had picked up the bark. She was staring at the scrawlings.

"Hello!" The muscular figure, Hernando, strode toward her. "Coming for a swim?"

She looked up, saw him, then looked back at the bark. Her gaze slid almost to Antonio; her eyes were puzzled. Again she looked at the bark, then shrugged and cast it aside. It fell to the sand waveringly, like a falling leaf. Now she looked at Hernando again, and smiled.

"Coming!" she called and ran toward him. He took her hand and, laughing, they ran together into the waves.

Just two more things happened.

Antonio watched them go, then he stood, brushing the sand from his thighs. He turned around and looked back at the cottages, with the mountains in the distance, and, nearer, the giggling group at the groyne. His emotions surrounded him like a cold mist. He thought for a moment, fought himself, then, unable to bear the pain any longer, reached down into his being, into some core of awareness deep inside him.

Help me, Little People, please help me!

Help?

Make me happy, now. I do not want to love.

They saw him standing like a rock; then they saw him relax and smile. He gave a little skip and turned, saw them and ran toward them, his heels throwing up puffs of sand. Now he was a carefree boy; he had cast love off like a hermit crab casting off an old shell that had become too confining. Laughing, he joined them at the groyne, shadowboxing, suggesting games. A couple of them became quiet, eyed him curiously, and continued to observe him covertly for the rest of the day. Antonio was a strange fellow. Unpredictable.

"He was a nice boy," said Ana again, remembering. "Why wouldn't you let me talk to him?"

"He had to be hurt, and I had to observe his reaction. It was a test. Love used to be a very powerful driving force in humans, and Antonio had love. Not many humans did, by that time. That's one of the reasons they lost the knack of Greataway travel. But Antonio was exceptional, and I had to know if the Macrobe gene was strong enough to defeat his love for you."

Ana said sadly, "He never really looked at me, after that."

"His Macrobes knew he could destroy himself for love of you. You were a very beautiful woman in those days," said Shenshi dispassionately.

"Some men think I'm not too bad right now," said Ana, annoyed.

"One thing I never knew. Why did you choose that name? What was wrong with your own name?"

"I didn't like what I was doing, Mother. I suppose I didn't want to associate my name with it."

"But why that particular name? It's not from this region."

"Bonnie? It's an old human legend I got from a terminal of the Rainbow. Bonnie was a cow with a human mind, and a man called Adam fell in love with her. I think the story was intended to mean that human love and sex weren't the same thing. Bonnie seemed an appropriate name, so I used it. Did you notice how Antonio's poem spelled it out?" Ana smiled.

"It will be a good thing when you lose your human emotions, Ana. Remember, you only have them because I gave them to you as a disguise while you live among these creatures. You will not have them much longer."

"Perhaps that will be my loss."

"When you reach my age, you won't even remember those emotions. However, young Antonio had them in full measure, and this was recognized by the Cuidadors. They came from the Dome and took him, and shipped him up to their People Planet. He was a perfect specimen from their point of view. He had love—so essential for their Greataway travel. Physically, he was acceptable.

"And most important, the Macrobes were in his genes. So they gained their foothold in the breeding program—unknown to the Cuidadors."

Ana said thoughtfully, "I haven't noticed much difference around Pu'este in the last thirty-five thousand years. The Wild Humans are still out here, looking more like barrels every generation. And the Domes . . . All I know about them is what Zozula tells me occasionally. I haven't heard of any big changes over the millennia. So what have the Macrobes done lately?"

"They haven't been very successful on the People Planet. Although they have a collective intelligence, their sense of self-preservation can lead them into mistakes. They started by neutralizing the human genes that cause ageing, thinking this would insure their survival. Maybe it will, but since their hosts never reach puberty, they cannot reproduce. A thousand of these creatures were produced before the True Humans realized something was wrong. They were placed in isolation in a corner of the People Planet, and as far as I can foretell, they will remain there until the sun goes nova. The Cuidadors call them the Everlings."

"Poor things."

"They were the Macrobes' first mistake," said Shenshi. "But the Everlings were of little consequence, compared to what the Macrobes did next . . ."

THE LOST NEOTENITE

••

*S*elena was carrying a memory potto on her shoulder, and the sight of it saddened Zozula, reminding him that the Cuidadors were getting older and having to rely on more and more artificial devices to carry out their jobs. The little primate stared at him with its huge eyes, seeing everything, hearing everything, remembering everything. It was telepathic, too, and whenever it sensed that Selena was groping to recall some fact or incident from the past, it would feed the memory to her as if it were her own. Selena was rarely without her memory potto, these days.

She saw Zozula looking at it. "There's so much to remember, up on the People Planet," she said defensively. "The display screens shift so fast . . . I don't have time to take it all in."

They sat around a table in the Rainbow Room. The atmosphere was gloomy. The search for True Humans in the ocean had failed, and meanwhile another seven neotenites had died.

"I've asked your man Brutus to make sure the nurses replace all sick neotenites immediately," Zozula said, and before Selena could object, he continued, "I'm aware that the recent deaths seem to be due to some kind of mental problem, but I want to make sure we're covering all angles. Brutus tells me there are thirty-four standby bodies in storage, and I told him to use them all."

"That doesn't allow us any spares for emergencies," said Selena, white-faced.

"You'll have to ship in replacements from the People Planet."

"They're not old enough! The rules state they have to be at least six months old before they're brought to Earth."

"We made the rules, Selena," said Zozula gently. "We can change them."

Meanwhile, Manuel, listening to the argument with half his mind, was watching the Girl on the other side of the Rainbow Room. She sat at the console, renewing her acquaintanceship with Dream Earth. A prehistoric scene was enacting itself under the vaulting roof of the room. A herd of mastodons strode in stately line along a valley bottom, and Caradoc sat on a rock nearby, bringing the Girl up to date on recent happenings. The Girl looked terribly vulnerable, a mountain of delicate flesh sitting beneath the stamping feet of the mastodons, albeit in another dimension.

She had been very kind to Manuel since the death of Belinda. Kind and sympathetic, and sad. In her present form, she thought, no young man would fall in love with her. (She had never heard the legend of Bonnie and Adam.)

Manuel, looking at her, experienced a rush of pity that made him forget his own sorrow. "There's only one thing to do," he said suddenly. "We've got to find out what caused neoteny in the first place. If we can do that, we might be able to discover a cure—or the Rainbow might discover it for us. It could be something quite simple, some little thing lost in history. But people didn't always have bodies like that," he pointed at the distant Girl. "Something caused it. So it can be reversed. But instead of getting to the bottom of the problem, we've been wasting our time running around looking for ready-made True Humans." Aware that he had been making a speech, he fell silent, abashed.

Selena said, "Neoteny happened over a long period of time."

"But it must have had a beginning," said Manuel.

"What I mean is, there's probably no cure. Humans simply changed, gradually, because they were in the Domes. It happens to animals, when you take the element of threat out of their environment. Juvenile characteristics are retained in the adult form—things like big eyes, high brows, plump cheeks and small noses."

"Why?" asked Manuel.

"I don't know. It may be that childhood becomes lengthened because there is no need for adulthood. It may be a survival factor because the childlike appearance is appealing. Look at that archetype that used to be popular in Dream Earth—remember when all those people were Marilyns? The Girl was one herself, once. Well, those Marilyns had a number of the characteristics of neoteny."

"I don't believe all that stuff," said Manuel. "You're just saying what your potto tells you."

Selena flushed. "The potto never makes a mistake." She reached up and patted the little creature reassuringly.

"The potto only knows what you once knew. You could both have missed something."

Zozula said quietly, "He could be right, Selena."

"There's nothing to miss. Do you think I haven't checked it all, hundreds of times? Neoteny was first observed in the hundred and sixth millennium, and the Cuidadors became so concerned about it that they founded the People Planet." Selena dropped all pretense of quoting from her own memory and closed her eyes as she allowed the potto's thoughts to reach her mind. "Then, around the year 108,270, things started to go seriously wrong. First the Everlings were created, then there was a rush of neotenite births. There have been very few normal creations on the People Planet since . . ." She opened her eyes, looking a little puzzled.

"There you are, then," said Manuel. "Something funny happened around 108,270. We have to find out what."

"I think . . . Yes, I've already tried. There are gaps in the records."

"We'll just have to fill those gaps," said Manuel.

Zozula was eyeing him curiously. "What's your interest in True Humans, Manuel? Why are you so anxious to help us?"

The youth hesitated. "I don't necessarily want to help True Humans. I think you're a bunch of snobs who refuse to admit that Wild Humans have taken over the Earth. No—I feel sorry for all those neotenites who could hardly walk if you unplugged them from Dream Earth. I feel sorry for the Girl." He watched as the Girl rose awkwardly from her seat at the console and walked heavily and painfully toward them. "Most of all, I feel sorry for the Girl," said Manuel.

Selena said, "I'll do my best."

At that moment Brutus arrived, in great distress.

✳

Brutus was a troubled gorilla-man. He did not know it, but in the Song of Earth he would become famous as one of the great human symbols of compassion, the Specialist who had attempted to save the lives of hundreds of neotenite babies instead of recycling them as he had been instructed to do by his True Human mistress, Selena. He had been caught out, and had received a severe reprimand. Now, still nursing his grievance, he had been helping the raccoon-nurses revitalize the standby bod-

ies. He was carrying out Zozula's instruction to replace the sick neotenites.

"It's inhuman, killing all those babies," he remarked to one of the
nurses. "There has to be a better way."

"Well," said the nurse in practical tones, "you can't know they'll turn
out to be neotenites until you've created them." She gave him a quick,
sympathetic raccoon smile.

"Maybe we should shut the breeding program down."

"Then you'll never create True Humans."

"We haven't been able to create a True Human for as long as I can
remember."

"You're a gifted man, Brutus. Don't throw your career away."

Brutus slid another hibernating neotenite into the revitalization chamber. "I'm beginning to wonder if my career is worthwhile. I have to go
through all this—the strange creatures on the People Planet, the disap-
pointments with every breeding cycle, the murder of babies whose only
crime is being born—all for the sake of True Human form. Well, I'm not
a True Human; I'm a Specialist. I have animal genes, and different loyal-
ties. Most of all, I'm loyal to life itself—that's why I do this job. I love
being a part of bringing new creatures into the Universe. But the disad-
vantages are beginning to outweigh all that."

The transparent chamber misted over but they could still see, faintly,
the first movements of the awakening neotenite. "We must stick to the
rules," said the nurse. "Try to remember that, Brutus, the next time they
give you a batch of babies for recycling."

The shelves in the hibernating room were all empty now, and Brutus
said suddenly, "I thought there was one more neotenite in here."

The nurse glanced at the indicator on the revitalization chamber. "You
must have miscounted. We've processed thirty-three."

Brutus, alarmed, was tapping at the keyboard. The screen showed the
number of neotenites delivered from the People Planet, the number of
those used as replacements in the Dome, the balance remaining. "Thirty-
four," said Brutus harshly. "It should be thirty-four. There's a neotenite
missing. Oh, Mordecai!" He used the Specialists' oath.

"Well, *I* don't know anything about it."

"And neither do I. But the Cuidadors will think I do, after . . . after
that other business." He stared wildly at the empty shelves. "How can it
happen? Where has it gone? *When* did it go?"

"It could have happened anytime," said the nurse, rolling the last
neotenite onto a trolley. "I don't suppose anyone makes a regular count

of the inventory here. It's only come to light because we've used our entire stock. For all we know, the shortage could have existed for centuries."

"But how?" Brutus stared at the last neotenite. It lay on the trolley quietly, a slack mountain of flesh, twitching a little. It had never received any stimulation of any kind. It had been kept in a coma since the day of its creation, brain activity maintained at the minimum level consistent with life, body growing until it reached a length of approximately one and a half meters. It was physically male, but it was not aware of the fact. It would only become conscious of its sex when it received a standard brain imprint and its mind entered Dream Earth to continue the wild imaginings of the neotenite it had replaced.

"We'll have to report this to the Cuidadors," said the nurse.

Although Brutus towered over her, he seemed to have shrunk. He crouched in an almost animal posture, making washing motions with his hands. "Must we?"

"If we don't report it, you can be sure the Rainbow will."

"Mordecai!" Brutus glanced involuntarily at the monitor in a corner of the ceiling.

"Get it over with, Brutus," said the nurse kindly. "We'll all back you up. There's no reason for them to blame you. Now get along to the Rainbow Room and tell Zozula what's happened. He's a good man. He may even know how to ask the Rainbow where the neotenite went."

"Yes, he may," agreed Brutus quickly. "He may." He took a deep breath, inflating his enormous chest, quelling the shivering. He gave her an overbright smile. Murmuring reassurances to himself, he lumbered from the room.

✳

Brutus had hardly begun his explanations when Juni arrived. It was almost as though she sensed trouble.

"*Another* irregularity, Brutus?" she said coldly.

"It's no fault of Brutus's," Selena explained. "Just a simple mistake in data entry, I expect. I'll check with the records on the People Planet."

"It couldn't have been anything to do with the Girl, could it?" asked Zozula. "Perhaps we forgot to record her release, when we removed her mind from Dream Earth and woke her up."

"That's what it is," said Selena in relieved tones.

"No, it's not," said Brutus.

"Speak when you're spoken to, gorilla-man," said Juni.

"What do you mean, Brutus?" asked Zozula.

"I checked the Girl out myself."

Juni was gazing sourly at Brutus. "It's funny how these things always seem to happen when you're around."

"That's enough, Juni!" Selena rose to her feet. "Come on, Brutus. It's time we got back to the People Planet. We have a lot of work to do. We can't afford to waste time arguing about a lost neotenite when we've got a whole breeding program to accelerate. We'll lose more than one body if we don't hurry up and restock the hibernation room—we'll start losing the minds in Dream Earth!"

She hurried from the Rainbow Room, and Brutus trailed disconsolately after her. During the ten-minute trip to the shuttle station she was silent, and Brutus found himself glancing at her often, trying to gauge her mood. Her lips were pressed together and her memory potto seemed ill at ease. It was trying to groom Selena's hair—a sure sign that it was being affected by disturbing thoughts from its host. Brutus was not sorry when they reached the station and took their seats in the shuttle.

The shuttle was a total mystery to the Dome's inhabitants—all except the two Specialists, Akela and Verna, who operated it. Knowledge of the shuttle's working had been handed down from one fox-human generation to the next since time immemorial.

"Greetings, travelers," said Verna, sidling up to them and smiling too brightly, like a member of some Wild Human love cult. Brutus snorted.

"Greetings," snapped Selena.

"Oh, no—now that won't do," said Akela softly. "That won't do at all, Selena. The shuttle must have harmony. The vibrations must be sympathetic. The secret is serenity and love."

"Well, that's not the way I feel right now. Get on with it, you two."

"I'm afraid we just can't." Akela and Verna, male and female fox-humans, stood close together, almost rubbing against each other, smiling and murmuring, flashing each other looks of embarrassingly open adoration. "We wouldn't like to take the chance. We could find ourselves losing control of the shuttle somewhere out in the cold Greataway, all because of your hate-thoughts. And you wouldn't want that to happen, would you?"

"Look at the Helix," said Verna, unclipping the golden object so that it sprang upright, man-height, bouncing slightly. "See how dull it is?"

"And the Chain," added Akela. "It's like putty. It has no strength."

He held it up for them to see—long, silver and tinkling. "This would never protect you from the winds of the Greataway."

"Nonsense," said Selena. "Mystical claptrap. This is just an ordinary Space shuttle and you're the pilots. Now get going before I report you to Zozula."

Brutus, sitting in the back seat of the tiny cylindrical vehicle, groaned. It was terribly unwise for Selena to threaten the pilots. If they chose to withdraw their services, the People Planet would be cut off. And that would be the end of everything for the True Humans.

Akela and Verna had walked away, ignoring Selena, and were now stroking each other near the airlock that led Outside. Brutus spoke quietly to Selena.

"Forgive me. But we really should compose ourselves for the journey." And because Selena didn't seem to have heard, he touched her on the shoulder.

She started, staring at him wildly as though he was a stranger, threatening her. For an instant, far behind her eyes, there was a flash of something very like fear. The potto jumped, too, twittering.

"Sorry, sorry, sorry," muttered Brutus, snatching his hand away and scratching himself.

Selena closed her eyes and took a deep breath, then let it out shakily. "I'm sorry, too, Brutus," she said. "It's been a bad day. I must pull myself together." And when she opened her eyes, the strange expression was gone. Akela and Verna, sensing that she was under control, walked toward them with dancing steps. Verna took the Chain and began to encircle the small, enclosed vehicle with it . . .

Fifty thousand years previously, any psycaptain would have recognized the actions of Akela and Verna. They were a long-standing tradition, refined by years of practice and codified by the Psycaptains' Guild, but they had died out during the Age of Regression, becoming almost extinct with the planting of the Hate Bombs.

They were the trappings of the Outer Think.

The Song of Earth relates that the Outer Think fell into disuse at the time of the Hate Bombs, and this is substantially true. However, the Song of Earth does not relate that one tiny thread of vulpids carried the knowledge and traditions through fifty thousand years and countless generations, solely for the purpose of operating the shuttle between Earth and the People Planet. The True Humans of the time did not know that the Outer Think was being used. Because the shuttle looked something like an ancient three-dimensional Spaceship, they assumed that was what it was. The fact that it never required fuel did not concern them; they left such details to the ship's foxy custodians.

Now the vulpids, hand in hand, were repeating the Psycaptains' Apothegm:

> *Take the Silver and the Gold,*
> *Take the power of the mynde.*
> *Learning new and knowledge old,*
> *Greataway and hearts entwined . . .*

In years to come, the Song of Earth would relate that the Outer Think was rediscovered by Manuel, Zozula and the Girl when they defeated the Bale Wolves and removed the Hate Bombs. Such is the accepted view, and the existence of the vulpids should not be allowed to detract from the Triad's achievement. So far as the True Humans were concerned, the secret was lost. However, the vulpids were not the only people still to possess some of the old powers, as we shall see. There was, for instance, an Everling known as Loanna, living on the People Planet, who . . .

But that is in the Ifalong.

CREATURES OF THE PEOPLE PLANET

••

*S*elena left Brutus at the fork in the trail. Hunched against the rain, she climbed the hill toward Boss Castle, where she lived. Brutus, big hands thrust deep into the pockets of his rainwear, plodded downhill toward the baby factory.

Selena was a little puzzled. As usual, the shuttle had landed close to the array of monoliths known as Horst's Stones, and the fox-human pilots had made it clear that they could not—or would not—drop their passengers off any closer to the Castle. So it was going to be a long, cold and wet walk home.

However, just before the shuttle had touched down, there had been a rare break in the clouds, and the sun had illuminated the landscape so that Horst's Stones glittered like diamonds. And the perspective had been wrong. Instead of seeming to be *down there,* on the surface of the planet, the Stones had somehow appeared all around the shuttle, as though they were a vast three-dimensional complex of which she, Selena, was a part. She had a sense of *belonging* to something so huge that her mind was incapable of grasping it.

She decided to talk to Mentor about it. Mentor was the most understanding person she had ever met and the only other True Human resident on the People Planet.

The door slid open and, gratefully, she entered the warm, bright interior of Boss Castle. Allowing a caracal-girl to take her clothes off, she passed through the sonic shower and into her private room. As she entered, the old guilt returned, and with it the old breath-catching excitement.

Mentor took her in his arms.

He had no real name; somehow she'd never dared to give him one. To her he was simply Mentor, and had been for the past eighty years: her mentor, her companion, and her lover. She had taken him as a child and raised him—mothered him and taught him—and as time went by their relationship had undergone a slow reversal, so that now he was the counselor and advisor and she the uncertain one, eager for advice. After all, he was several hundred years younger than she, and he had no need of pottos. He had grasped the workings of her Rainbow terminal as a child. He was strong, healthy and skilled in the practice of the Inner Think. As he held her, the guilt faded. And as he carried her to their bed, guilt became meaningless, an instrument of self-torture that she could lay aside at any time. So, for a while, she immersed herself in the joy of reunion.

Afterward, one of the many facets of guilt returned.

"Mentor," she said. "Don't you get lonely while I'm away?"

He smiled at her. "I have the Rainbow and the caracal-girls. Why should I be lonely?"

"You're a True Human. You should be with other True Humans. But you've never even seen one, apart from me."

"Humans are humans," he said with naive wisdom.

"The caracal-girls are just . . . Specialists. Not that there's anything wrong with Specialists, but . . . Mentor, you're a real person and you have a mind of your own. Don't you ever feel you need some real, challenging True Human company? Don't you ever wonder what it's like on Earth?" *Say you don't want to know,* she thought. *Say I'm all you need.*

"The Rainbow provides more challenge than True Humans ever could. And the caracal-girls provide more fun."

What about me? "What about me?"

He kissed her gently. "You are all the True Human I need."

"You're only saying that. You probably think the caracal-girls are better. All I can say is, you'd better watch out for those caracal-men. They may be small, but they're vicious brutes."

"Selena, Selena. You've only just got back."

Just a touch of the Inner Think, and she laughed. "Sorry, Mentor. I'm just a silly old Cuidador who can't believe she's so lucky. If they ever took you away from me, I don't know what I'd do."

"They'll never find me, so they'll never take me."

Selena bit her lip. "Brutus discovered a shortage among the standby neotenites today. It's just possible he could follow it through, if he felt like it. There could be some awkward questions."

"You've always told me what a good man Brutus is. Surely he wouldn't cause trouble?"

"At one time I'd have said he wouldn't, but now he resents me. I'm frightened that if he ever found out about you, he might do anything!"

"Calm down, my love. How could he possibly resent you?"

So she told him the terrible story of how Brutus, full of love, had been unable to recycle the neotenite babies; how for generations he and his ancestors had been setting the babies free to drift down the river Outside in little boats, hoping some kindly Wild Humans would find them and care for them; how, in the gorilla-peoples' minds, anything was better than feeding living, crying little babies into a recycling machine.

"Mordecai!" murmured Mentor. "The poor man."

"I felt so sorry for him. But I had to reprimand him in front of the Cuidadors. What else could I do? Juni wanted to recycle *him.*"

"I'm glad I've never met Juni," said Mentor.

She hugged him. Then, as often happened, she found herself gazing over his shoulder at a picture on the opposite wall. It was a portrait of a young girl with an intelligent, lively face; a small plate attached to the frame bore the simple caption SHE. Four other paintings hung on the walls of Selena's quarters, all of the same girl, but all completely different in execution, as though the artist had been experimenting with styles, using the same model.

Yet the artist had no model. He was an Everling. In over twenty-six thousand years of exile on the People Planet, he had seen no True Human woman apart from Selena. He had painted the same girl, over and over again, several hundred times. Selena looked at the picture. She'd always wondered who this mystery girl was; now, for the first time, she could see something familiar in that pretty face. She decided she must visit Joe, the artist, as soon as possible. The Everlings' latest creative cycle was coming to an end, and she was looking forward to seeing Joe's latest portrait. In the past, each one had been slightly different from the last, slightly improved, as though a real character was forming behind the pigments. The last SHE was a perfect work of art. Could Joe possibly have improved on it?

She would have to see him soon, because each of the Everlings' thirty-year cycles of creative activity was terminated by an orgy of destruction.

She must save SHE from the fate of all the other artwork. They were a curious race, the Everlings.

Indeed, everything about the People Planet would seem curious to a visitor from Earth. It was a rain-sodden world with just one island large enough to support life, where creatures of various types lived.

Of the Second Species of Man—those who called themselves True Humans—there were only two: Selena and Mentor.

Of the Third Species, the animal-people created long ago in the laboratories of Mordecai N. Whirst, there were many.

Of the Fourth Species, the neotenites, there was a fluctuating number. They were produced at regular intervals—and just as regularly shipped off to Earth for recycling, because rules concerning births and deaths were very rigid on the People Planet. If a count were not strictly kept, the Specialists would be smuggling them into their homes and raising them.

Of the Sixth Species, the Everlings, there were eighty-three.

And finally there was the creature that the Specialists lived to serve. Hua-hi was its name, and it was a giant aquatic mammal created by the kikihuahuas. It was a gift to Mankind from those tiny, kindly aliens, designed for the complex needs of the breeding program.

There was a time, before the moment of our story, when certain humans became skeptical about the integrity of the kikihuahuas. Here were these aliens (they said) who were reputed to be totally good, who never killed a living creature, who existed only to help others, who never even used metal or fire or any other sharp cruel element; instead, who gently created other animals to help them—from the Space-bats, with their thousand-kilometer wingspan, to the tiny sapas that wove cloth for the beautiful Ana.

"So how can you create new life-forms," the skeptics asked, "without vats and tubes and generators and wires? Even the great Mordecai N. Whirst, who created the Specialists, needed vats."

The answer, as humans eventually discovered, lay in the Beast with Two Mouths, which the kikihuahuas called the Hua-hi.

Before human history began, the Hua-hi was a terrified little running animal on a world called Ach. The Hua-hi had many enemies, but it also was a predator in its own right and chased and ate creatures smaller and weaker than itself, which likewise hunted smaller creatures still. There were no plants on Ach, and at the bottom of the food chain sat tiny flightless mosquitoes, carpeting the ground and drawing nourishment from the soil through threadlike probes.

By the time the kikihuahuas arrived on Ach, there were seventy-two basic species of predator, evolved through the ages, and one oddity, the Hua-hi. The Hua-hi had not evolved by natural selection. Instead, it absorbed the best survival characteristics of its prey and passed them on to its young. At first the kikihuahuas thought that the fifty or so varieties of Hua-hi were different species, because they were so disparate in size, appearance and behavior. Only years of observation enabled them to distinguish true, evolved creatures from Hua-hi imitations, and to realize that the Hua-hi, dissimilar though individuals might be, was a single asexual species.

When a Hua-hi killed its prey, it ate most of it in the normal manner. But a small part was ingested through a separate orifice, the maga. The tissues were broken down and analyzed, and their best genetic survival characteristics were stored until a Hua-hi decided it was time to give birth. Then they were used, and each child of a Hua-hi emerged a different creature from its parent.

The kikihuahuas found that the Hua-hi was well on the way to becoming the dominant predator on Ach, because it was gaining the ability to kill animals larger than itself, and even to prey on its own species—a habit that gave it the prospect of achieving almost infinite savagery. The kikihuahuas, kindly creatures, shivered . . .

But later, when the kikihuahuas began to develop their Examples and to shun the use of fire and metal, they remembered the Hua-hi. They brought a Hua-hi into their society and showed it their ways, meanwhile keeping it safely confined. In due course a heroic kikihuahua called Ahia sacrificed himself to the Hua-hi, which then produced an intelligent and gentle offspring and died.

To the Hua-hi's offspring they brought another creature, a telepathic bat-thing called Sa. With Sa as a medium, they set up scenarios in the Hua-hi's imagination: mind-pictures of the Greataway and of other worlds, and of the needs of the kikihuahuas. The Hua-hi would go into a trance while it "believed" the scenario, whereupon the kikihuahuas would feed it selections of desirable genetic material.

Thus the Hua-hi was persuaded that the creation of certain life-forms —those the kikihuahuas wanted it to create—was essential to the survival of its species. Sometimes a growth factor was added; in this manner the Space-bats and the beacon hydras were created. When the Hua-hi began to age, it was easily persuaded that death was undesirable, so it produced an immortal duplicate of itself.

The telepathic Sa lived and died, but the Hua-hi lived on, helping the kikihuahuas to fulfill their Examples. Sometime around the 110th millennium Cyclic, when Earth appealed for help in its breeding program, the kikihuahuas produced a Hua-hi suitable for the People Planet. Then they drifted off into the Greataway in their Space-bats, immune from the Hate Bombs because of the physical nature of their travel. By the time the Cuidadors discovered that their human genetic material was imperfect, it was too late to recall the kikihuahuas.

THE BEAST WITH TWO MOUTHS

•••

*T*hey say you were disgraced," said Alice the next day. "Is it true?"

"It's true," muttered Brutus, examining the birth tubes of the ocean cow where they projected through the thick transparent wall of the delivery room. On the other side he could see the hide of the vast creature itself, stirring slightly with the waves as it lolled on the continental shelf.

"Why didn't you tell me you were trying to save the lives of those babies? I'm your wife, aren't I? Do you think I wouldn't have approved?"

Brutus sighed and faced this woman of surpassing ugliness with whom he spent his days and nights. "I didn't want to involve you. It's been going on for generations—my father and his father. It's a man's problem. A man's secret."

"Mordecai!" Alice roared, her voice carrying to the far reaches of the chamber and causing distant dolphin-people to look up from their work. "Only men could be such fools! Don't you realize every Specialist on the People Planet would have been behind you, male or female? Don't you know how our people feel? Don't you understand how we prize children —we, above all other humans!"

"It's our code."

"It's more than our code! It's in our genes and it's in our laws, and in the True Human laws, too. Why do you think the True Humans restrict our ability to have children, Brutus?"

"Well, to keep the population down, of course. We're hardly self-supporting. Most of our food is shipped up from Earth."

"That just shows how much you know. They curb our own natural instincts so we'll have more time for *their* children, don't you see? The whole Specialist population on this planet is conditioned to love True Human children, Brutus. You can't be blamed for what you did. True Humans made you that way!"

Brutus sighed again. Three of the birth tubes were swollen and pink-tipped, signifying the imminent arrival of babies. Behind the wall the ocean cow pulsed with muscular contractions, green-grey and immense, longer than the half kilometer–long window.

"We've been through all this before," he said.

"Well, you're going to hear a lot more. The people are furious, and there was a meeting this morning. They say the True Humans have disgraced us all by reprimanding you. Any one of us would have done what you did. We're going to be taking some action, Brutus, believe me!"

"I hope not," said Brutus quietly.

He was saved further discussion by the arrival of a baby. Outside the window, a birth tube thickened suddenly and a bell rang. They hurried down the chamber, and Alice, with surprising gentleness in one of such ferocious appearance, took the tube, which more than anything resembled a green elephant's trunk, in her hands. Rippling contractions convulsed it as the bulge moved through a grommet where the tube passed through the window. Alice gripped the end of the tube tightly, so that it would not damage itself lashing about. Other Specialists arrived at a run: raccoon-nurses and delphids, pushing trolleys. Rhythmically thrusting, the tube pushed the bulge toward Alice's hands. A nurse was murmuring a ritual prayer.

The baby was born.

It was a tiny sexless human, but whether it was a True Human or destined to become a neotenite, only time would tell. It lay in Alice's huge hands, coughed, and cried. There was no umbilical cord, no blood. By human count, it was already two weeks old. Selena would give it a sex if it was True Human—which was very unlikely.

"Good luck, little one," said Alice, laying it gently on a trolley.

Then she looked at Brutus. "Our people look on you as their leader," she said. "Did you know that?"

✳

Brutus, moved as ever by the birth of a baby, hurried away before she could see the tears in his eyes. Confused emotions caused him to mumble to himself and he barged heedlessly through a door, almost knocking over a young dolphin-girl. Yelling some apology—too loudly—he raced up the stairs. *I am not a leader,* he told himself. *I do not want to lead. We are a team with a job, we Specialists. We do not need a leader. The laws are enough.*

He paused, greatly embarrassed by what he was shortly to do. He leaned his massive fists on a window ledge and stared across the endless, storm-ridden sea of the People Planet. The baby factory consisted of a series of interlinked caverns. Southward the caverns became smaller and tunneled up to small outcropping rooms and entrances. Here people lived, a few hundred Specialists in a tiny and strictly regulated society. When the True Humans decided that a bloodline was becoming too inbred, they shipped up fresh Specialist stock from Earth.

Somewhere at the back of Brutus's mind was a feeling of vast injustice . . .

He watched the heavy rollers that smashed into the cliff fifty meters below. Occasionally they left a trough low enough to reveal some part of the ocean cow, looking like an encrusted reef. Half a kilometer north lay an island that was the creature's breathing apparatus, a knobby projection spouting a steamy spray. Brutus pounded his fists on the stone ledge, grunted, wheeled round and opened the door of the Records Office.

The long-faced clerk looked up. "Ah. Brutus. I . . . I'd like to tell you how sorry . . ."

"Yes—I can't understand how everyone got to hear about that so soon," said Brutus hurriedly. "Anyway, that's not what I came about. I want to see the production records."

"You *what?*" The horse-man's sympathy evaporated.

Brutus explained the discrepancy in the Dome. "The inventory was short one neotenite."

"I can assure you my records are in perfect order." The clerk's neck lengthened as he stared at Brutus in outrage.

"Well, *somehow or other,*" said Brutus forcefully, "there's been a mistake, and I'm not going to take the blame."

"Nobody's blaming you."

"I'm going to get to the bottom of it. There's a body missing and I need to know why." He moved close to the horse-man, overpowering him with his presence. It was against his nature to threaten, but it was the only way to get cooperation.

"If there's a body missing, then, by Mordecai, we must find it," agreed the clerk quickly, horny fingers prodding at his console. The screen lit up. Figures trotted across it like mounting arguments. Clone bank accumulations were checked with usage. Stocks on hand were checked with physical counts. Usage was checked with birth counts. "See, there's nothing wrong," said the clerk.

"Earlier years, please."

The headings changed. *143,622. 143,621. 143,620.*

"Just search for discrepancies," said Brutus.

There were none. *143,427. 143,426 . . . 143,000.*

"That's enough," said Brutus. He didn't know whether to be relieved or not. "Perhaps a baby died once, and they covered it up for some reason." Perhaps a Specialist-nurse was to blame.

"We haven't finished yet," said the horse-man slyly.

"It couldn't have been more than five hundred years ago. It would have been discovered."

"It could have been quite recent," said the horse-man, "if the gene material didn't come from the clone bank."

"Where else could it have come from?"

"It could have been fresh tissue. There have been certain experiments in the past . . ."

"Show me."

Now the record of births was checked against the record of shipments to Earth, and Brutus, fingers twisting, watched the screen intently.

143,600. 143,550. 143,545 . . .

"Stop!"

143,545.

"Please leave me alone for a while," said Brutus.

"But . . ."

"Do what I say."

Clearly disappointed, the clerk left. Brutus played at the keys, his big fingers surprisingly nimble. His heart was thumping. 143,545. Discrepancy—one child. Why had no one noticed before? Because it was not listed as a discrepancy—it was shown as a shipment, but not to Earth. That baby had been transferred within the People Planet, to . . .

Selena!

What had she done with it? And, perhaps most significant, why had she wanted it? Brutus played with the keys. He dipped into forgotten intricacies of the Rainbow, he discovered ancient programs, he unlocked forgotten memory banks. And he found the answer.

"Oh, Mordecai," he whispered.

*

So the bewilderment changed to understanding, and after a while, the understanding changed to a slow anger. Selena knew the answer. Selena knew that Earth was one neotenite short, and that it had been for almost eighty years. But when the discrepancy had come to light—when the assembled Cuidadors had turned accusing eyes on Brutus—Selena had not spoken. She had sat by, secure in her position as a True Human, and allowed suspicion to surround Brutus like an animal stink.

Brutus growled.

In the Song of Earth, as in all of Mankind's legends, revenge is accepted as natural; the ability to harbor a grudge and act upon it is something that distinguishes humans from animals. Only in everyday life is revenge condemned. Yet Brutus the animal-man thought of revenge, that day.

He had two courses open to him. The first concerned Selena and the lost baby. The second was more far-reaching, and it had the additional advantage that he could change his mind at any time. So Brutus, full of mighty rage, chose the second course.

He would physically remove the data crystal dealing with the early days of the neotenites, effectively preventing the True Humans from learning about this period and—possibly—finding a cure for neoteny. He, Brutus, would call a halt to neoteny research until he felt good and ready to allow the True Humans to continue . . .

He could almost hear the Rainbow creak as it dealt with the unfamiliar instructions. Brutus was no genius, but he knew his way around this section of the Rainbow better than any Cuidador. And it crossed his mind that nobody had researched neotenite history before because nobody possessed the necessary computer skills. Whatever the reason, the neotenites were still neotenites, and Brutus intended to make sure they stayed that way for a while.

The Rainbow gave the location of the data crystal.

Brutus left the room accompanied by the horse-clerk, who by now was almost prancing with curiosity and frustration. He made his way to the vaults.

"What are you looking for?" asked the clerk, as Brutus touched his fingers to the codepad and the door swung open. Now the clerk was whinnying with excitement; Brutus and Selena were the only people on the planet with authority to enter the Rainbow's innermost parts. Afraid of being excluded, he crowded Brutus through the doorway. "What's happening? What's going on?"

"Stay here." Brutus walked on, entering the memory bank, where over

35,000 memory crystals, containing everything that had happened on the People Planet since it was founded, sat in rows like bright and perfect teeth, occasionally glowing and winking when the Rainbow, in its endless deliberations, called on one for data. Brutus began to search the earlier crystals, running a thick finger along the rows, lips moving. Soon he found the century he was looking for, then the decade.

And there was one crystal missing.

It could not be coincidence. The cube for the year 108,285 Cyclic, which the Rainbow had defined as being crucial to the history of the neotenites, had been removed . . .

Only one person could have done that. Selena.

Therefore she must have outguessed him and taken the crystal for safekeeping.

His anger changing swiftly to guilt, Brutus rushed for the exit, almost bowling over the horse-man, who had crept forward to peer over his shoulder. "Tell nobody we were here!" he growled. "Nobody at all. Do you understand?" He seized the clerk by his loose tunic and stared ferociously into his eyes.

"I understand, Brutus," replied the clerk.

Brutus was about to re-emphasize his warning, when the bells started ringing, and in his remorse he uttered a sudden roar that caused the horse-man to scream with fright, thinking he was about to be attacked. For an instant they clung to each other, struggling and bellowing.

Then Brutus tore himself free and ran for the stairs.

✳

Alice met him in the delivery room. She was talking wildly. ". . . you weren't here, you see, and I couldn't hold it—I didn't have the strength." She was weeping, her huge face wet and crumpled like a crushed fruit.

"What happened?" And then he saw.

One of the birth tubes was missing. The ocean cow had dragged it through the great window, and the grommet had snapped shut. Water seeped to the floor. "That's no big problem," he said. "Somebody can go out and guide it back through. We've done it before."

"But . . ." She pointed speechlessly.

Outside, the tentacle waved aimlessly in the surging green of the ocean. Beyond it, through the mist of silt and plankton, Brutus could see the bulk of the cow. It was moving, turning. Slowly, it was rolling away from the caves of the baby factory. The other birth tubes were stretched taut.

Nurses were clamoring. "It's pulling away from us!" one of them cried, seizing Brutus's clothing. She was a delphid, but for once she was not smiling. "Do something, Brutus! We'll lose it!"

"I don't understand," Brutus muttered, scratching himself wildly. "It has no reason. It can't be hungry. And it's in the process of giving births." He collected his thoughts. "Unless it's in pain." He peered through the window.

A few meters away, close to the limits of visibility, he saw a bulge in the loose birth tube. A series of muscular spasms radiated from the bulge across the expanse of the hide, like ripples in a lake.

"That's it," said Brutus. "It's a difficult birth. The baby is stuck." The next thought was completely automatic. "I must go out there and free it."

"Not you," said Alice.

But Brutus was hurrying away from her, out of the delivery room, making for the waterlock and shouting for a delphid to follow him.

As the endless flank of the ocean cow slid past him, his mind was still on Selena and the way she'd allowed Juni to blame him for the missing child. He saw Selena in his mind's eye, slim and elegant—which his Alice was not—and, usually, kind and fair-minded—which Alice was. Many times, Selena had shielded him from Juni's cruel shafts. Even on that dreadful occasion when he'd been discovered in the Dome's lower reaches floating the neotenite babies Outside in little boats, Selena had tried to be fair.

So why had she not admitted to taking that baby? After all, it had happened eighty years ago. Presumably she'd wanted it for purposes of research and it had died. That was sad, but not criminal. So why not admit it?

Brooding, cocooned in his pressure suit, Brutus swam downward. He was alone. The delphid, who could hold his breath for half an hour, needed no suit and had gone on ahead. They would try to get the end of the birth tube back through the grommet so that the baby could be born in the delivery room.

The ocean cow shifted perceptibly, narrowing the gap as Brutus swam between the creature and the cliff. Soon the window of the delivery room came into view. Faces crowded against it, mouthing soundlessly. He saw Alice looking scared and chewing her knuckles. He passed the first birth tube; it was stretched slender. Watching it go through the grommet, he saw that the nurses had gotten ropes around the tip and were pulling.

Other teams hauled at other similar ropes down the length of the delivery room. It was a futile exercise. Out here, he was very much aware of the vast bulk of the cow. If it decided to roll, nothing would hold it. As he watched, he saw teams of shrugleggers being led into the room. They were quickly harnessed to the ropes, backs to the window. They leaned into their work, their muscular thighs straining.

The delphid tapped him on the arm, pointing. A tube hung loose, thrashing, and the bulge of the baby was halfway to the tip. Now a new worry seized Brutus. The obstruction seemed to have cleared itself, but unless they got the tube back through the grommet, the baby would be born underwater and would drown.

The tip slapped him across the side of the head and, spinning, he caught it. The delphid swam up and got an arm around the tube. Together they tried to maneuver the tip toward the grommet. Brutus shouted soundless encouragement into his helmet. The tip touched the grommet, then jerked away. The strength of the tube was fearsome. It lashed sideways and rammed Brutus against the window, squeezing the breath out of him. He shook his head, gasping, hoping the helmet's tiny oxygenator had not been damaged.

Then the wall of the ocean cow rolled in toward him, pinning him against the window, upside down.

He got his knife against the cow's hide and pushed, but he might as well have tried to stab Azul Dome itself. The cow was like a smooth rock, insensitive to localized discomforts. His legs trapped, Brutus yelled into his helmet.

The delphid swam below him, gesticulating in the dark tunnel formed by the ocean cow and the cliff.

Apart from its one free tentacle, the cow was comfortable again, lolling up against the window with birth tubes hanging limply inside. That free tentacle flapped past Brutus's face and he caught it, hoping it might pull him free. But it too went limp, giving one last spasm.

And a baby floated before Brutus's face.

The Song of Earth makes much of this moment. The minstrels sing of the trapped Brutus, symbol of compassion and one of the great heroes of all time, picturing him as some kind of dumb animal whose actions were governed by instincts of beauty and purity, picturing him as anything but what he was: a Specialist of average decency with admittedly, a strong sense of duty and a love of children—but above all, an intelligent man.

Gorilla-man, gorilla-man, what terror holds you
*   now?*
Scream you now for someone else beside the ocean
*   cow?*

And the listeners draw near, wide-eyed and wondering, awaiting the minstrel's next words, knowing the outcome because the song has been sung a million times, yet every time seeing it afresh in their mind's eye: the green surging water, the mountainous ocean cow, the tunnel formed by the cow and the cliff, the simple man pinned upside down, and the baby.

✳

Brutus thought of the Greataway and the places far beyond Earth and the People Planet. He thought of something the Rainbow had told him, one cool day of autumn when he was exploring the memory banks and he came upon the story of the Hate Bombs and the humans trapped on the far side of them, unable ever to return. He wondered if perhaps they thought it was Earth that was trapped, because *they* were still free to explore the whole Universe if they wished.

He thought of another day when he'd been unhappy and restless and he'd wandered the tiny confines of the island and found himself among Horst's Stones. He'd heard a footstep and turned quickly, expecting a gang of playful Everlings to mob him with their small bodies, prepared to defend himself without hurting them if possible. But it had been an old woman, a stranger in a cloak that clothed her like night.

"I want to tell you about the Ifalong . . ." she had said.

She had spoken of the Galaxy and the Hate Bombs, and of a mighty creature she called Starquin. She had told Brutus he was a necessary element in a great Purpose, and that he should do certain things and make certain choices. In particular, she said, he should act with great compassion when faced with certain problems.

Brutus thought of the babies in the little boats and the reprimand he had received.

"And above all," the woman had said, "you must protect your own life, because you are essential to the Purpose. On some happentracks you will die, and it is important that those happentracks be few."

Brutus thought of Selena and the breeding program, and of all those years since there had been a True Human born, and of the slimness of chances. He wondered what the point of it all was, striving after an ancient form when quite obviously the human race had evolved beyond that form.

And the baby's mouth opened as it tried to take its first breath.

With a mighty shrug, Brutus got his hands around his helmet and ripped it off. He held it right way up and it filled with air, beginning to spill bubbles from the bottom edge. He took the baby and put it into the helmet. Then he handed the baby and helmet to the delphid.

The delphid, expressionless, began the half-kilometer journey along the tunnel to the waterlock.

✳

And? asked the listeners.

On many happentracks, the minstrels tell how the baby became the first True Human born for many years: a child of surpassing brilliance who singlehandedly solved the neoteny problem, analyzed and removed the Hate Bombs and freed the Almighty Starquin to roam the Greataway once more.

The minstrels tell that because that is how the legend goes. Such an act of heroism as Brutus performed must have been successful, otherwise his death would have been in vain and the whole legend would have had little point. And—such is the infinite nature of the Ifalong—on a few happentracks the minstrels were right.

But on most happentracks they were far from the truth.

THE DAY OF DESTRUCTION

Out with the old and in with the new.
There's only so much that an artist can do.
— Cyclic Everling adage

*T*he horse-clerk had smiled ingratiatingly. "As I understand it, Brutus discovered one of the data crystals was missing. He left only a moment ago—didn't you hear the alarm?"

"I'm sure Brutus is capable of dealing with any emergency," Selena had said coldly. She didn't like the clerk; of all the Specialists, the horse-people were the one race she could say she disliked en masse. They were small-minded, unintelligent and sly. They were, however, very good at their jobs. And now, she guessed, this wretched long-faced man was implying she ought to leave him alone and go and check on the delivery room.

"Perhaps you should—"

"Which crystal was missing?"

"Brutus made it very clear that he wanted nobody to be told about this—"

"You've already told me, you fool. And I'm in charge of this Station, remember? *Which crystal?*"

"It seemed to be around the early part of the hundred and ninth millennium," the man had said sulkily.

So, like Brutus a short while before, Selena had found her investigations into neotenite history blocked at the crucial year. She'd played with the Rainbow for a while but, lacking Brutus's skill and unwilling to ask the clerk for help, she had been unable to establish the significance of the year 108,285—or even to call up the events of the preceding years.

Frustrated, she had decided to take Mentor's advice. She would ask the Everlings if they remembered anything about that period.

It was a bad time to visit the Everlings.

As Selena dismounted from her shruglegger, she could already hear the yells of satisfaction as the immortal children rampaged through their village, indulging in one of their insensate periods of destruction. As she hesitated, a small deerlike creature appeared from behind a corrugated-iron shed. It was beautiful and graceful, and there was fear in its wide eyes as it stepped along quietly, obviously hoping to reach the safety of the hills. It glanced at Selena in passing, a long-lashed timid look that tore at her heart. Then a sudden yell of discovery made it bound forward.

"Come here, you bugger!"

A child ran round the corner of the shed, grinning ferociously and brandishing a club. "Got you, hah!" he shouted, chasing after the deer and leaping nimbly over the heaps of accumulated garbage, the wrecked statues, half-finished vehicles and mysterious, incomprehensible inventions that littered the landscape of the Everlings' territory.

The tiny deer bounded into Selena's arms and huddled there, trembling.

"Give me that!" The Everling's face crumpled in frustration. "It's mine!"

"Do you have to destroy it? It's such a beautiful thing."

"Well, *I* made it."

In reasonable tones, Selena said, "But it has freewill. It doesn't *want* to be killed. Can't you see that? I don't want you to kill it, either. It's one of the nicest things you Everlings have ever made."

"All the more reason to destroy it!" So saying, the child reached up and dragged the little creature from Selena's grasp. Throwing it to the ground, he swung his club in a powerful arc, catching the deer on the shoulder and splitting it open. Delicate electronic components spilled out. The next blow tore into the mechanical parts—the wires and cogs, spindles and chains. Screaming wordlessly, the child jumped up and down on the remains, kicking and stamping, reducing the deer to unrecognizable wreckage, scuffing the brown pelt into the mud.

Only the head remained. "Now," gloated the Everling. He raised his club, paused for an anticipatory second, then brought it down with such force that his feet left the ground.

The head split open and Selena uttered a little scream of dismay. Blood and pale organic matter splattered her cloak. "It's . . . it's got a brain! How could you *do* this?"

"We're very clever people," said the child, suddenly still. He seemed abashed, ashamed of what he had done, as he stirred the remains with his toe. "Oh, what the hell," he muttered. Then he brightened up. "Jacko's got a Crystal Palace to pull down," he confided. "He says he'll let me help him."

"You're Tom, aren't you? How long has this destruction been going on?"

"We started this morning. It's taken me all this time to catch my deer. I'm through with organic stuff for a few cycles, I can tell you, Selena."

"I'm very pleased to hear it."

"Jenny's been breeding electronic guinea pigs. You should see the little buggers go! We've been mostly into livestock, this last cycle. It makes a change from pure art. Nature is Art, anyway—so Georg said a few hundred years back."

"*Breeding* electronic guinea pigs?"

"You want to see? I don't think she's smashed them yet. Come with me!" He took her hand and led her into the village.

The Everlings' village consisted of a single street of tumble-down buildings that looked as though they had been dumped there by the last hurricane. All manner of construction materials were used, but the principal ingredient seemed to be flattened works of art. Selena saw a crushed copper shield used as a door; it had been inlaid with a ceramic design and some remnants of its beauty could still be discerned. A window was framed with a picture frame, wonderfully carved and decorated with peeling gold leaf. Selena couldn't help but wonder about the painting that once sat in that frame, and to lament its destruction.

"Better wait," said Tom suddenly.

A large statue stood at the end of the street. It was in heroic Greek style, a perfectly proportioned nude male in full color, with a victor's crown of leaves, holding a bow, a quiver slung across his back. It was in the act of reaching for an arrow, frozen in a timeless moment of grace. Selena felt tears prick her eyes as she looked at it. *This* was the True Human form. *This* was what the Cuidador's duty was all about. Just for a moment, the clouds parted and the sun shone, and the statue appeared to be bathed in glory, glowing against the backdrop of the angry sea.

"Ned spent fifteen years on that," said Tom reverently.

"It's beautiful."

"And that's not all."

There was a sound of trumpets. By now all the Everlings had gathered in the street, watching the statue. This was clearly a big event. Unhappily, Selena waited for the beautiful creation to explode, or melt, or whatever childish fate the Everlings had in mind. The trumpets called again.

The statue's arm moved. Slowly, gracefully, it reached behind its back and grasped an arrow. The crowd hushed. The arrow was drawn out smoothly and, with precision, fitted to the bow. Muscles tensed, perfectly proportioned, perfectly realistic. The string was drawn back. For an instant the statue was motionless, sighting along the arrow at some distant, unknown target. Selena held her breath. The suspense in the onlookers was almost palpable.

The strong fingers released the string; the sudden twang was shocking.

The arrow shot backward. It struck the hero in the groin. For the first time, Selena saw that the genitals were oversize, out of proportion. The arrow lodged there, quivering.

There was a single yelp of laughter from an onlooker, quickly hushed.

The statue swung its body, tilted its head, looking down at itself. Its lips moved.

"Oh, bugger it," said the statue.

Meanwhile, a group of Everlings scattered, leaving behind a richly detailed bronze cannon from which a wisp of smoke trailed. While the crowd was still rocking with laughter, the cannon roared, and Selena caught a glimpse of a large ball catching the statue squarely in the buttocks and propelling it off the plinth. Yelling realistically, it lurched forward, clutching itself front and rear, staggered to the edge of the cliff and fell out of sight.

By now many of the crowd were rolling in the mud in agonies of laughter. "That's the best ever!" cried Tom, tears flowing down his cheeks.

Losing control for quite a different reason, Selena snapped, "It's the most disgusting thing I've ever seen!"

"Eh?"

"Mocking the True Human form. Don't you have any respect for—" Her next words were unheard as the cannon itself exploded, filling the air with whizzing shrapnel and causing the few members of the audience who were still standing to fling themselves to the ground. "It's so childish!" said Selena from her prone position.

"Well," retorted Tom viciously, "we *are* children, and we always will be, and ask yourselves who were the buggers that made us this way?"

"But you're intelligent people, Tom."

"That has nothing to do with our fun."

"Your idea of fun is too destructive for my tastes."

"Oh, is it?" His face was twisted with malice as he jumped to his feet. "Too destructive, is it? Well, let's get on with it, shall we? I was going to show you Jenny's guinea pigs. I'll guarantee you won't find *them* destructive."

With some foreboding, Selena followed Tom into a nearby shack, where a small urchin sat. Clearly, Jenny had not been watching the exhibition in the street. All around the walls of her shack stood gleaming machinery, but the only item Selena could recognize was a computer keyboard. On the dirty floor lay a mess of broken machinery, which Jenny, sitting on a rough chair, was rhythmically pounding with a mallet.

"You've smashed them all," said Tom, disappointed.

She flashed him a guilty look from dark eyes.

"You haven't?" Tom brightened. "Selena here would like to see them breed."

Slowly Jenny rose and from a cupboard took two small creatures. She laid them on the floor. They sniffed around, noses twitching. "I was going to smash these, too," said Jenny. "I really was."

"Is there anything . . . organic in them?" asked Selena cautiously.

"No."

The guinea pigs were now sniffing each other. Tom uttered a little sneeze of laughter. Jenny glanced at him gravely, pulling a box out from under a bench. The box was full of minuscule glittering things. The guinea pigs sniffed the box. They stood on their hind legs to look inside, then dropped back to all fours, regarding each other stonily.

Then abruptly they reared up and, prancing on hind legs, sang in tinny little voices:

> *We're two little guinea pigs all alone.*
> *We have no food and we have no home.*
> *All the same we're full of joy,*
> *'Cos I'm a girl and he's a boy!*

The last line rose to a squeal of triumph and the guinea pigs scrambled into the box and began to forage among the tinkling objects. Picking up tiny tools in nimble fingers, they set to work in a blur of motion, singing all the while:

> *Screw little guinea pigs, screw all day.*
> *Screw at work and screw at play.*
> *Screw for the future, screw for the fun,*
> *Screw for the good of everyone!*

"It's an allegory," said Tom, suddenly grave. "It could be one of the most powerful works the Everlings have produced. Almost a pity it has to be destroyed."

Selena watched, her lips tightly compressed, saying nothing. It had become clear what the guinea pigs were doing. With incredible rapidity they were constructing duplicates of themselves from the components in the box. Soon they were finished. They rose on hind legs and began to dance again. To an accompaniment of tinkling and smashing components, they sang:

> *Four little guinea pigs learning fast,*
> *How to make resources last.*
> *Crawl into a Dome and start anew,*
> *And if things get worse we can always screw!*

Now the box was a whirl of activity as the four guinea pigs duplicated themselves and, having done so, spilled out of the box while they assembled a creditable miniature of Dome Azul. All this time the relentless chorus hammered at Selena's ears until, to her fury, she found her foot was tapping with the beat. *Screw for the good of everyone!* Then the dancing resumed.

> *Sixteen guinea pigs full of cheer.*
> *Getting a little crowded here.*
> *Hate Bombs above and Hate Bombs below,*
> *Blasters at the ready to exterminate the foe!*

"I suppose that's all," said Selena grimly.

"There's more," said Tom. And there was. The jingling chorus had resumed, and the guinea pigs were working again. Selena backed away as a furry tide spread in ripples toward her. Menacing little globes materialized in midair. By the time their chorus had reached "Screw for the future, screw for the fun," it was almost deafening, like an advancing army of starving rats.

Soon the guinea pigs had finished their work. They covered a large portion of the floor, but now they were moving much more slowly. Due to their dancing and trampling, many of their number had been constructed of damaged components. Some lay motionless, and the final verse assumed the quality of a dirge.

> *Two-fifty-six little guinea pigs now.*
> *We'd like to sail the Greataway but we've*
>   *forgotten how.*
> *Some are dumb neotenites and all are under stress,*
> *If screwing's not the remedy, then please clean up*
>   *this mess.*

With this, the guinea pigs self-destructed, collapsing in little explosions of components. The tiny Hate Bombs fell and burst open, and the Dome fell in. Within seconds the floor was carpeted with small parts and Jenny was sweeping them together, glancing shyly at Selena from under a lock of lank hair.

"You do understand," said Tom.

"More than you think," said Selena tightly. "But what I don't understand is what's got into you people, this last cycle. I remember when I looked forward to my visits to the Everling village because of the works of art I'd see. You'd be creating poetry, literature, music, paintings—beautiful things. And you did it all for the pure love of creating. But now . . ."

"We're going through a period of social comment," said Tom sulkily. "The purpose of Art changes. True Humans aren't handling things well. We're pointing it out through our Art."

"Garbage!" Selena found herself trembling with temper and struggled to control herself. "What you're hitting at is not True Humans. It's *sex*—and there's no way you can say True Humans invented that. Everything I've seen since I arrived has been aimed at degrading sex—because we can experience it and you can't. Well, too bad. But you can keep your nasty, sniggering little jealousies to yourselves from now on. I don't have to see it."

"But Selena—"

"And another thing!"

"There's more?"

"Instead of creating for the love of it, you've started creating for the fun of smashing. These works of art are no better than firecrackers—all the excitement is in watching them destroy themselves. Do you know what will happen next? You'll lose all your artistic ability because you've forgotten that love and art can't be separated, whereas love and sex can!"

"We lose our ability at the end of every creative half-cycle, every sixty years. But it comes back."

"The time will come when it doesn't come back," said Selena angrily. "And what will be the point of your existence then? What will you do, for the rest of Time?"

✳

It had been sixty years since she'd seen Joe, and her memory potto had to prompt her several times as she climbed into the hills behind the village, following the twisting trails. A cold wind swept in from the sea, driving the rain into her clothing and soaking her, chilling her to the bone. Above her, the towering form of one of Horst's Stones pointed starkly at the sky. She found its permanence reassuring after the rampant destruction in the village—but whether it could be considered Art, she doubted.

She found Joe's shack on the sheltered side of a natural outcropping of granite, leaning into the rock and, unlike the village shacks, constructed mainly of driftwood and moss. The interior was similar to Jenny's, however. The tools were there: the lathes and lasers, the minipile and the computer. Joe sat before a flickering fire, gazing into the flames, holding on his knees a framed painting.

He brightened when he saw her. "If you hadn't come, I'd have had to destroy it," he said. He laid the painting carefully aside and stood, clasping her hands. He was a good-looking child, dark and intense—and according to some versions of the Song of Earth, genetically identical to Antonio the Poet.

"Show me," said Selena.

He handed her the painting and she turned it to the light. A small sigh escaped her. She knew she was looking at the pinnacle of Mankind's achievement in this particular field.

In appearance the girl portrayed was unexceptional—a True Human with none of the wild beauty that characterized legendary Specialists such as Captain Spring or Karina. She was pretty and her hair was a medium brown. Her nose was a little too short and her best asset was her smile, wide and delighted and lighting up her eyes, as though the artist had just told her he loved her.

Such was the latest painting of the mysterious She, and unlike the others, it was somehow complete. The girl, the whole canvas, appeared to be suffused with a glory that could not be duplicated, much less improved on. Suddenly, Selena felt sorry for Joe.

"This is the last one?" she asked.

"I think so. Next cycle I'll try something else, as the others always do. Anyway, my potto died, and She seems kind of unreal, now. I've lost track of how many times I've painted her, but one thing I do know—each painting took me thirty years. That's a long time."

"You don't remember how or when you met her—or even if you did meet her?"

He shrugged. "I lost that memory a long time ago. For some reason, one of my pottos didn't pass it on to its successor."

"I wish I had them all—all those old paintings. Those I saw were all beautiful, and I'd have liked to trace the progression. It's almost as though you were working toward a perfect woman, but seen from one very private viewpoint." She glanced at him and suddenly chuckled. "And it can't be your own viewpoint, either. Do you realize just how *sexy* this girl is?"

Joe smiled too, regretfully. "I wouldn't know."

"Well, she is. She's the kind of girl that a man would fall completely in love with. She's good and kind and giving, too—her whole personality comes right through." Again Selena felt that regret. "Joe—why did you destroy the others? Can't you see how stupid it was? You're different from the other Everlings; you don't have to act like them."

Joe said thoughtfully, "We're all humans, and human art has definite limitations. Artists strive for a kind of private perfection, and being human and fallible, the time comes when they think they're close to it. And from that point on, their work ceases to be art in an understandable form. It turns in on itself and becomes a struggle, and increasingly incomprehensible to anyone but the artist himself. We've had it happen here, many times, even with the thirty-year cycle. An Everling produces a series of poems, each more beautiful than the last. But then, gradually, there is a falling-off. The poet himself doesn't know it; he thinks he's getting better all the time. But his listeners can't understand him any more, and they drift away. The work, whether it's literature or sculpture, painting or music, whatever art form it is, becomes private, introspective and abstract.

"That's why Everling culture insists on the cycle. We create for thirty years, then we destroy it all and spend thirty years in manual work, during which time any form of art is prohibited. Then we create again, but starting from scratch, so we have nothing to build from. It takes human art thirty years to flower; anything beyond that is repetition and introspection—which is the last thing we need, being immortal. If it weren't for our cultural cycle, I think we'd go mad. Look what's happening on Dream Earth."

Selena said, "But you keep producing the same painting, and you're not mad."

For a moment Joe looked puzzled. "I can't think why not. I've finished now, anyway. There won't be another *She.* And my potto accidentally died. I'll start the next cycle with a fresh mind, and maybe try music."

"The others don't use pottos."

"It's against the rules, for obvious reasons." He sighed. "That's why I live alone up here. Now, maybe, I'll go and live in the village."

Before Selena left she asked about Horst. "Why isn't he subject to the cultural cycle? Why aren't his Stones destroyed every sixty years?"

Joe laughed. "We may be artists, but we're practical. It takes Horst thirty years and God knows how many shruglegger-hours to carve one of those Stones, bring it from the quarry and set it in place. It would take quite some time to destroy one, and we get sick of destruction after a couple of days. So we let them stand. I'm not sure they qualify as art, anyway."

With the painting under her arm, well wrapped against the rain, Selena mounted her shruglegger and left. Joe had been her last hope, and the death of his potto meant that nobody had the capability of remembering what had happened to the crystal missing from the Rainbow.

It was a frustrating day. When she reached her quarters, she found a deputation of Specialists waiting outside. Their mood was angrier than she'd ever known.

Alice acted as spokeswoman. The others, Specialists of many varieties, ranged themselves behind her. She began abruptly: "There was an accident."

"Is anyone hurt?"

"Brutus is hurt. My man, Brutus. He might have died, but we pulled him into the delivery room through a grommet." Her voice was cold and flat as she described the events leading to Brutus's final act of heroism. "Brutus saved a baby that would have drowned. He did this because he's been led to believe it's his duty to do such things. He's a very clever man, but he's simple, too. He saved a baby that will almost certainly be no use to anyone, and that you will make him destroy in a year's time. You are very complicated people, you True Humans, and you're taking advantage of us."

"How . . . how badly is he hurt?"

"You're not listening."

"I'm listening," said Selena tightly, "but for me it's more important to know how Brutus is. And because I'm the boss, you'll tell me. Then we'll talk about the other stuff."

Alice glanced around as though seeking support, then said reluctantly, "Brutus's hip is broken. Doctors are looking after him. He'll live, but I can't believe that is of any interest to you."

"Brutus is my assistant," snapped Selena. "He's my friend, too. When an accident happens in this place, I like to receive a proper written report —not a whimpering rabble. Now, tell me something else. Was the ocean cow injured?"

"The delphids had to cut it, to get Brutus away. It moved, but it's still in position. We want to speak to you, we Specialists. We want a full discussion about our situation here on the People Planet."

"Tomorrow," said Selena. "First I have to see Brutus, then I must Fastcall Earth. Tomorrow evening at this time."

Ignoring the angry murmurs, she strode off toward the sick bay.

Brutus appeared comfortable, but her problems were not over for the day. She visited the Fastcall room, where the telepathic bat-creature relayed her thoughts to Earth, informing Zozula of Brutus's injury and asking for a replacement to be sent up. After a pause, the creature's medium—a humanoid invention of the kikihuahuas—said to her in Zozula's voice: "I'm sorry about Brutus. Of course we'll send up Shelma right away—she's had plenty of experience. And the three of us will be coming along, too."

"The three of you? What three?" The Triad had not achieved the same significance in Selena's mind as in Zozula's.

"Manuel, the Girl and I, of course."

"I see no need—"

"I'll explain when I see you," said the medium, and it was clear to Selena that Zozula would not accept any argument.

She walked back to Boss Castle, shaking with anger, and even the presence of Mentor failed to calm her.

"He's *never* come here before. The People Planet is *my* province. Doesn't he trust me? Does he think I'm not trying my damnedest to get to the bottom of the neoteny problem?"

"It could be some quite different matter," said Mentor.

"And to bring those other two!" raged Selena. "A Wild Human and a neotenite—it's an insult!"

"I thought you told me they were nice people."

"That's not the point. I don't want them here, or Zozula either, poking their noses into my business and interfering. What will the Specialists think? Damn Zozula. Damn him!" She regarded Mentor speculatively for a moment. "This means you'll have to go into hiding, of course."

"Go into hiding?"

"Well, you can hardly stay in Boss Castle with Zozula prowling around here. There are some caves down the coast."

"Caves?"

"You can take a shruglegger; it won't be missed. And that reminds me of another thing: The records clerk told me that Brutus has been checking on the neotenite quantities. He's onto something, I'm sure. And a terrible thing happened a little while ago. When Alice told me Brutus had been in an accident I . . . I think I hoped he was dead. That would have solved all my problems. What a dreadful thing to think."

Mentor, who had been looking increasingly despondent at the idea of roughing it in a cave, pulled himself together and took Selena's hand. "We can't control what we think," he said, "any more than we can decide whom we fall in love with."

He meant well, but it was an unfortunate statement, given Selena's present frame of mind. She flushed and shot him a look of suspicion, wondering how much he'd guessed about his origins and whether he was laughing at her behind her back, the way the caracal-people did.

THE LEGEND OF LOST LOANNA

I sing the Song of Earth as we know it to be: an epic tale involving many heroes, many heroines and many strange creatures. The story of the Triad is one part of the Song but because there are infinite happentracks, there are infinite versions of the Triad's quest. On some happentracks, the Triad failed in their quest, and the Hate Bombs were not removed, and Starquin remained trapped for varying periods of time.

Another tale of failure is the legend of Lost Loanna, and on a distant happentrack it is a familiar tale because of its poignant quality, and because it involves immortals. Immortals are always popular figures in legends, because the listener can tell himself they are probably still around, walking incognito.

Horst and Loanna were immortal children created by Mankind from the flesh of an ancient called Antonio, descendant of John, son of Karina, descendant of Captain Spring. Although Horst and Loanna could never reach maturity, an extraordinary thing happened to them one day. They looked at each other, found their emotions had changed in a subtle way and realized they were in love.

Like the immortal children around them, they played at creating works of art. There was one special talent they alone possessed, however, and they used this talent like a game. In their game of hide-and-seek, one would slip into another dimension of the Greataway and the other would try to hunt the hider down. It was great fun. It was in fact a version of the Outer Think, the art of which was gradually being lost.

Horst and Loanna would have been very happy, but for one thing. Loanna put their discontent into words. One day she said, "I wish I could have a baby."

"Only mature humans can have babies," said Horst. "Let's play hide-and-seek."

"I'm tired of games," said Loanna. "They're for the other kids. We're different. I love you and you love me. So give me a baby, the way the adult humans do."

"It just won't work," said Horst unhappily. More than anything in the world, he wanted to please Loanna. "We're not built right, inside."

And Loanna sighed and began to lose interest in life. Horst watched her pining, feeling somehow responsible but unable to help her.

✳

One day while Loanna was moping about in the rain, Horst had an idea. At the other end of the island was a palace, and in the palace, Horst knew, they made babies. They grew them in vats, and every so often they shipped them to a world called Earth.

Horst decided to steal a baby for Loanna.

That night he walked across the island and slipped into the palace, unseen. He found himself in a huge room with rows of containers full of liquid. At the bottom of each container lay a baby. Horst began to move along a row, intent on picking out the most beautiful baby for Loanna.

But when he reached the third container, the baby leaped out and seized him by the throat.

It was the most dreadful creature, tiny and hairy, dripping wet and with a chillingly evil face. Horst fought it, but it was incredibly powerful, its skinny little fingers like pincers biting into his flesh. From the corner of his eye, Horst caught sight of other, similar little demons jumping from their vats. He fell, and the vile babies swarmed all over him, snapping and clawing, screeching.

Then, as he felt his senses slipping away from him, the baby at his throat relaxed its grip. It smiled into his face, showing fangs. It spoke.

"We don't want you to die," it said. "That would be no fun at all."

What followed was the most terrible night Horst had experienced. The hairy babies were able to summon up every fear he'd ever known, and play on it, and amplify it, terrifying him systematically, laughing all the while. As he screamed, so they laughed, a shrill cackling not unlike his screaming.

"Why are you doing this?" he asked them at one point, sobbing.

"Because we are evil," said the baby. The hair was not the only grotesque feature of these babies. They were thin and wiry and their noses were pointed. Their heads were narrow and their eyes red. Horst had never dreamed that any living creature could be so ugly, or so cruel.

When dawn came they released him, simply because they were tired of him. It pleased them to think he would never sleep easily again, and for that reason they let him live.

*

When the humans saw the appalling monsters that had appeared spontaneously in the cloning vats, they were horrified. By noon the creatures had locked themselves in and were feeding on the tissue banks, fouling what they could not eat. There was a fear that they might start on the normal babies next. They were growing fast, and becoming more terrible by the hour, and the whole region around the palace held a miasma of corruption.

Light-years away, the leaders of Earth considered the situation. They recognized the creatures as the biggest threat they had faced since the Red Planet's Weapon.

"We must destroy the People Planet," they said.

An objection was quickly raised by the scientists. "Our only sound genetic material is on that planet. You know the problems we've been having recently with the gene bank. If we destroy the People Planet, we could be destroying the future of the human race."

By the time they'd finished discussing that point, the monsters, fully grown, had broken out of the palace and were holding the entire planet hostage. Word came of torturings and killings, and unimaginable cruelty.

"We must talk to them," said one of Earth's leaders. "We must try to make them see reason."

The fox-people took him to the planet, and he met with the monsters. His message was quite simple: "Either you allow us to remove you to exile on another world, where you can live without troubling us, or we will vaporize this planet, its people, its genetic material and yourselves. In other words, we will cut our losses."

For the leaders of Earth had recognized that they had created, unwittingly, the most terrible creatures the Galaxy had ever known, who were purely evil and who would, if unchecked, spread through and dominate the entire area within the compass of the Hate Bombs. Humans could not run from them, because they were trapped by their own Bombs.

And although the monsters could not use the Outer Think because the psetic lines rejected their evil presence, they were already beginning the construction of their own three-dimensional Spaceships according to an ancient design. They were incredibly quick and clever, and it was rumored that they could jump between happentracks at will, stealing a thought from here, an invention from there. In due course they would discover an anti-Greataway, which would allow them limited local travel.

The monsters spoke, realizing Earth meant business.

"How can you send us into exile? The Greataway rejects us."

"We will parcel you up in a drogue, and our most capable psycaptains will pilot you."

The monsters cackled. "You know what we will do to *them*, once they land us on our new world."

And Earth's leader said, "We must accept the suffering of two humans as a small price to pay for ridding ourselves of you."

The monsters laughed even louder. "Yes, but will *they* accept that?"

"I hardly think humans are so selfish as you creatures," said Earth.

So they asked the vulpids, who replied: "This is a True Human matter and we want no part of it. Why should we die helping you solve a problem of your own making?"

So they found a handful of cat-people who still remembered something of the ways of the Outer Think, and asked them.

And the cat-people replied: "When you True Humans threw up the Hate Bombs without warning, you trapped our best pilots outside, in the distant Greataway. We would not help you True Humans, even if we could."

The leaders of Earth searched the nearby inhabited worlds, and they searched the Rainbow, and finally they found the only True Humans who might be able to help. Obtaining a special dispensation from the monsters, they approached Horst and Loanna.

"You're asking us to die?" asked Loanna.

The emissary said, "For the good of the human race. And we must not forget the possibility that the creatures will let you go."

"I doubt it. We've seen what they are like."

"Yes, they hold you prisoner at present. Is what we are asking much worse than that?"

"A lot worse. On this planet, the monsters have a lot of people to keep them busy. We don't see them very often. You are suggesting we take them to a world where we will be the only humans."

"For the good of the human race."

Loanna said finally, "I suppose we have no choice."

But nearby, Horst trembled as the nightmares rode through his mind.

The fox-people trained Horst and Loanna in the ways of the Outer Think, because up to now the lovers had only been playing at Traveling. Within a week they were ready and, according to instruction, Loanna encircled the Bale Wolves with the silver Chain, while Horst prepared the Helix.

They also took all records of the events of the past weeks, because Earth wanted the memory erased. Earth was ashamed of the creatures, guessing that they represented all that was evil within Mankind itself, distilled into semihuman form. Earth did not want future generations to know what had happened in the cloning vats that terrible night.

Horst and Loanna spoke the Apothegm and closed their eyes.

Nothing happened.

The creatures, endrogued, capered and spat. The lovers tried again. Again they failed. "I can't understand it," said Loanna. "We've never had any difficulty before."

"It's my fault," said Horst. "I can't do it. I'm frightened of the monsters." That night in the palace had affected his mind. The proximity of the creatures terrified him, and he could not achieve the serenity that Greataway Travel demands. He never would, as long as he lived.

And Loanna, brave Loanna, said, "Move away from the Helix, my darling."

Horst, not for a moment divining her intent, stepped aside.

And Loanna disappeared, all by herself, with the cargo of monsters.

When Horst realized what had happened, he was overcome with guilt and wept for a week. A kind of madness overtook him and people began to avoid him. He thought it was because they despised him, but in fact it was because he no longer behaved rationally and they were frightened of him. He took to wandering alone in the endless rain of his planet, crying out to his distant love. At night he would lie on the ground and watch the sky and imagine Loanna on that alien world, surrounded by the monsters forever, because she was immortal and the monsters would never kill her, for they enjoyed inflicting pain.

Years passed, until quite unexpectedly it became necessary to Starquin's purpose that Loanna return one day. However, it was occupying all of Loanna's mynde to fight the pain inflicted by the monsters, leaving her with no mynde for practicing the Outer Think. As long as they kept torturing her, she could never slip from their grasp.

One day an old woman appeared to Horst. "Loanna will return," she said.

He was insane, and her words hardly registered. "How?" he asked at last.

"You will help her."

He struggled to understand. "I need to know where she is."

"She is far away. She passed through many Pockets and took many different psetic lines before she reached her destination. You could not visualize enough of the Greataway to be able to link your mynde with hers."

"So how can I help her?" asked Horst.

"You will build a map," said the Dedo.

And so, once every sixty years, the Dedo appeared before Horst and led him through the rain. After a while she would stop and tap the ground with her stick, saying: "Build here." So Horst would take teams of shrugleggers to a distant quarry, and erect on the spot indicated by the Dedo the biggest monolith that the shrugleggers could drag, and it would take him thirty years to do it. Then he would camp beside it for another thirty years, trying to reach Loanna with his mynde, knowing that every moment lost was a moment of torture for her.

Millennia went by, and every sixty years Horst would expect the Dedo to say, *The map is complete. This stone represents the location of Loanna, and the psetic lines run so, and so. Sit down, Horst, and allow your mynde to flow along those lines, until you meet the mynde of your lost Loanna. Then help her to return.*

But instead, the Dedo would say, "Build here."

ARRIVAL OF THE TRIAD

Selena would never have guessed how lonely Boss Castle would be without Mentor. After she had visited Brutus and found him resting comfortably—although, alarmingly, unable to look her in the face—she returned to her quarters to await the arrival of Zozula. Shortly before noon, following a period during which her imagination had run riot and she had decided that not only Brutus, but Zozula, too, knew about Mentor, she summoned a caracal-girl by the name of Felicity.

"Do you people have regular contact with the baby factory?" she asked.

The girl was lithe and slender. She was pretty, too, but now her face twisted in disgust and she almost spat the words, "Contact with those dumb Specialists? Not us!"

"I think Brutus suspects the existence of Mentor. Could any of you have told him?"

"No. Why should we? You treat us well, and my father told me that we should never speak of what happens inside this place. It was a part of our original contract when our people became your personal attendants." There was pride in Felicity's voice. The caracal-people were fierce and clannish, which was why Selena had chosen them for their present duties.

"What about your menfolk?" she asked.

"There are only three. They would die rather than talk to others about Mentor. You ought to know that."

"Yes, I ought. I'm sorry. It was a bad day yesterday, and today may be worse. Zozula is arriving from Earth."

"Zozula? He's the head Cuidador from Dome Azul, isn't he? What does he want?"

"I wish I knew. He's bringing a Wild Human and a neotenite."

"To the People Planet?" Felicity was outraged, her fingers bent claw-like. "It's an insult to you—to all of us!"

"We must try not to see it like that," said Selena, and by the time the Triad arrived an hour later, she had been able to compose herself. Felicity brought the three Travelers in, and Selena greeted Zozula calmly.

"Welcome to the People Planet," she said.

Zozula was shaking water from his cloak. "I'd forgotten what a godforsaken rock this is," he said sourly. "Does it ever stop raining?"

"I saw our sun for at least three minutes yesterday. Did you have a good journey?"

"Tolerable, although I'd feel a little happier if those vulpids cut out some of the mumbo jumbo. It seems to me that every profession has built up a mystique around itself over the years. I sometimes think the sole purpose is to make it difficult for us True Humans to maintain control. Do you ever have any problems up here?"

Zozula's question had emerged so naturally out of his remarks that she had to assume there was no ulterior meaning. "Not usually," she said. "But Brutus's injury triggered a reaction. Suddenly the Specialists are complaining about everything, and they've demanded a formal discussion. We're meeting later this afternoon." She went on to describe the circumstances surrounding Brutus's accident.

The Girl spoke for the first time. She looked even paler than usual. "Brutus sounds like a very good person."

"Well, he could make us very bad persons in the eyes of the Specialists. I can't think why he took such a chance. After all, what's one neotenite more or less?" The moment Selena said the last words, she regretted them.

"Watch your tongue," said Manuel, giving her an angry look.

Selena swallowed. How could a Wild Human speak to her like that? As the frustrations of the past days came rushing back to her, she found herself very close to tears. "Who do you think you are?" she asked unsteadily, "Coming to my world and—"

"Hold it, Selena," said Zozula quickly, before matters could get out of hand. "Let's get to the purpose of our visit. How are you getting along with your neoteny research?"

It was the wrong question, and too abruptly put. "I'm getting no-where," Selena snapped. "Weren't you listening? The Specialists are using Brutus's accident as a lever to get concessions and promises out of us. I'm getting no cooperation at all."

"I'll deal with the Specialists," said Zozula tactlessly.

"Over my dead body!"

"Well, I thought you said—"

This time it was Manuel who came to the rescue. "I'm sorry if I was rude, Selena," he said with surprising humility. "Now, it's really important that we talk about the neoteny problem. You see, two days ago we hooked up the Girl to the Diagnoser, and the results weren't good. It seems neotenites aren't suitable for leading a normal life, even if they've got plenty of courage, as the Girl has. The Diagnoser says the Girl is simply wearing out and she'll be dead within the year. So, as I said, it's really important we stop quarreling and talk about this problem."

The shock of Manuel's statement had the desired effect, and Selena said quietly, "I'm sorry, Girl. I didn't know."

She explained about the missing crystal. "I've wondered whether Brutus took it, but I don't think he did. It's lost, and that's all there is to it. I went to see the Everlings, but they don't use memory pottos. There was just one Everling who might have helped—an artist called Joe." She nodded at the painting, which she had hung on the wall that morning. "He painted that, as a matter of fact."

Zozula glanced at the picture. "Nice. Pretty girl."

Manuel looked at it, and kept looking. "Who is she?" he asked at last.

"I don't know. Joe lost the memory."

Manuel said slowly, "I've never seen anyone so beautiful in my life."

"What about Belinda?" asked the Girl in surprisingly acid tones. "What about Polysitia, and all that? It seems to me you're rather fickle, Manuel."

"It doesn't matter," said Manuel. He watched the painting greedily, as though he expected the model to step off the canvas. "She's so . . . real."

"Joe didn't paint her for himself," said Selena. "Perhaps he painted her for you, Manuel."

"Nonsense!" said Zozula briskly. "So the artist couldn't help you, Selena?"

"No . . ." Selena was still watching Manuel, and a puzzled look crossed her face. "It's strange . . . From some angles, you look very

much like Joe, Manuel. Older, of course. But you look the way I think
Joe would have looked, if he'd ever grown up."

"And they have the same taste in girls," said the Girl.

"Joe was the last one you talked to?" asked Zozula. "There are no
other Everlings who might know something?"

Selena thought. "Well, there's Horst, of course, but he's quite mad,
poor fellow. I don't suppose he has a potto."

"We will see Horst," said Zozula.

"We'd be wasting our time."

"We have to explore every possibility. That's why we're here, Selena.
We're not implying any criticism of you. The neotenites are dying and we
have to find a cure quickly, before we lose them all. We've come to help."

Somewhat to Selena's surprise, Zozula insisted that she sit in the center
of the stage while he sat well to the side. The Girl and Manuel waited in
the wings. Zozula refused to explain his strategy. "It's best you act naturally," he told Selena. "I know the way these Specialists' minds work.
Don't worry if the meeting seems to be going badly. It'll come right in
the end."

The meeting was being held in the small theater used by the Specialists
for their frequent music and dance performances; the delphids, in particular, were famous for their spectacular ballets. The theater was full. All
the adult Specialists were present except for a skeleton crew attending to
the ocean cow's needs. Several hundred people faced Selena, talking quietly to one another. Probably a dozen races were represented in the
audience. Each race had its traditional duties in the care of the ocean cow
and the babies, and the maintenance of services.

"The meeting is open," called Selena. For a moment she regarded the
crowd, regretting that this situation had arisen, still seeing them as her
friends and workers. Then Alice stood, her huge face set in a ferocious
scowl, and Selena knew she faced her enemies.

"Fellow Specialists," said Alice. "I'm speaking on behalf of our leader
Brutus, who is too sick to attend this meeting. Brutus was injured saving
a baby from drowning. The baby will almost certainly prove to be a
neotenite, and therefore useless. Brutus risked his life needlessly, as a
result of his conditioning by True Humans." Now she turned and faced
Selena. "If Brutus had died, the True Human race would stand accused
of murder."

There was a roar of agreement from the audience. Selena replied.

"Brutus was not conditioned, as you call it. He received standard training for his job. You can't blame the whole True Human race for an accident that happened to one brave man."

"Our training may be standardized, as you say," shouted Alice, her huge shoulders hunched, her jaw thrust forward. "But the conditioning takes place throughout our lives. You don't allow us to have the children we want. We come of partly animal stock, and some of us have bodies equipped for multiple births—your own caracal-people, for instance. We're built for reproduction, but you restrict us, only allowing us two children each. It's unnatural! And what is the purpose of this restriction?" She swung round and faced her audience. "Its purpose is to foster within us an exaggerated sense of the value of children, any children— True Human children! Its purpose is to compel us to perform exactly the kind of senseless, heroic deed that almost killed my man Brutus!" Tears were running down her dark, downy cheeks and her sincerity was apparent to everyone there.

For a while the meeting was in disorder while Specialists shouted and Selena pounded with her gavel. Eventually Zozula stood and walked slowly to the center of the stage. His action had the effect of calming the audience, and when he spoke, they listened.

"I'm from Dome Azul, as you know," he said. "There are a number of Domes on Earth, but my Dome is responsible for this planet and its breeding program.

"You've probably wondered why the breeding program is set up here on this lonely world, instead of on Earth. The reason is ancient, and concerns the years when babies were produced directly in the vats, before the coming of the ocean cow. Unusual breeding experiments were carried out in those years, and it was feared that a virulent disease, or even a hostile and powerful creature, might evolve. It was decided that breeding should be carried out in isolation, as a safeguard.

"But the People Planet is not self-supporting. Crops do not grow well on your rocky, rainy island. Fishing is restricted, since the ocean cow needs all the food it can get. So almost all your food and other materials must be imported from Earth. The resources of Dome Azul are small and the present population of the People Planet stretches them to the limit. If breeding among Specialists were allowed to go uncontrolled, your children would starve."

A horse-man called, "Get the food from the other Domes!"

"We have no transport between Domes. We can communicate through the Rainbow, but that's all."

"I hear the land around Azul is fertile. Grow crops there and ship them up! Why must you depend on the Dome's machines to produce food?"

Zozula appeared to get flustered. "There's a primitive tribal society Outside, composed of Wild Humans. You all know that. We do not have the manpower to grow crops, let alone protect them from the depredations of savages!"

At this point some of the audience heard a shout of anger from the wings, but they forgot about it when Alice began to talk again. "Excuses! You True Humans are always full of excuses when it comes to making changes. So here we work, as our forefathers have worked for twenty-six thousand years, trying to re-create what you people call the True Human form—and getting a little worse at doing it, year by year. That's a disheartening existence, don't you agree?"

She lowered her voice, darting cunning glances around her. "But suppose we succeeded? Suppose, suddenly, the babies began to breed true? Where would that leave us? In a few years the neotenites in the Domes would have been replaced and the need for the People Planet would end, and we'd be out of a job. What then, True Humans? Would you continue to support a world for which you had no further use?"

Selena said, "We'd relocate you all on Earth, of course."

"What? Set us down among the Wild Humans? Turn the savages loose on us?"

What happened next was never forgotten by those who saw it, or by their children and their children's descendants, because it became a minor legend among the Specialists on the People Planet. What happened next was that two people emerged from the wings. Legend tells that they moved in stately fashion, halted center-stage and delivered polished monologues. The truth was, Manuel came storming into view in the full flood of fury, unceremoniously dragging the Girl. The audience didn't know who they were, of course. That was the shock effect Zozula had been counting on. The audience saw a tubby, muscular young man with a shock of black hair and a murderous expression, pulling behind him a strange fleshy creature.

"I'm a Wild Human!" the young man yelled, and looking at him, the audience believed him. Moderating his tone, Manuel continued, "I live in a house by the sea that I built myself, and I keep two tame vicunas. I'm an artist. I own a machine called a Simulator and I use it to create mind-paintings and I've seen *this* man—" he stabbed a finger toward Zozula "—cry when he looks at them. The people in my village grow crops and tend animals, and in the evenings they sit around and talk. I've never known them to make war on another village. Right now they're getting ready for their Horse Day celebrations. People come from all around to take part—even Specialists from the Dome. We're not savages. We're human beings living the way humans were meant to live—on Earth, in the open air!

"And you!" He pointed at Alice. "You have the gall to say a neotenite baby is useless? How can you say that? Everybody has a purpose—to grow up and be a part of society. Neotenites grow up, too." He indicated the Girl. "This is a grown-up neotenite!"

They hadn't guessed. They'd never seen one before. The babies had been taken to Earth when they were one year old—when they still looked like ordinary babies. Most of them were then recycled. It hadn't occurred to Specialists to wonder what the remainder grew up to be like. Perhaps they hadn't wanted to wonder. Now, faced with the indisputable presence of a real live adult neotenite, they were silent. Some of them turned away. There was a low murmur of pity.

Manuel said, "We call her Girl, because she refuses to take a real name until she's earned it. She had the guts to leave Dream Earth, where she could have everything she wanted, and live in the real world. And she's going to pay for it, because she's wearing out and she'll be dead soon. You think you've got problems? Take a look at the Girl. Look at her body."

The Girl made a little movement, trying to drag away. "No, Manuel," she whispered.

"Look at her arms, look at her legs. Just imagine how it hurts her, just to move around. But, of course, you can't imagine that. You're Specialists. You're physically perfect. Well, I'd like you to help the Girl to be as perfect as you.

"I'd like you to carry on with the breeding program for her sake, and for the sake of those like her. Forget about your problems here—because I'm quite sure there's no quick answer. Just work toward the day when you can give the neotenites real bodies—and let's try to make it soon, because the Girl hasn't got much time. Then you can all go down to Earth if you want to and live among us Wild Humans. I give you my word we'll make you welcome."

There was a long silence while the audience waited for a lead. People glanced at one another and nobody spoke, although from somewhere the sound of muffled sobbing could be heard. Most people were looking at the Girl. There was an almost physical aura of pity in the theater. These people loved babies; whether or not they had been conditioned to have this love was beside the point. And here was the biggest, saddest baby of them all.

Finally there was a movement from the audience.

Alice lumbered to the stage, her eyes fixed on the Girl, trying to understand the manner of creature her world had been creating, seeing the physical reality and beginning to get some inkling of the suffering behind that shapeless exterior. She climbed onto the stage and put out a hand, touching the Girl's hand. Then, impulsively, she hugged her.

"We'll do whatever we can, my dear," said Alice.

HORST'S STONES

●●●

*T*he following morning they rode shrugleggers into the Everling village, where the rain fell heavily, as though to wash away the debris and the memory of the destructive orgy. The Everlings remained indoors, composing themselves for thirty years of dull, repetitive labor. Selena caught sight of Jenny through an open door and waved, but the little girl ignored her. All the equipment had been removed to a central storage place, and the shack was empty of all but the most rudimentary furniture.

With giant strides and thrusting thighs, the shrugleggers carried them up the hill toward Horst's Stones. Joe's cabin was empty; the artist was walking in the rain somewhere, coming to terms with himself. It was a time of reflection for the Everlings, a time for unwinding.

When they reached the top of the ridge, they found one Everling still working. The squat figure of Horst could be seen beside a monolith over ten meters tall, chipping at it with a chisel. The faint clicking of metal on stone carried across the basin to them.

Even Zozula was awed by the sight of the Stones. "I've never seen them from this viewpoint before," he said, as they paused to allow the shrugleggers to recover their breath. "It's a hell of an undertaking. What is it all for?"

"I've no idea," said Selena, rather shortly. She felt strongly that the journey was pointless. "And neither has Horst, I suspect. The poor child is mad."

"But still possessing certain skills." Zozula gazed across the wide, shallow basin, where over five hundred Stones had been erected in a seemingly random arrangement. The rock on which Horst worked was the most recent; it was the only one without a heavy covering of lichen and moss. "Let's go and talk to him," said Zozula, kicking his mount forward.

But Horst ignored them. "I'm almost finished now, my love," he was murmuring in tones of quiet exaltation, tapping with obsessive care at the rock. Up close, they could see that the Stones were not smooth. Horst had chipped a number of indentations into the surface, again placed randomly—or perhaps in accordance with some design known only to his fevered mind. "It won't be long now," he said.

Zozula, becoming impatient, dismounted and laid a hand on Horst's shoulder. The Everling jerked round to face him. "How long have you been putting up these Stones?" asked Zozula.

"Who wants to know, tell us that?" said Horst with a sly look; then, glancing at the sky, he continued, "We won't tell them, will we, my love? We won't tell them anything. That way they can't hurt us."

"We don't want to hurt you, Horst," said Selena. "We just want to know if you remember anything that happened a long time ago. Back in the beginning."

"We don't remember, do we? We will not remember." But it seemed that Horst couldn't help remembering something, because his face crumpled and he began to cry. "So sorry, my love," he sobbed. "So sorry. I tried. I tried so hard, but . . ." And his eyes widened, and a look of staring fear was there, so dreadful that Zozula swung round, half expecting to find something hideous crouched behind him.

Selena said to Zozula, "I told you we wouldn't get anything out of him. Whatever happened in the past cost him his sanity. The poor fellow refuses to remember."

"All we need is a telepath," suggested Manuel. "Maybe the Fastcall creature could help."

"I don't think it's that simple," said Selena. "If he really has hidden information he doesn't want to remember, it could well be blocked from a telepath, too. They can only skim the surface of the mind . . ." Her voice faded away. She was staring across the basin. Was that someone standing beside a distant Stone? She thought she saw a figure in black, and a raised hand, beckoning. An instant of dizziness took her and the view before her shifted slightly, as though she had slipped into an adjacent happentrack. But the Triad was still there, in discussion.

The Girl said, "When we saw the Stones from the ridge, they reminded me of something. It's right on the tip of my memory." She frowned, annoyed with herself. "It was the way they were set out. That pattern is familiar."

"How can a pattern of five hundred rocks be familiar?" asked Zozula sceptically.

"It's finished!" shouted Horst, so loudly that they jumped. He flung himself to the ground weeping, caressing the base of the rock as though it were a woman's skin. After a moment he appeared to pull himself together and began to babble some kind of incantation, over and over again, with a queer desperation.

"What the hell is he gabbling on about?" said Zozula disgustedly.

The Girl said, "It sounds familiar."

"Everything's familiar to you, today."

"No—listen. Where have I heard that before? Quite recently."

Manuel said, "It's like the mumbo jumbo the vulpids say before the shuttle takes off."

"That's right!" the Girl cried. "And—"

The Stone lit up.

The Triad backed away hastily, but Horst uttered a cry of delight and sprang to his feet. The Stone glowed with a pulsing bluish light that seemed to emanate from the areas around the circular depressions. Horst was silent now, his hand pressed into one of the dents, his eyes closed and an expression of rapt attention on his face. Then he nodded and babbled again and stared up into the sky while the rain poured down his face.

Then he began to run. Bounding across the rough ground, leaping boulders, arms flapping like wings, he reached the next nearest Stone. Even at a distance, he communicated a breathless excitement to the onlookers. Zozula was puzzled, but Manuel seemed to be feeling a quiet empathy.

"After all this time . . ." the young man murmured, gazing around the at immensity of Horst's work.

"After all this time, what?" asked Zozula, unimpressed by Horst, but still wary of the Stone glowing nearby. So far, it had shown no sign of actually exploding, but that was not to say he trusted it.

"To be finished. I can't imagine what it must be like." Manuel had spent several days perfecting his major mind-painting, *Belinda: the Storm-Girl,* but Horst's work was beyond his powers of comprehension. The monoliths towered all around him and extended into the distance. They possessed a massive poetry of their own. There was something cosmic about them. Manuel could sense it.

"Yes," said the unimaginative Zozula patiently, "but *what* has he finished? What's it for? Is it art? If it is, then explain it to me, Manuel."

"It has to do with the Greataway," said Manuel. "And it's very important to Horst—there's a kind of urgency about it. And there's love there, of course."

"Important to Horst but nobody else," Zozula snorted. "It's as Selena was saying last night—something that Everling Joe told her? About art getting introspective after thirty years. Well, Horst's been building this for twenty-six thousand years. In my uneducated opinion he's been wasting his time."

"Look at that," said Manuel.

The second Stone glowed. Horst, yelling encouragement, ran on to the third.

The Girl said with sudden certainty, "Next, he'll go to that one over there." She pointed. "To the left, there."

And sure enough, Horst did. And soon the Stone lit up.

"Now that one," said the Girl, pointing again.

"How in hell do you know that?" asked Zozula.

The Girl smiled. "Not so long ago, we followed the same route. On a larger scale, of course." She looked around. "Selena, I think we should—" She broke off, puzzled.

Selena wasn't there. Her memory potto sat on the ground, shivering unhappily.

"She'll be back," said the Girl, picking up the little creature. She set it on her shoulder and sat down on the wet ground to watch Horst making his zigzag way among the Stones.

"Won't someone tell me what's going on?" asked Zozula plaintively.

Selena stood before the old woman. There was a dreamlike unreality about the scene, as though the two of them were surrounded by a mist that isolated them from the Triad, Horst and the Stones. One Stone remained; the one beside the old woman. And now Selena saw that this one was different from the others. No lichen grew on it, no cracks disfigured its surface, and yet it bore an air of unimaginable age.

"Who are you?" asked Selena.

"I am Shenshi."

"What are you doing on my planet? How did you get here?" It was impossible that this old woman should be standing here. "Are . . . are you human?" Selena asked finally, guessing part of the truth.

"Not so human as you, my dear. That's why I've come to see you. I have scanned the Ifalong, and I believe that you could shortly be making a decision of Galactic significance. Through a series of related events, the results of your decision will affect the health and sanity of a great Being to whom I am responsible. It is my duty to insure your decision is the right one."

"Oh," said Selena. There seemed to be little else to say.

"Tell me what your plans are."

"Well . . . It's a long story."

"You may assume that I know everything that has happened so far."

"Oh. Well, we're looking for a lost data crystal that may hold the clue to neoteny."

"I can give you that crystal."

"You can?" And the mists cleared for a moment. Selena saw Horst running, running and shouting, bounding among the Stones, and every time he touched a Stone it glowed. Over half the Stones were glowing now and . . . Selena stared, then decided it was an optical illusion caused by the mist. But it seemed to her that the glowing Stones had left the ground and now hung in the air at varying heights. "Can I have the crystal, then?" asked Selena, holding out her hand. She wanted to get away from here. Strange things were happening.

"Very soon. I must warn you, though, that the crystal will be no use to you unless you make the correct decision."

"Just tell me what decision you want me to make," said Selena, more sharply than she intended. She was becoming very frightened.

"I can't do that. It would presume an exact knowledge of the future that I do not possess. I can say in general terms that the decision ought to have been made already, and that the reason you have procrastinated is because the decision is a very difficult and—you may think—personal one. But the decision is too complex and the Ifalong too uncertain for me to tell you exactly what it is, and when it should be made."

"I don't know what you're talking about," said Selena.

"If one thing in the Ifalong was certain," said Shenshi, "it was that you would have said that. Always remember, the same decision will be before you, time and again, until you die. So decide soon, at the next significant branching of happentracks."

There was a long silence. At last, quietly, Selena said, "How will I know when that is?"

"Everybody knows when happentracks are about to branch. You can feel it within you," said Shenshi. "So don't deny it when you feel it."

Then she touched the Rock and was gone.

*

"Where have you been?" asked the Girl. "I've been looking after your potto for you."

"I . . . I'm not sure," said Selena. What was that, a residue of a memory in her mind? Something about an old woman and a decision? She shook her head and placed the potto on her shoulder. Most of the Stones were glowing now, and they really did seem to be hanging in the air. In point of fact, she decided, they were being reflected from the clouds. She stroked the potto, determined that from now on she would always keep it with her. She was getting old, and human memories could play tricks.

"Horst has almost finished," said Manuel.

"And what happens then?" asked Zozula. "Will that be all? The Stones he touched first have stopped glowing now." Those Stones stood cold and dead, barren chunks of granite.

"I'm sure it will be worthwhile, after all this time," said Manuel. "He seems to be working his way over to that far side. Let's go, shall we?" Not wishing to miss anything, the young man hurried to the other side of the basin. A Stone stood there that was a little different from the rest.

The Girl followed on her shruglegger. "This will be the last one," she said confidently.

When Selena arrived she regarded the Stone curiously, chasing an elusive memory. Her potto could not help her. The little animal shivered suddenly.

"This had better be good," said Zozula.

Horst arrived, breathless. He flung himself at the last Stone, yelling. His hands sought the indentations while his gaze roved wildly over the clouds. He calmed himself, muttering incantations. His young face was contorted with emotions too strong for his small frame to contain, and he seemed to radiate a vital, desperate energy. "Come to me, my love!" he shouted finally.

And she came. There was a sound like a thunderclap and a young girl materialized beside the Stone.

She had dark hair and a pretty, immature face that bore no sign of the tortures she had undergone. She glanced briefly at the Triad and Selena, then her gaze rested on the Everling. She smiled.

"We did it, Horst."

"We did." But he stood apart from her, not meeting her eyes.

"Kiss me, Horst."

"I'm not worthy."

"Oh, don't be a damned fool, Horst," said Zozula briskly, intruding on the scene with clumsy impatience. "Kiss the girl. Then tell me what all this is about, for God's sake."

But Horst stood where he was, until Loanna stepped forward and, taking his face in her hands, kissed him firmly on the lips. Then he grinned briefly and took her hands, staring at her greedily.

"I can't believe it," he said. "Those demons. How did you give them the slip?"

"Oh, they were all around me. It seems they always have been." Her face clouded as she remembered. "Hairy and evil, like humans who have been made wrong . . . and I always kept seeing little bits of myself in them; that was the worst part. If they hadn't always made it clear that I was their enemy, I might have ended up believing I was one of them." She shuddered. "But then, today, I thought I sensed you out there, Horst. I couldn't believe it—it was the first time I'd felt anything like hope for thousands of years. And suddenly this old woman appeared, right there, among the monsters. She said, 'Horst has come for you. Link your mynde with his, Loanna.' Just like that. And the monsters seemed to freeze, as though time had stopped for them."

"An old woman?" repeated Selena thoughtfully.

But Loanna wasn't listening. She was looking at Horst, holding his hands.

"We ought to go," said Manuel.

"Wait a moment," said Selena. Addressing Loanna, she said, "We're seeking knowledge from a long time ago. Do you have anything for us?"

Loanna managed to disengage a hand long enough to reach inside her cloak and bring out a glittering crystal.

"Thanks" said Selena shakily, taking it and holding it carefully. "I think that's all we needed. We'll leave you alone now."

Mounting their shrugleggers, they rode out of the basin of dead Stones.

SELENA'S CHOICE

*T*he wind was strong that evening, and Selena had to cling tightly to the shruglegger's neck as the massive creature bore her along the cliff path. Below, the dark waters thundered. It was an hour before she reached the appointed place: a cleft where the path descended to a narrow beach and the waves boomed hollowly among caves.

Mentor stepped out of the darkness and lifted her down from her mount. They kissed, and she tasted salt on his lips. After a while they entered a nearby cave illuminated by a small glowpile.

"I've missed you," said Selena. "It's been hell, trying to act normally in front of those people. Never knowing if a caracal will let something slip. Always scared I'll use your name by accident."

"I've missed you, too," said Mentor shortly.

Selena held him at arm's length, looking into his face. "Is something wrong?"

"Of course something's wrong. I'm wet and I'm damned cold, and I'm getting a little tired of this cave. If you'd given me more notice, I'd have been able to stock it up with food and drink, and maybe a caracal-girl. Look at it!" He gestured at the streaming walls, the puddled floor, the pale crawling things. "This is no place for a True Human!"

"It's only for a short time, my love. And anyway, I'm here now. Let's not quarrel."

"I'm not quarreling, I'm merely stating facts. How much longer am I going to be stuck here? Is Zozula satisfied with what he's seen?"

Rather acidly, she said, "He didn't come here to criticize. We have problems, and he wanted to help."

"That's not what you told me before."

"I was wrong. What does it matter? Today we found the data crystal, and tomorrow I'm going to get Brutus to install it and call it up on the keyboard."

"Couldn't you have done that tonight?"

"My God! I wanted to see *you*, don't you understand? And you have to realize, Brutus is very sick. If it weren't for the urgency, and if it weren't for *you*, I'd have let him rest for a couple of days."

"Well," grumbled Mentor, "why don't you do just that, if he's so important to you? Just send me a caracal-girl with some supplies."

"I will *not* send you a caracal-girl," she snapped. "Are you telling me *I'm* not good enough?"

"I'm telling you you're not here often enough. I get lonely."

"Well, that's just too bad. You'll have to sit it out for a few days."

"Perhaps I won't."

"What do you mean?" There was an edge of alarm in Selena's voice.

"I have freewill. You don't own me. I might just make my way back to Boss Castle."

"You wouldn't!"

"I might."

"But . . . It would be the end of us. You couldn't . . ." Aware suddenly that she was beginning to plead, she said harshly. "They'd recycle you."

"Oh, no they wouldn't. I'm a perfectly good True Human. One of the last. I could be very valuable to the human race—much more valuable than I am as your plaything." The words began to come fast. Obviously he'd been brooding about this for some time. "I've sat in your quarters for eighty years, do you realize that? Just wasting my time and growing old. You've kept me a prisoner."

"You've had everything you wanted, and you've been outside often. And you've never complained before." She felt the tears coming. "How was I supposed to know you felt like this? When I first took you, you were just a baby. I fed you and looked after you, and I thought you were happy. And then, later . . . You grew up so tall and handsome . . . I *love* you. Can't you understand that?"

"Then send me a caracal-girl."

For the first time, she thought: *He's immature, and he always will be, unless he's exposed to real people. But all he's had is the caracal-girls and*

*a few trips into Dream Earth. I made him this way. He is the same flesh as
his vat-father, but he is quite a different person. It's my fault. And now I
may lose him.*

"I'll send you a caracal-girl," she said.

✳

Lying in his hospital bed, Brutus couldn't understand what was going on
around him.

After the initial pain had subsided and he was able to think coherently,
he had experienced a flush of pride. He had saved a baby from drowning.
Once again, he had dealt capably with an emergency and justified his
position as Selena's right-hand man. He lay there smiling for a while.

Then Alice had arrived and it emerged that he was not the hero he had
thought himself to be. Instead, he was a stupid ape, a lackey of the True
Humans, possessed of unthinking animal obedience. He went to sleep
with that thought, and he awakened in a fine rage.

When Alice came next she was curiously reluctant to discuss the matter, however, and avoided his eyes when he began to rail against the
unfair treatment of the Specialists. Then she did a complete about-face.

"We're all working toward the same objective," she said.

Brutus had stared at her and had not pursued the matter. He didn't
know what had happened to change her mind, and obviously she didn't
want to tell him. She began to talk about their work and the progress of
the latest crop of babies as though nothing had happened. By the time
she left, he was totally confused. He tried to work it out, but the only
issues he could comprehend were his own grudges: the episode of the
babies in the boats, the missing neotenite and Alice's criticism of his
bravery. So he thought about these matters for a long time, scowling.

Eventually Selena arrived.

Selena was not in the best of tempers, either. Mentor was childish,
selfish and getting out of hand. And now she had to go crawling to
Brutus, whose recent attitude had been one of sullen resentment and who
probably knew about Mentor, and ask him to replace the crystal and
access the data. By the time she reached the hospital, she'd convinced
herself that Brutus would bear watching while he fixed the Rainbow. She
wouldn't put it past him to sabotage the entire data bank.

She opened the door and saw him lying there, scowling brutishly. She
hesitated, fighting a moment's pity at seeing his gigantic frame so helpless, then strode forward, holding out the crystal.

"I'm sure you know what this is," she said.

Brutus assumed she'd found it somewhere around the factory. And he assumed that she would think he'd hidden it so that they wouldn't be able to solve the neoteny problem.

"It looks like some kind of glass cube," he said sulkily.

"You know damned well what it is."

"Yes, I do. And I did *not* remove it from the Rainbow."

"I never said you did. That's the trouble with you Specialists. You're always so damned defensive. Always harboring imaginary grudges."

Brutus's temper began slowly to rise. He could feel it happening and he made a conscious effort to hold himself back—because he knew that his anger could be a frightening thing to other people. But Selena's attitude was too much for his self-control.

"Perhaps *you* took the crystal," he said.

"Don't be ridiculous! Why should I do that?"

"You might have something to hide!" shouted Brutus before he could stop himself. His great fists were clenching and unclenching as though seeking something to crush.

"Just exactly what do you mean by that?" asked Selena, white-faced.

"You stole a baby, you . . . You True Human!" roared Brutus. "You stole it—and let me take the blame!"

"If you mean I requisitioned a foetus for research," said Selena icily, "you are quite right. But it has nothing to do with this crystal. The data here is ancient." *Oh, dear God,* she thought. *Can he see me trembling? Can he read my mind?*

"So where is the baby now?" asked Brutus in dead tones, suddenly ominously calm.

"That has nothing to do with the crystal." Stupidly, she brandished it in support of her argument.

Brutus's hand flashed out. He took the crystal. He said, again, "Where is the baby now?"

She shrugged. "I don't know. What does it matter? What's one baby more or less?"

With a roar of rage, Brutus crushed the crystal in his huge fist. Little shards tinkled to the floor and lay there glittering. The memory of what happened in the year 108,285 winked out.

Those events occurred on countless happentracks. A whole new branch of the Ifalong arose as a result—a branch on which the Triad did *not* discover the cure for neoteny and did *not* defeat the Bale Wolves or remove the Hate Bombs. On those happentracks Starquin remained a prisoner. The Dedos were instructed to investigate other possibilities, and the members of the Triad went their separate ways. Crucial events in Earth's Ifalong were delayed by twenty thousand years. Alpacas and jaguarundis became extinct.

And the Song of Earth told of different triumphs, different heroes. All because Selena had been unable to make the decision that Shenshi wanted.

But on countless other happentracks she *had* been able to—like this: She opened the door and saw Brutus lying there, frowning unhappily. She hesitated, her irritation turning to pity as she saw his gigantic frame so helpless. She walked to his bedside.

"How are you feeling, Brutus?"

"I'm fine," he said. "I'll be up in a day or two."

"That was a very courageous thing you did."

His frown lifted. "Thank you."

"I realize you people sometimes get disheartened because the babies don't turn out right. I'm hoping we'll be able to change all that, soon. We've found a crystal that I think will help us a lot." She related the events of the afternoon at Horst's Stones, concluding, "So as soon as you feel well enough, I'd like you to replace the crystal and access the data for us."

Brutus watched her.

"And there's something I've been meaning to tell you," she said. "A long time ago I did a very foolish thing. Worse than that, it was an illegal thing . . ."

✳

The events resulting from Selena's first choice drift into an uncertain Ifalong where only the principal events are known through the Rainbow's projections. The events resulting from her second choice are well known.

Both choices are often compared by the minstrels and poets, and the whole incident is used as a cautionary tale.

> *For anger at a crucial time can alter Fate's intent,*
> *And set in motion happentracks that wisdom*
> *might prevent.*

So runs a couplet in the Song of Earth.

WHAT HAPPENED IN THE YEAR 108,285

Mankind is one of the few Galactic races that distinguishes Good from Evil. To take it a stage further, Mankind is one of the only intelligent species that assumes that there is something intrinsically and cosmically *wrong* with that which it does not like. Mankind, for instance, classifies the creatures of the Red Planet as evil because once they cut a swathe through the Greataway with their Weapon. In contrast, Mankind sees the kikihuahuas as good because they are helpful and agreeable.

However, if this matter was put to either the creatures of the Red Planet or the kikihuahuas, they would simply say they were trying to survive with the best means at their disposal. And they would grant their enemies the same motives.

This odd trait of Mankind—the concept of Good and Evil—makes it inevitable that, if a creature such as the Bale Wolf should evolve, it would happen within Mankind's orbit.

Many centuries before the time of our story, when humans were beginning to lose the capability to build, service or even understand their own machines, the kikihuahuas developed a simple little animal from the same stock as the memory potto and presented it to Earth. It became known as the saybaby. It had a mind of great logic but extremely limited intelligence, and it had been indoctrinated with computer and human language. It worked in conjunction with the Rainbow, taking instruction from its human masters, quickly analyzing the available data, sorting it into logical order in human language and verbalizing it.

So when Brutus replaced the data crystal and gained access to it through the keyboard, he did not need to devise a complex program in order to extract the specific happenings that might relate to neoteny in their correct order of causality. He didn't have the skill to do that, anyway. Instead, he summoned the saybaby, which condensed weeks of work into an hour.

Brutus, Selena, Zozula, Manuel and the Girl were present when the saybaby finally turned away from the flow of aural and visual displays. These displays had been far too rapid for the humans to understand, but the saybaby had seen them all with its goggling eyes, heard them all with its outsize ears, rejected what it did not need and sorted the remainder. Now it was ready to speak.

First, it cleared its throat with a tiny cough and gaped a couple of times as though practicing. Then it spoke in a piping voice.

It spoke of the Macrobes and the second mistake these little parasites had made. They had discovered through the Everlings that immortality was not necessarily the key to survival. They had observed human history and noted the natural appeal of juvenile characteristics: the plumpness, short limbs, snub noses, the innocence, and that natural *goodness* that triggers the protective instinct in adults.

"The Macrobes decided that the key to survival was *to be loved,*" piped the saybaby. So the Macrobes went back into the genes of their hosts. They identified those genes that were responsible for behavior, and they split the gentle from the aggressive. They identified the genes responsible for physical characteristics, and they split the rounded from the angular, the babyish from the adult, the pretty from the ugly. They did a very thorough job on the human form, and they accomplished this separation throughout the gene bank.

"The next time the vats were used, two distinct groups of creatures emerged. One was a gentle, lovable thing totally unsuitable for survival in any normal environment. The other was a cruel, violent demon.

"The Macrobes had made another mistake, but this time it affected the whole human race. The People Planet was the repository for the only remaining True Human tissue hardy enough to breed true and to survive. The samples had been gathered from Cuidadors long dead. And now the Macrobes had polluted the bank. It was a sad year for the True Human race.

"The evil monsters were sent into exile, and it is hoped that they remain there. But the neotenites will be there to rebuke Mankind until the last True Human dies and the People Planet closes down and Earth is left in the hands of the Wild Humans and the Specialists." Having finished, the saybaby closed its eyes.

"So *that's* how the neotenites came about," said Selena.

The Girl said, "The evil monsters . . . You know what they are, of course. They're the Bale Wolves. Do you remember, Manuel? When we were on the Skytrain, the passengers were scared of meeting the Bale Wolves. I thought it was some kind of legend, but maybe they're the real thing."

"I'm sure they are," said Manuel. "And I tell you who's seen them."

"Who?" Brutus asked the question so sharply that they stared at him. He began to twiddle his fingers in embarrassment.

"Loanna," said Manuel. "The girl Horst brought back. She described them, remember? Hairy humans, nasty as all hell? Those are the Bale Wolves, for sure."

"This Loanna," said Brutus, "she's an Everling?"

"That's right." Manuel described the events at Horst's Stones while Brutus nodded rapidly, again and again.

"Does this get us any further?" asked the Girl.

"Now we know the cause of neoteny," said Selena. "It's a step in the right direction."

"Yes, but surely they'd have found the cure for neoteny back in the hundred and ninth millennium—if there is a cure." The Girl sounded despondent. She had hoped the crystal would reveal a little more.

Zozula said, "I don't suppose they even tried to find a cure. They blamed themselves for not policing their research more closely, and their main concern was to get the Bale Wolves out of there, fast. And then they probably closed down the vats for several generations. By the time they got back into production, the details of the Bale Wolves' creation had been forgotten. They *wanted* to forget it."

"They were so horrified by what had happened that they shipped off the data crystal with Loanna," said Selena. "It was an indictment of their stupidity. They knew that the crystal would only return if the Bale Wolves were safely isolated."

"But what are we going to do now?" asked the Girl.

Brutus said, "There's only one thing we can do."

"What is that, Brutus?" asked Selena eagerly. Zozula, looking at them, suddenly knew where the real power on the People Planet lay; he offered a silent prayer for the True Human race.

"We must obtain a genetic addendum to replace what the Girl and the other neotenites lack."

"That's easily said." Selena was disappointed. "You know as well as I do, the science of synthesizing genes was never perfected. Where do you suggest we obtain the addendum from?"

Brutus bared his teeth in a smile without humor. "From the obvious source. The Bale Wolves themselves."

TO CATCH A BALE WOLF

*T*here was a silence while they regarded Brutus, who became nervous after a while and began to scratch himself.

Eventually Zozula spoke: "We don't have the knowledge to prepare a genetic additive, even if a Bale Wolf were available. It's a good suggestion, but it's not practicable, I'm afraid, Brutus."

The gorilla-man said, "The Rainbow has the knowledge. The creature Caradoc in Dream Earth can probably help me find it. He is very knowledgeable."

"And Brutus certainly has the ability to carry out the laboratory work," added Selena.

"And where would we obtain our Bale Wolf?" asked Zozula sceptically.

"From the Nameless Planet," replied Brutus.

"Do you really suppose he would volunteer his services?"

Brutus scowled. "I'm just a Specialist, trying to help you True Humans. I'm telling you that if you give me a Bale Wolf, I can probably cure your neotenites. I'm not going to catch a Bale Wolf for you; that's your job."

"Watch your tongue!" said Zozula imperiously.

Manuel said, "It's no business of mine, because I'm just a savage Wild Human. But it seems to me that Brutus has a point. If you are to do your duty, as you so often call it, you must get hold of a Bale Wolf, Zozula. I'll help you."

"And how would we find our way to the Nameless Planet, Manuel? Tell me that!"

"Loanna will show us the way."

The Girl said uneasily, "You remember what they said on the Skytrain? The Bale Wolves are the most terrible creatures in the Galaxy. Nobody has ever survived meeting them."

"Except Loanna. If she can survive, we can. And anyway," said Manuel, warming to his theme, "they're only another kind of human being. It's not as though we were thinking of attacking the Red Planet."

"How can anyone capture a Bale Wolf?" asked Zozula. "They can jump happentracks. As soon as we tried to get a net over it, or whatever, it would disappear into the next happentrack, if it didn't kill us first."

"Loanna will know a way," said Manuel confidently.

Selena, who had been listening quietly, said, "We have no alternative, Zozula. None at all. This is the only chance the neotenites have."

Loanna couldn't understand what had gone wrong.

What was the matter with Horst? Why, after all these millennia, wouldn't he speak to her? After the others had left, they had walked together to his shack, she talking brightly, half crying, immeasurably relieved to be back in the company of a real human being again. At first she had taken Horst's silence for a quiet joy; but then, as the hours went by, it became clear that it was sullenness. He answered her questions in curt monosyllables and he seemed to flinch from her touch. In a moment of quick irritation—had she waited thirty-six thousand years for *this?*—she asked, "What the hell is the matter with you, Horst?"

He glanced up at her, then glanced away.

"No, look at me." She insisted. "I really want to know."

"You're back, aren't you?" he said at last. "Isn't that enough? You beat the Bale Wolves, Loanna. You must be very proud. You certainly ought to be."

"It's not enough."

"What more could you want?"

"You, Horst."

He looked at her, a look of sudden wild misery, then jumped to his feet. He made a sound something very like a sob, then set off into the rain at a stumbling run. After a while, she left the shack, too, with some vague idea of finding him later, but initially with a desire to be alone to think.

Thirty-six thousand years was a long time, and it was conceivable that

Horst had fallen out of love with her. Maybe he was involved with some girl from the village. But if that was so, why had he gone to the trouble of constructing his astral chart? When first she had seen that monumental undertaking, she had taken it as a measure of his love for her. Now, she wondered if he had built it out of some dogged sense of obligation.

Loanna walked through the rain and soon reached the top of the cliff. Below her, the water surged against the rocks, and as the heavy swell rolled into a cave far below her, the ground trembled. A few stones rattled down the cliff face. The land was under siege and within her lifetime would yield to the ocean. She would see the factory crumble and fall, and she would see the True Humans and the Specialists evacuate to Earth and the ocean cow bellow its death cries into the wind. And, perhaps, she would leave for Earth herself.

But all that was a long time in the future, and there was an infinity of chances of accidental death before that happened, before the People Planet became a world of water. For instance, she could slip and fall from this cliff . . .

She got a grip on herself and came to a decision. She would tackle Horst and find out what his problem was. After all, at one time they had shared every thought. It was ridiculous to be frightened of finding out the truth. She had survived far worse things.

And with that last thought the nightmares came flooding back like a tide, and the shivering started. The Bale Wolves . . . For thirty-six thousand years she had clung to the memory of Horst, shutting out the memory of each previous day's torture because she knew that if she allowed the effects to accumulate, she would go mad. And the imperfections of her own mind had helped her, as the creatures had slapped her and hissed at her and sucked her blood and done whatever their limited imaginations permitted, because she began to forget specific incidents. Once they built a baby and cooked it and ate it in front of her, and she didn't forget that. But otherwise one day was much like the last, and after a while one torture was much like the last, until eventually she was able to treat each day as it came, with Horst the only bright beacon in her memory. Horst, always Horst; her one love, her one hope.

She stepped back from the cliff. She turned her steps in the direction of the Stones.

Horst was not in sight, but she heard his voice from inside the shack and she felt a glow of joy.

Someone else said, "So you see, it's important to the human race that we get hold of a Bale Wolf. We thought probably Loanna would be able to take us to them."

And then Horst's voice. "I'm sure she'll take you."

Then a voice that she recognized as the pathetic neotenite they called the Girl. "It's a lot to ask. We'll understand if she can't face them again."

Horst said, "Loanna isn't afraid."

Loanna felt a blinding flash of rage. Hardly aware of what she was doing, she strode into the shack and confronted the meeting. Zozula was there, and Selena and the young Wild Human and the Girl, all sitting on the floor around Horst.

"You have a damned nerve, Horst!" she said, furious. "If you think I'm going anywhere near those Bale Wolves again, whether the future of the human race depends on it or not, you're crazy! You simply don't know what I've been through. And now you want me to go back?"

"What's the matter?" mumbled Horst. "Are you frightened of them?"

"Of course I'm frightened of them!"

"Well, you didn't give that impression when you took off with them."

"They were safely in a drogue! Horst, you spent a whole night with them. You know what they're like!"

"I thought you were braver than I."

"Well, I wasn't. I hadn't been in their clutches, that's all. I hadn't been affected by them. Now I have—and I'm not going to let it happen again! I'm sorry, you people," she addressed the others, "but I won't take you. I can't. I wouldn't be able to compose myself for the Outer Think. It would be impossible!"

Horst's demeanor changed. He took a deep breath and his shoulders lifted as though shrugging off a burden. "Impossible?" he repeated.

"Well, you know that, Horst. Look what happened to you."

"Maybe I was a coward."

"Cowardice had nothing to do with it." She was talking more quietly now. Hesitantly, she sat beside Horst. "Is that what you've been thinking?"

"For a very long time."

"Don't think it anymore." She took his hand. "I know what you went through, that night at the baby factory. And I know you did it for me, because we couldn't have children. You're no coward, Horst, and neither am I. There are certain things that we simply can't do, no matter how much we may try. We can't be blamed for that. Blame the structure of the Greataway, if you like, but don't blame yourself."

She kissed him.

Manuel cleared his throat and frowned at the others. Quietly they got to their feet and left.

✳

It was a silent party that rode back to Boss Castle. Even the shrugleggers seemed depressed, plodding dismally through the rain, sensing the disappointment of their riders.

As they dismounted, Manuel burst out: "Well, you can hardly blame her!"

The Girl said sadly, "You're right, Manuel." A caracal-man helped her down from the shrugleggger, grinning slyly. They walked through to Selena's quarters.

Selena herself seemed ill at ease. Manuel drifted over to the painting of *She* and stood regarding it. The Girl snorted unpleasantly, and it was Zozula who finally spoke.

"Nobody could have done more than we have. Nobody could have tried harder."

Selena said heavily. "It's the end of everything. We might as well close the People Planet down, now. I feel sorry for our Specialists. We're taking away the whole purpose of their existence. But we can't justify maintaining this place on the basis of the occasional fluky True Human birth —not now that we know what the real problem is."

"I feel sorry for us," said Zozula. "There's no reason for our existence, either, now."

Manuel swung round from the painting. "You True Humans give up easily, don't you?"

With heavy sarcasm, Zozula said, "Perhaps you'd be good enough to tell us what you have in mind, Manuel. Have you rediscovered the Outer Think all by yourself? Don't keep it a secret. By what means are we going to locate the Bale Wolves?"

"The Celestial Steam Locomotive," said Manuel . . .

"Oh, no," said the Girl softly. She remembered Dream Earth and the terrible creature who had held her prisoner, that black-cloaked monster who still tapped his way through her dreams with a white stick and dead eyes. "Oh, no, Manuel."

"I'll look after you, Girl."

"The Locomotive, eh?" said Zozula pensively. "Now, that's not a bad idea, Manuel. We have nothing to lose. Unless they've already met the Bale Wolves and been wiped out. The Locomotive may no longer exist."

"I think . . ." Manuel struggled to find the right words. "I think the

Locomotive always existed and always will. I don't think it's connected
with Time, the way we are, Zozula."

"You could be right. And right or wrong, it's our only chance," Zozula's mood became buoyant. "Selena! We will depart for Earth immediately—Manuel, the Girl and I. Let those fox-people know. And I'd like
you and Brutus to stay here and prepare for the Bale Wolf."

"Can I speak to you in private for a moment?" Selena took his arm
and led him into the next room, closing the door behind them. Here a
huge window looked out over a vast expanse of tossing grey broken only
by the island of the ocean cow's breathing apparatus a kilometer away.
She stood with her back to Zozula, watching the waves. "Do you remember . . . a long time ago, when we found something was wrong with the
tissue bank, we decided to use samples from our own bodies. We thought
we might clone ourselves, as a last resort."

"Yes, but it didn't work. We probably left it until too late—we were too
old. And it wasn't an ethical approach, anyway. Our duty hardly includes populating the world with duplicates of ourselves. We should
never have tried it."

"But we did try it."

"What are you getting at?"

Selena took a deep breath and swung round from the window, facing
him. "It didn't fail completely."

"Oh? I didn't realize that. But it doesn't matter. As I said, it was
unethical."

"It was very unethical, Zo. And I was the guilty one. You see, I took
the only successful baby we produced and raised it myself."

"What!" He stared at her. "You mean there was another True Human
up here, that we didn't know about? But how did you manage to conceal
it? What happened to it?"

"He's alive."

"Where?"

"Here."

He flushed a little, still staring at her. "Look here, Selena, this is
unforgivable. Why did you do it?"

"Oh . . ." She shrugged. "I don't know. At first it was a kind of
superstition, I think. I had an idea the baby might turn out well, so I
didn't want to entrust him to the Specialists. I know that doesn't sound
logical, Zo. After all, they're trained for the job, but . . ." Her voice
trailed off.

"So you and the caracals raised it in secret?"

"Him. He's male. You make it sound so . . . furtive, Zo. Really, it was more like research work. That's how I thought of it . . . *Tried* to think of it. Oh, I know I've done wrong. All I can say is, it won't happen again. It was a mistake, because the man has grown up a little narrow in his outlook. It's time he saw something of Earth."

"I'll say it is," said Zozula grimly. "How old is he?"

"Oh . . . fifty years or so."

"What!"

"Well, I . . ." Again she shrugged helplessly. "You'd better see him," she said.

She opened a door. "You can come and meet our head Cuidador now," she called.

Mentor entered, smiling, saw Zozula and stopped dead.

"My God," said Zozula.

For a while there was silence as the clone-relatives stared at each other. Then, as if seeking an explanation, they turned to Selena.

"Don't say it," she muttered, close to tears.

"No." Zozula frowned thoughtfully. "It's interesting. In a way, it's a little eerie, but I suppose this is what cloning is all about. I must say," he walked around Mentor as though he were a specimen, "He's a fine-looking fellow."

"You were a fine-looking fellow yourself at that age, Zo," said Selena desperately.

And Zozula still studied his double. "I'd like to think so."

Mentor said, "You must be my clone-father. It's good to see another True Human."

Selena turned away from them.

She heard Zozula say, "We have a lot to talk about. When we get back to Earth, I'll introduce you to the Rainbow, and to Caradoc, our agent in there. You'll find we have an interesting setup. Perhaps I should take a direct interest in your education. But first, I have two young people I'd like you to meet. Don't be surprised at their appearance . . ."

Selena found herself alone. The moment she'd dreaded for many years had come and gone. Had it come? Had it gone?

Watching the waves roll in, she whispered, *"Zozula, will you never realize?"*

HERE ENDS THAT PART OF
THE SONG OF EARTH KNOWN TO MEN AS
MANKIND'S CRADLE

OUR TALE CONTINUES WITH THE GROUP
OF STORIES AND LEGENDS KNOWN AS
THE OUTER THINK

where the Triad
again rides behind the Celestial Steam Locomotive,
then does battle with the Bale Wolves
and secures the release of Starquin
the almighty Five-in-One

LEGENDS OF DREAM EARTH

•••

What should we call you?" asked Zozula. "We can hardly address you by my own name. That could cause some confusion." He was in high good humor.

"Selena called me Mentor."

"Mentor it is, then. Now, this is the Rainbow Room. It's our access to the knowledge in the Rainbow. That's Cytherea over there."

Mentor was impressed and a little frightened. Since arriving in the Dome his senses had been battered by new impressions, chief among which was the awesome vastness of everything. And now this Rainbow Room. It was enormous, filled with people indulging in some huge and noisy bacchanal. "Which one is Cytherea?"

Zozula was smiling tolerantly at Mentor's amazement. "Cytherea's the one at the console. The others are all Dream People."

"Dream People?"

"Inhabitants of a part of the Rainbow known as Dream Earth."

"You'd better explain. I can't take all this in."

"Well, you saw the neotenites—those people who looked like the Girl, here, all asleep on benches. There are ten thousand of them, and they're all plugged into Dream Earth. It's an imaginary world created by the Rainbow, where the neotenites' minds can live whatever lives they please."

Mentor watched the people. They were without exception beautiful and they wore flowing robes. A few animals were there, too—sleek cheetahs and lean running dogs with jeweled collars. The 83rd millennium was in vogue.

"They don't look like neotenites," said Mentor.

"They can adopt any form they choose, by means of a process known as a Bigwish. It takes a lot out of them, though. When they change bodies, they deplete a spiritual quality we call psy. It takes them at least fifty years to build up their psy sufficiently to change again."

"What about those animals?" Mentor pointed at a pride of lions lazing at the foot of a classical column. "Are those people who've Bigwished?"

"They might be, but it's unlikely. I expect the animals are smallwishes, just like that pavilion over there. Smallwishes don't need so much psy. They're used for creating background scenery. You see that?" Totally anachronistic, a hot-air balloon floated into view, garishly painted. A group of yelling Neanderthals hung over the rim of the basket, dropping objects onto the orgy beneath. These proved to be bags of a bright saffron powder that burst open on contact, dyeing the revelers and obviously producing an unpleasant smell. Confusion reigned. Guns appeared out of nowhere and the balloon came under heavy fire. For an instant it sprouted flames, but then it metamorphosied into a huge bird that flapped heavily away, bearing the cheering primitives on its back. The partying resumed, the participants gradually shedding their yellow dye.

"All done by smallwishes," said Zozula.

Mentor regarded the Girl. "You actually lived in that place? What was it like?"

"Too easy," she replied.

"What do you mean?"

"You could have anything you wanted, just for a smallwish. You wished, and the Rainbow set it up for you. You could never come to any harm, not unless you managed to achieve Total Death. There was no challenge. People do the craziest things in there, simply because they get so bored."

"What kind of things?"

"When they're really tired of it all, when they've done everything and seen everything, they take a ride behind the Celestial Steam Locomotive. And I have a suspicion they never come back."

Manuel said, "It's not that bad. We rode the Train once, and we survived. And look—there's Caradoc and Eloise. What could be more normal than that?"

The scene had shifted, drifting away from the noisy party, as Cytherea scanned soft hillsides and valleys, homing in on a stone cottage set among elms and chestnut trees. Two horses stood in a cobbled yard. Caradoc and Eloise were emerging from the cottage, dressed as Terrestrial Protectors of the 92nd millennium.

"Now there's a good-looking couple," said Mentor.

The story of Caradoc and Eloise is one of the classic legends of the Song of Earth, and it goes like this.

Once there was a Mole. The Mole was a grotesque thing, deaf, dumb and blind, the only son of an influential Wild Human called Lord Shout. Lord Shout loved his son dearly, but could not communicate with him, until one day they met a wild neotenite telepath called Eloise. Eloise dug into the Mole's thoughts.

She told Lord Shout that the Mole had a brilliant mind, but no way of using it. So Lord Shout asked Zozula, a Cuidador, if the Mole could be placed in Dome Azul and his mind allowed to wander free in Dream Earth, where at least he would be able to converse with other people's minds. Zozula agreed, partly from pity, but also because he believed the incisive brain of the Mole could benefit Dream Earth.

Meanwhile the Mole had fallen in love with Eloise, and she with him. Or perhaps their minds fell in love, because they were both very ugly people. Then Eloise fell sick and died, as is the way with neotenites.

The Mole carried the memory of Eloise with him into Dream Earth, and he re-created her with a smallwish. But the Eloise he created was not a neotenite. She was exceptionally beautiful, even in a world where beautiful people are the norm. This was because Eloise, when describing herself to the blind Mole, had cheated on him. She had made herself out to be far prettier than she really was. It was simple vanity, and quite excusable.

And the Mole became Caradoc, a fine young man, brilliant and athletic. This was Eloise's doing, too. She had persuaded him that he, too, was beautiful, but this time she acted out of love rather than vanity. She took the elements of his character—the kindness and the intelligence—and she expressed them in physical form, the way an artist creates a mind-painting. And she told him, telepathically: *This is the way you are, Mole.* So the Mole Bigwished himself that way, and became Caradoc.

The minstrels of later years forgave Eloise for deluding him:

> *Come, hear about the forest nymph who met a*
> *crawling Mole,*

*And with the fabric of her love she made his body
whole.*

Eloise stayed with Caradoc for a thousand years, sharing his adventures in Dream Earth until his real body wore out and he suffered Total Death. They lived happily, though sometimes they quarreled, of course—a thousand years is a long time. But they never parted. How could they? Caradoc couldn't get Eloise out of his mind. She'd arranged it that way.

There was a happentrack on which Zozula appeared before Caradoc and said, "We've solved the neoteny problem. We have a good, strong body all ready for you. You can come back to the real world, now."

And Caradoc looked at Eloise, who was watching her reflection in a pool. She glanced up at him, brushing the hair from her eyes, and smiled. *She is a creature of my mind,* thought Caradoc, *and if I leave Dream Earth, she will cease to exist.*

"Thank you, Zozula," he said, "but I'll stay here where I am."

Other legends have come out of Dream Earth, and some of them are not so happy as the story of Caradoc and Eloise. One of these legends concerns a creature so vile that he could not have existed in the real world, because he would have been quickly killed. He came into being during a period when life was dull, the Dream People having exhausted their imagination for a while. The monsters had become bigger, and their claws sharper and their teeth more numerous, and they thundered through Dream Earth while the people clung to one another in joyful fright. But the fact that the monsters could not actually hurt people caused their demise. They became parodies of themselves as people began to wish humorous appendages onto them. This culminated in the preposterous creatures known as the Tyrannosaurus Wrecks, a shambling herd of gap-toothed carnosaurs that were the butt of the Dream People's insults for several centuries, until someone took pity on them and smallwished them out of existence. Clearly, something more subtle was needed in order to give the people the frisson of terror that they craved.

Now, the Rainbow cannot read people's minds; it can only record what they do. Many of the legends surrounding the creation of that misshapen and terrifying creature, Blind Pew, arise out of supposition and not fact. It is fact, however, that for centuries the loathesome figure of Pew tapped his way around the dimensions of Dream Earth, black-cloaked, stinking and indescribably evil. He filled the Dream People with a very real dread, partly because he was created out of their own innermost fears, but also because he achieved such stature that he *could not be wished away.* Countless smallwishes had gone into his creation, until he became a cesspit of the unconscious, a repository into which anyone might unload their secret terrors and feel a little lighter for it. It would take more than a mere smallwish to dispose of Blind Pew.

The Dream People tried, but at first their efforts were uncoordinated. By the time they thought to assemble a group of people rich in psy, for the purpose of jointly smallwishing Pew out of existence, it was too late. The blind man had developed his own defense—which was to anticipate, by a fraction of a second, the actions of others. He could dodge bullets and meteorites, and for a while it seemed that he would stalk the reaches of Dream Earth forever. Then somebody hit upon the idea of tricking him onto the Skytrain.

The driver of the Celestial Steam Locomotive, himself a slippery character, was able to maroon Pew in that strange corner of the Rainbow known as the Land of Lost Dreams, where he remained, tapping his way among other stranded creatures and screaming oaths at a magenta sky, for many millennia.

And during this period the Girl had fallen into his clutches.

She outwitted him and escaped, but he followed her to Dream Earth and, for a short time, held her captive again until she was rescued by Caradoc. Terror is a subjective thing, and different people have different fears, but when the Girl dreamed of Pew, which was most nights, her terror could be compared to that of Loanna when she dreamed of the Bale Wolves.

✳

"I don't think I'll come with you into Dream Earth," said the Girl casually. "You don't need me. I'll stay in the Rainbow Room and monitor you. Someone has to do that."

"Cytherea can do it," said Caradoc. The young man's image, four times life-size, stood before them. This was one of the unexpected benefits of the Mole's entry into Dream Earth. He had discovered a way to communicate directly with the Cuidadors in the Rainbow Room.

"I've been trained to operate the console," said the Girl. "That's why you brought me out of Dream Earth in the first place, wasn't it, Zozula?"

Zozula said, "You have a knack with the Locomotive. We need you with us, Girl. Remember what happened last time? We'd be riding the Train still, if it weren't for you. You must come."

Now Manuel spoke, annoyed at the insensitivity of Zozula and Caradoc. "Where's Blind Pew?" he asked Caradoc.

"The last time I saw him, he was back in the Land of Lost Dreams. You don't need to worry about Pew, Girl. He's a spent force."

"Are you sure?"

"Of course he's sure," said Zozula confidently. "Anyway, Pew's only a smallwish. He hardly concerns us. It's the Bale Wolves we must concentrate on."

"I can't help you there," said Caradoc. "They're out of reach of the Rainbow. But as for the Celestial Steam Locomotive—so far as I can tell, it's always here within the Rainbow, in spite of the fact that it's always out in the Greataway, too. It exists in strange dimensions, does the Locomotive. I can get you aboard without any trouble. What happens after that is not my responsibility."

The third legend of Dream Earth has no end. It starts with a Dream Person whose name is lost in antiquity and who was doomed to Total Death for certain reasons. This man wished to create a single thing of beauty before he died. After many failures, he finally conceived the idea of recreating a machine of the 51st millennium—a machine that had the power to touch men with an indescribable magic.

He created a steam locomotive in accordance with ancient plans in the Rainbow. He created it in such minute detail that it took an enormous amount of psy, because each rivet required a separate smallwish to drive it home. After a while he was helped by other Dream People, and the locomotive became the big project of the age. The creator died before it was finished, but he would have been proud of the result. For centuries the locomotive stood as a monument to human achievement of the machine age, a thing possessing a grace and artistry unrivaled by the starships and brontomeks of later periods.

The creator would not have been proud of what happened in the end, when the natural boredom and petulance of people who could have everything they wanted caused them to tamper with his dream.

The locomotive became a magnet for meddlers with psy to spare. Tracks were laid and a long train of carriages added, and spectacular accidents were staged, with countless imaginary casualties. Soon even this became dull and the train began to set off on more unusual journeys, unconfined by track. In the end, loaded with smallwishes and sustained by the powerful composite belief of its passengers, it slipped out of the normal boundaries of the Rainbow and into the dimensions of the Greataway. The Celestial Steam Locomotive, as people began to call it, became a bastard version of the Outer Think.

It was an ironic result of an unselfish concept, because the train attracted passengers of a particular kind—pleasure-seeking, world-weary, sometimes vicious—far removed from the gentle people for whom the creator had built the Locomotive.

And the legend has no end, because the Skytrain still thunders among the stars in a timeless dimension of the Greataway where everything happens at the same instant, and will always do so.

On the Skytrain

•••

*T*he Train flew through the Greataway, and the stars flickered past like lighted windows seen from afar. The passengers were preoccupied with their own affairs: drinking, playing cards, doing whatever people do to kill time when there is excitement in prospect—because the driver of the Celestial Steam Locomotive, one Long John Silver, had promised them a meeting with the Bale Wolves.

"By Jove, I'm looking forward to bagging a brace of those rascals!" said Sir Charles Willoughby-Amersham, baronet.

Mentor sat by himself. He had boarded this outlandish Train alone, and he wished he knew what had happened to the others. The conversation of the past two hours had been ominous and he badly needed reassurance. "We could be making a big mistake. That robot over there said we could be facing Total Death. I . . ." He gulped uncontrollably. "I want to get off."

"Well, don't tell the driver that, dearie," whispered Blondie Tranter, a buxom woman with bedroom eyes.

"It'll all come right in the end," added the little brown girl, Bambi. "It always does, you know."

"I wish . . ." Mentor's voice trailed away, as he realized his words could be overheard and misinterpreted.

"I wish I knew what happened to those people who were with me," he said eventually.

"What people, I wonder," said Bambi.

"A man who looked like me, and a plump girl. And a young Wild Human. They said they'd been on the Train before—you must remember them."

"It's best not to think about it," said Bambi, turning to the window. "Much nicer to forget. Oh, look—a falling star!"

"She means we don't talk about people who disappear," Blondie Tranter explained quietly. "Not on the Train. You'll get used to it."

"But why do people disappear? Silver won't allow smallwishes; he says he needs all the psy we have, just to keep the Train—" he gulped again "—in existence!" The flamboyant figure of the Locomotive's driver had terrified Mentor.

Blondie looked cunning. "Sometimes people become a liability. They have a negative effect on the Train. They become skeptical and that threatens us all. It's better that they disappear."

"But how, if—"

"Silver shows them the footplate of the Locomotive . . . and the controls . . . and he introduces them to the fireman." She had said all this quickly and jerkily with eyes closed. Now she snapped them open and continued, "There, I've said it. Now let's forget all about it."

But Mentor couldn't. The suspicion was growing within him that he was stranded on the Train, at the mercy of Silver and his ghastly stoker, who had consigned Zozula, Manuel and the Girl to some kind of nondimensional limbo. Anything was possible in this unpredictable place. And if this were not bad enough, there were the Pirates . . .

The Pirates swaggered around the carriage, a group of picturesquely clad rogues who had apparently known one another for a long time. In their chosen period of history, they were close to Silver's time, but it was noticeable that the driver ignored them, stumping rapidly past them whenever he made his way down the aisle. The Pirates, for their part, lost no opportunity to bait Silver, on one occasion toppling him to the floor by kicking his crutch as he went past.

And they had noticed Mentor.

He saw them talking together and glancing at him from time to time, and he guessed what would happen next. They would stroll down the aisle in a body, cram themselves into nearby seats and subject him to that mental torture beloved of Dream Earth deadbeats: talking at, rather than to, him, humiliating him with veiled insults, taunting him with painful little smallwishes. And if he retaliated, any one of them looked quite capable of coming back at him with a Terminal Bigwish.

He'd recently witnessed the effects of a Terminal Bigwish while Zozula was showing him the workings of Dream Earth through the scanner in the Rainbow Room.

He'd seen a villein, sitting in a medieval inn, teasing a serving wench. (Why anyone should Bigwish themselves into a serving wench was beyond his comprehension, but the passage of a few thousand years inevitably produces oddball wishes, out of sheer boredom.) The villein had caused the wench to spill pottage down her apron, had tripped her and fondled her roughly and had finally poured beer down her cleavage. The only possible explanation for such behavior was Temporal Insanity—or, conceivably, that the villein thought the wench was a composite smallwish.

And the wench had finally reacted.

She followed him outside. There was a village green and stone cottages and a few sheep. Willow trees leaned over a pond fed by a meandering stream. People went about their tasks amiably, greeting one another in the street. It was a pleasant place, and people who wished into it often stayed for a long time. The villein lay down beside the stream intending to doze in the sun.

He never had the chance.

The wench Bigwished herself into an allosaurus. It towered above the cottages on legs like oaks. It gazed questingly this way and that, sighted the villein—he being the nearest morsel—bent down and devoured him.

There was panic in the village.

(There was panic among the Keepers, too. Cytherea had been on duty at the Rainbow console at the time, and for a moment she'd been unable to recollect the correct procedure for such emergencies. Dream monsters usually presented no problem; they were smallwishes and couldn't hurt. Dream People almost never Bigwished themselves into animals—it was tantamount to a life sentence, since animals do not have the intelligence to wish themselves back into being humans. But now Cytherea was confronted with a monster that, by Dream Earth standards, was quite real. It had imposed Total Death on the villein by extinguishing his psy. Zozula, Juni and Husto came running. The monster was looking around for further delicacies. Cytherea's hands flickered over the tactile surfaces. The monster snatched the thatch roof from a cottage in a giant mouthful, exposing the terrified people beneath. Then the training of many centuries imposed its discipline on Cytherea, and she made the correct moves.)

As Mentor watched, the allosaurus had flickered out of existence. Composite Reality adjusted. Somebody smallwished the thatch back on.

But nobody could wish the villein back. He was Totally Dead, and in another dimension, his plump body was disconnected and recycled.

So Mentor had seen the terrifying reality of violence, and his mind balked at contemplating it again. Coming to a quick decision, he made his way down the aisle and slipped through the corridor connector. He could retreat the whole length of the train, if need be. He had no idea how long the train was, but suspected it might be at least ten carriages. In fact, he was short by thirty-two kilometers.

He slid aside the door to the next carriage—and stopped dead. The carriage held witches, dressed in black with tall pointed hats, and druids in coarse robes. The carriage was huge, wide and high, and contained a small-scale Stonehenge set atop a grassy rise. The witches and druids danced and chanted within this diorama, the centerpiece of which was a stone slab. A maiden lay on it, dressed in white. A priest stood near, knife in hand. The chanting was reaching a crescendo.

Mentor shut the door, blocking out the scene. He wondered at the kind of people who boarded the Train. He wondered what it was like, to have been everything and done everything, your Humanity leeched away by experiences, century by century, until you finished up something less than human. He wondered if innocence was synonymous with Humanity and that question frightened him, because it seemed to hold out no hope. He had to get off this accursed train. Beside him was a door. He tried the handle, but it was locked. In despair he flung himself against the door once more, and this time the handle seemed pliable and warm. It yielded readily, and the door swung open.

Space roared like a thousand lions. Tiny pinpoints of light flickered past. Yet he could breathe. Holding onto this one Reality, he told himself: *Everything I see is an illusion. I am on Earth, and I can do anything I want. I may be a little new to this, but I'm not asking for a Bigwish. All I want is enough moxie to get off this damned Train and back home. The Girl explained how to do it.*

He concentrated, summoned up his psy and prepared to jump. He thought the act of jumping would trigger an adrenalin surge that might, in turn, boost his unpracticed psy.

He shouted, "Here I come, Earth!"

And a voice close by said, "Not so long as my name's Silver, lad."

A hand closed around his arm like a tourniquet.

THE CRASH

So what might ye be planning to do—might I make so bold as to ask?"
Silver's voice was deadly polite. His hamlike face was ruddy with the
effort of dragging Mentor back aboard.

"I wanted to get off, that's all."

"Ye scurvy dog! Desert the ship, is it? I tell ye, mister, I've had a
bellyful o' whimpering dogs." Silver's temper was unleashed, and he
shook Mentor with a menace that brought back all the fear of physical
violence.

"Let me go! You don't need me. I don't even know how to smallwish!"

" 'Tis a matter of . . . Belay there, messmate." The eyes became
shrewd. Silver paused, thinking. He scratched his head, tilting his hat.
"How did ye open yon door?" His voice was quiet, now. "Tell me that,
shipmate. Did ye wish it open? Becuz that'd take a powerful draught o'
psy, lad. More'n ye're capable of, I'll lay to that!"

"I don't know. Let me go, will you? I just turned the handle, that's all.
It felt kind of soft."

"Ah-hah!" Silver was silent for some time, thoughts flittering across
his face like shadows. Eventually he released his grasp and made some
ineffectual gesture toward dusting Mentor off. "Beggin' yer pardon, shipmate. Seems like old Barbecue's jumped the gun again. Never intended
no harm. I get these headaches, y'see, and with them comes the most
powerful evil nightmares. I see things'd turn yer blood to ice, I do."

"You do?" Mentor found these sudden changes of mood hard to keep up with and very unsettling. He wanted to get away, but he feared another outburst if he tried. "W-what kind of things, Silver?"

"Ghouls, lads. Ghouls the likes of that no-good stoker in the cab, all dressed in black—'cept they be women. 'Tis a deadly circle, lad. I drink the rum to shut out the fear and get me some sleep—then with the sleep comes the dreams. Women, all dressed in black, a-pointin' at me and a-tellin' me to drive on, to keep going no matter what, like as if 'twere the most important thing on Earth. I got them both. There's that devil in the cab, stoking like as to send us all to Perdition, and when I get me some sleep, there's the women. There's no rest on this Train for an honest man!" And his lips trembled, and for one moment Mentor thought the driver was going to weep in self-pity. The smell of liquor was pungent on Silver's breath.

"I'm sorry. I . . . I wish I could help."

"Mebbe ye can, lad—mebbe ye can." Silver's tone became wheedling. "The troubles of this Train are more than one poor body can bear. Mebbe if ye just . . . keep yer eyes peeled, keep yer ear to the timbers and report back to me the minute ye smell a rat. There's people aboard this Train," continued Silver portentously, "who wish us no good, and ye and me is a-going to winkle them out, by thunder! A bargain's a bargain—and in return I'll see no man lays a finger on ye, lad!"

"It's a deal." There was little else Mentor could say. Silver shook his hand and slid back the connecting door, and together they walked forward.

✳

To Mentor's infinite relief, Zozula, Manuel and the Girl had arrived during his absence. He sat down beside them. "Where have you been?" he asked querulously.

"Who knows?" said Zozula. "Time plays funny tricks on the Train. These passengers—" he waved an arm "—they're exactly the same as we left them, when we were on the Train before. Even the blackjack game is still going on. Yet by my measurement of Time, a couple of weeks have passed."

Confirming his statement, Blonde Tranter leaned across. "So Long John Silver wouldn't let you off the Train, dearie? That's too bad. Still, the journey is fun, isn't it?"

Bambi said, "I'm so glad you decided not to leave us."

The Girl yawned, her psy exhausted. The image of Blind Pew was with her, tap-tapping his way around the Land of Lost Dreams. Her body ached and she was utterly spent, and she didn't have the energy to run from him. She closed her eyes, needing to sleep but knowing that Pew would find her in her dreams.

Mentor said, "Let's get back to Earth. I'm going to throw up."

"For a clone of mine you don't—" began Zozula irritably, but Manuel dug him in the ribs. The Girl was dozing, her body twitching restlessly, and she was mumbling to herself. Manuel took her hand and slid his arm around her elephantine body as far as he could, comforting her.

"She's not well," whispered Manuel. "Her body isn't strong enough for what she wants to do, and her heart isn't strong enough for her body. She needs to rest, but you won't let her." Gently he stroked the Girl's hair and began to sing a lullaby from his childhood, softly drawing a sad nostalgia from the words of long ago:

> Hey, little baby, don't you cry,
> Lift your head and watch the sky,
> Float like a feather up on high,
> While the guanaco clouds go by.

And the Girl's eyelids fluttered open and she smiled. Then she slept again, more easily now. Zozula sniffed. Mentor started as Silver went stumping by with an expression of urgency, the parrot clinging unsteadily to his shoulder. There was some kind of commotion at the back of the carriage; then shortly afterward Silver returned to the cab. A sudden explosion startled everyone. Conversation ceased. The Train rushed on, faster than ever, swaying wildly. A light bulb came loose and dropped to the floor, shattering. The sliding door crashed open.

Silver stood there. There was a wild excitement in his face. "We've run through a signal, shipmates! There be detonators on the tracks but we can't pay them no heed—not us. We needs must keep a-going, leastways if we don't want yonder black stoker to blow us all to Kingdom Come—that's the short and the long of it!"

"But . . . The signal must have been against us for a *reason.*" A Neanderthal woman spoke quietly to Manuel.

Little brown Bambi overheard her. "Everything will turn out fine in the end!" she said gaily. "It always does. Except just once . . ." And she went quiet, suddenly quiet, remembering one Dreadful Thing that she always tried to forget and that she'd never told anyone.

Another detonator went off. "How realistic can you get?" Zozula's comment was in tones of the utmost cynicism.

Silver flipped a small seat out of the wall and sat on it, swaying, regarding the passengers with a strange intensity. " 'Tis a mighty dangerous thing we do, to be sure. His gaze wandered to Zozula, who stared back blandly, with a faint smile. The wheels screamed as the train hit a curve.

"Very convincing," said Zozula.

Suddenly the noise stopped, as though switched off. Manuel grabbed his seat as the Train seemed to rise into the air. Somebody screamed, and Sir Charles exclaimed, "By God—" pulling himself to his feet. The carriage tilted abruptly and he fell, smashing his head against a steel seat support. Now the carriage tilted end over end and Manuel ducked as Silver's crutch came skimming overhead. Beside him, the Girl was falling toward the roof. People were screaming. Bodies tumbled in all directions, arms thrashing, legs kicking. A series of shuddering crashes jolted the carriage. Manuel hung onto his seat, letting it all happen around him, hanging onto the Girl's waist. Then, his grip broken by her weight, he too fell, landing heavily on his back, the Girl on top of him. The carriage came to rest on its roof. For a shocked instant there was silence.

And Silver still sat on his seat, now upside down. Manuel followed his gaze. Above him Zozula sat, unmoved also, seeming to hang impossibly from the upside-down seat, regarding Silver steadily.

Silver said into the stunned quiet. "Ye be the queerest passenger I've ever sailed alongside, and that's a fact."

"Not so queer as you, I'll be bound." Zozula's smile held no joy. He twisted around and, holding the seat, lowered himself until he stood beside Manuel. "Where's Mentor?" he asked.

"He's all right." Manuel helped the Girl, shocked from her catastrophic awakening, to her feet. "The door's open over there, see? Let's go and find out what's happened."

"If we can believe what we see." Zozula picked his way through the milling, chattering crowd of passengers, following Manuel to the door. On the way he passed Sir Charles, who was staring incredulously at the blood that was smeared, wet and warm and red and *real,* on his hand where he had touched his head.

THE LOST ARMY

Manuel stepped down onto pale sand that felt insubstantial under his bare feet. He turned and helped the Girl out, saw Mentor emerge with Zozula, then walked away from the upturned carriage. He had the strangest feeling that he was walking on top of a flat cloud. The sand stretched into the distance, rising slightly to the horizon, featureless and smooth. The whole scene was bathed in a soft light with no visible source.

The carriage lay stark and black and wrecked. Bodies lay all around. Some of them moved, others were motionless and the force of their impact had half buried them. Manuel ran to one of them, a woman who lay twisted, her blood staining the sand. She whimpered softly as he turned her into a more comfortable position, straightening her legs and heaping sand into a pillow for her head. Nearby the Locomotive stood unscathed, majestic, making quiet steamy sounds of impatience. A cowled head looked out of the cab in silent contemplation.

"Water . . ." The woman's voice was so faint that Manuel had to lean close.

"I'll get you some. You'll be all right." He hurried up to Silver, who leaned against the carriage side, smiling.

"I reckon ye be wastin' yer time, lad."

"Just a glass of water, that's all. Where can I get some?"

Zozula approached. "I don't think you can help, Manuel. I don't think anyone can."

"We can't just leave her lying there! And what about all the others?" Too much death, too much horror. He seemed to hear the woman's voice in his mind, pleading. He looked around frantically. The other passengers from Manuel's carriage had by now climbed down and were wandering irresolutely among the bodies, occasionally dropping to their knees to feel a pulse or murmur a word of encouragement.

Manuel ran to the Locomotive and clambered up the steps. The cab was quiet, the gauges still. The fireman still gazed out of the window, his back to Manuel. When the boy tapped him on the shoulder, he didn't move, but Manuel jerked his hand away, fingers tingling with a strange, psychic shock—not heat, not cold, but some sensation unlike any he'd ever felt before. He couldn't bring himself to touch the fireman again; neither could he speak to him. The hooded creature's very presence aroused a superstitious dread, the sight of his back was a hideous menace. Manuel swallowed, shivered and looked for water. He found a tap set into the tender, ran a trickle of brown, lukewarm water into a dirty cup and quickly left.

The woman was gone. The sand was smooth, as though she'd never been there.

The Girl stood nearby, with Zozula and Mentor.

"Where did she go?"

"I . . ." The Girl gulped. "I wished her away, Manuel. I couldn't watch you upsetting yourself. I'd wish all the others away, too, but I can't spare the psy."

"But she was dying!"

Zozula took Manuel's arm. "She wasn't real, son. None of them are. Neither is the crash real. It's all staged, all circumstantial evidence to reinforce people's belief in the Skytrain. Soon they'll start putting it all together again, and we'll be on our way." Indeed, breakdown cranes had already arrived and were swinging the carriages back into position.

"There's a track . . . rails—look!"

"Why not?" Zozula smiled. "It doesn't take much imagination. Look around you, Manuel. This place is an empty stage with a minimum of props. Just sand, track and Train. And a few bodies to occupy people's attention."

"It's cruel. Why do they have to use death to convince us?"

"Maybe it's the one thing everyone believes in."

Farther away, Silver was directing a crane, his crutch planted firmly in the sand, waving imperiously with his free hand and uttering a string of nautical oaths. Overhead, a boom swung ponderously and hooks were guided into position, engaging with projections on the upturned carriages. A railroad engineer might have objected to the methods used, but they were convincing enough for the passengers, who gathered around Silver, offering suggestions and encouragement.

Away on the horizon, the rim of sand became blurred.

Manuel saw the little brown girl standing nearby and joined her. She gave him a quick glance from doe eyes and said, "Isn't it just awful? But it'll be all right soon, you just see. Look, they've got our carriage back on the rails already."

"So what's going to happen about all the dead people?"

And Bambi said, "I don't see any dead people."

Manuel thought: *Maybe it's me. Maybe this scene is designed to give everyone what he needs to see—and for some reason I need to see cruelty. But haven't I seen enough, Belinda?*

Silver went hurrying toward the Locomotive, swinging along energetically, leaving no trail in the sand. "All aboard, shipmates! Look lively, now!"

"But . . ." Manuel looked around in bewilderment. Bambi was already climbing into the carriage. The cranes were gone. The sand was taking on the texture of mist. The Train, tidy and straight, stretched into the distance.

And descending the slopes from the horizon, moving diagonally toward the Train, came a vast multitude. Thousands upon thousands of people, clad alike in drab clothing, converging silently upon the Train. The sight of them, unhurried and relentless in their advance, sent a shiver down Manuel's spine and looking around, he saw Silver leaning from the cab, watching them, too. Silver saw him and motioned him urgently to get on board. Manuel paused, uncertain, wondering who all these people could be, and almost curious enough to find out . . .

The phenomenon known as the Lost Army of the Greataway has been observed many times. It was first documented around 92,700C during the short years of the Outer Think before the war with the Red Planet. In the words of Psycaptain Go: "We had paused for revitalization—not more than five Earth minutes, I should say. We hung in a convenient Pocket and joined hands. Pride and Speedy were tired, although I could probably have gone on. Perhaps we relaxed the Sac [Invisible Spaceship]; I'm not sure. Anyway, suddenly, there they were, looking in. Hundreds of them, humans in the middle of Nothingness, just hanging there with limbs loose like dangling puppets. I must have clenched up with shock, because the Sac began to turn opaque and the faces faded. Since we were revitalizing, it was not convenient to ask the others if they'd seen what I'd seen. But Pride and I are empathetic, to a degree, and I sensed some surprise there. The situation was extremely dangerous because I'd lost concentration and, as I say, the others were tired. We had a drogue and a great responsibility, and here was I, unable to get these faces out of my mynde! The faces were expressionless only on the surface—because, behind that blankness, I sensed an unvoiced Need, almost, I think, a Question. In some unimaginable way, all those suspended people *wanted in.* We couldn't take anyone, of course; to break the Sac, even in a Pocket, would have been fatal. So I tried to shut my mynde to them—one face in particular, that of a child of about five physical, occupied a portion of my mynde for months afterward, impairing my efficiency—and in due course I was able to Think again, if sporadically. Who were those people? Were they memories of all the faces I'd ever seen, dredged from my mynde by some quirk of the Greataway? I don't think so, because Speedy remembered seeing the child, too. Were they the faces of the human dead? Such a notion is overly superstitious and also unlikely. The human dead over the ages are numberless, but there was a feeling of *finiteness* about the number of the people I'd glimpsed. And I saw no alien dead. So it remains a mystery, I'm afraid, and likely to remain so. Current theory precludes any rupture of the Sac."

So said Psycaptain Go, a long time ago.

Knowing nothing of this, Manuel decided to board the Train.

It is probably fortunate that he did.

Departure of the Pirates

Silver sat on his folding seat, leg outstretched, regarding his passengers benevolently. "We met a deadly test, shipmates, and we showed our true colors." There was a roar of acclamation from his audience—and none were more enthusiastic than the Pirates, who set up a cry of yo-ho-ho! as they milled around at the rear of the carriage. Manuel noticed that Mentor had changed his seat. Now he sat several rows behind them, quite close to the Pirates. These rowdies were now stamping and yelling, and the rest of the passengers began to take up the cry.

"Splice the mainbrace!" shouted Silver suddenly. "Up spirits, me lads!"

"How lovely," said Bambi.

Silver produced a large bottle of dark rum; others were handing around foaming bottles of champagne. Zozula and the Girl refused their bottles, passing them on. Mentor drank. Manuel held his for a second, looking longingly at the cool, bubbling liquid spilling down the neck, then handed it to Blondie Tranter, on receiving a sharp glance from Zozula. Silver drank ostentatiously, throat working, then jerked the bottle from his lips with a sucking noise and began to sing.

"Broach me a bottle of Old Jamaica."

And the passengers joined in, "Heave-ho! and down she goes!"

"Drink with the Devil and meet your Maker!"

And the response roared back, "Heave-ho! and down she goes!" And on the ho! Silver slammed his crutch against the wall, raised his bottle

and drank again. Somewhere in there Sir Charles could be heard saying
". . . finest body of men it's ever been my pleasure to . . . ," while
beside Manuel, Blondie Tranter gulped down her champagne, a fair
quantity bubbling down her chin and over her breasts, like a mountain
stream over smooth boulders. Manuel laughed. The fun was infectious,
and it seemed to him that Zozula and the Girl were spoilsports, sitting
there disapproving like old Chine himself. He grinned at Blondie and she
grinned back, and just for a second he was far away, remembering his
childhood and Horse Day celebrations, the people of Pu'este all drinking
kuta, laughing with one another, dancing in strange costumes that were
obscurely frightening—just as these strange passengers were—but all the
more fun for being scary.

It ended suddenly with a roar of rage, the way those Horse Day celebrations used to end, all too often.

Silver lurched to his feet and swung down the aisle, an expression of
terrifying malignancy on his face, all clowning finished. He hurled his
bottle and it shattered against the rear door that had slammed shut an
instant before. "Avast there, ye mutinous whelps!" he shouted.

The door slid open again before Silver reached it, and Mentor staggered through as if pushed. He fell into Silver's arms and they tottered as
though trying to fit some crazy dance step together, then crashed to the
floor. Silver was up immediately, levering himself on his crutch. He
threw himself at the door, tugging at the handle.

"Well, will you just look at that," said Blondie Tranter in tones of
amazement.

She was staring out the window. Manuel followed her gaze and saw,
among the stars, a mechanical device encapsulated in a golden corona so
that it shone brightly against the dark backdrop of the Greataway. It was
receding fast, but before it became just one more speck among the stars
he was able to make out the angular shape of a railroad handcar, a flat
platform on wheels and attached to it a long bar with handles at the
extremities, pivoted on a central fulcrum. Pirates grasped these handles,
three at each end, working them frantically up and down, propelling
themselves and their bizarre carriage into nothingness. As they went they
changed color, the golden glow deepened to green, then blue. Finally, a
tiny purple spot, they winked out.

Silver turned back from the door, a jovial smile fixed on his face. He
dragged Mentor to his feet and dusted him off with brutal blows. Still
smiling, he said quietly through his teeth, "We had a deal, me lad. As I
recall, ye were to report any goings-on, and in return I'd steer ye clear o'

stormy weather. Well, ye shirked yer duty, lad, and now a bunch o' lily-livered whelps have deserted the ship. And deserters they may be, but they had a power of psy, ye may lay to it! They *believed*, lad. They believed."

"I'm . . . I'm sorry."

"And sorrier yet will be." Silver thrust his huge face close. "Because ye're no use to man or ship, lad. Ye're useless dunnage. I've a mind to be rid o' ye. 'Tis time ye met the stoker on this here craft."

Mentor swallowed involuntarily; what had the Tranter woman said? *He introduces them to the fireman* . . . "Listen," he said urgently. "I'll—"

But Silver had whirled around and was stumping forward. About to disappear into the Locomotive, he suddenly paused and swung round to face the passengers, the smile intensified.

"Shipmates! The song!" Pounding with his crutch, he led the passengers into the chorus:

> *We're all aboard for the trackless night.*
> *(Close your eyes and believe! Believe!)*
> *Wheels a-clanking and the firebox bright . . .*

The lusty song faltered and faded out. Someone gave a small scream. Silver's voice petered out too, in bewilderment and anger. Then he followed the direction of everyone's gaze. He turned round.

Standing beside him, in the passage between the carriage and the Locomotive, was the fireman. Silver backed away with a groan of pure terror. The black-cowled figure advanced two measured steps, then stopped, scanning the passengers silently from under a cowl that held all the emptiness of Space.

Silver bolted past him toward the cab of the Locomotive.

Zozula regarded the fireman for a moment, but quickly averted his eyes as a deep cold seemed to flow down his spine and a wild fear grew within him that threatened to burst from his lips. He swallowed heavily and turned away, fighting the urge to jump to his feet and run. After a while he became aware of Mentor crying weakly, and embarrassment temporarily took the place of fear.

"He's a coward," he told Manuel, "a damned coward. I can't believe he's a clone of mine."

"He's never had to take care of himself. You must be fair to him,

Zozula. You've had hundreds of years of responsibility, in charge of the Dome, giving orders. So of course you've grown up differently."

"Nonsense!" Trying to forget the faceless fireman, Zozula threw himself into the argument. "Mentor comes of excellent genetic stock. He must have suffered a mutation. It's not apparent on the surface but it's there inside him—a weakness. A rot. Look, the Girl's gone over to comfort him. She's *mothering* him, for God's sake."

But Manuel wasn't listening. He, too, was watching the Girl, and surprised by the sudden expression of terror on her face, wondered what she was looking at. It wasn't the fireman. It was something else, something outside the window.

Then he saw it too.

THE FIRST BATTLE WITH THE BALE WOLVES

••

*S*uddenly, the Girl felt cold. The stars no longer flittered past the windows; instead, a pale mist swirled around the carriage. The Train slowed in its headlong flight through Space.

The Girl remembered seeing an eye. She didn't *see* an eye. She never saw it. What happened was that a recollection of having seen an eye appeared in her memory. The eye was red and fierce, with a pinpoint black pupil.

The Girl screamed. Simultaneously Manuel started. Zozula gasped, then said, "It wasn't there."

As if in answer, a voice suddenly shouted, "AH, HAH!", and a figure bounded through the wall of the carriage and landed nimbly in the aisle, bouncing lightly on its feet, crouching, darting fiery glances around at the passengers.

The Girl had never seen a more fearsome creature in her life. It was man-sized and hairily naked, with bowed, sinewy legs and a squat torso with massive shoulders, giving the initial impression of a hirsute, muscular toad. It was its face, however, that filled her with dread and nausea— because that face was almost human, yet inhuman to an unimaginable degree, a brutish travesty of Humanity. She found she was still screaming. Everybody was. The creature was a toad, an alligator, a cobra, everything she loathed. It was a Bale Wolf.

Yet the other passengers saw different Bale Wolves . . .

They were jumping to their feet, running, colliding with one another and the carriage fixtures, beating off assailants that only they could see.

"She's going to blow!"

Silver stood in the doorway, face working. Then he saw the confusion and his gaze slid this way and that, finally fixing on a spot in midair, near a window.

"Ah, no . . ." he murmured, eyes wide, backing away. "No, no . . . No you don't. NO YOU DON'T! !" And he was screaming too, whirling his crutch like a propeller, his gaze fixed on a dreadful invisible thing.

The Girl's Bale Wolf was sidling toward her.

Its face . . . low-browed, cunning little eyes bloodshot, thick nose almost a snout. And somehow most terrifying of all, the mouth . . . Wide and fringed with hair, like a muzzle, forward-projecting, agape and gleaming with pointed, yellowing teeth.

She was trapped in her seat, pinned there by her own fear as the beast scuttled down the aisle, then swung itself, monkey-like, over the intervening seats. The Girl's fingers closed on something hard. A weapon.

The Bale Wolf crouched on the next seat, bobbing on its haunches, stinking. Then suddenly it ducked its head.

Ages later the Girl brought her hand up and with all her strength swung the fire extinguisher.

The Bale Wolf didn't even blink. The extinguisher flew out of the Girl's hand and passed straight through its head. For an instant, the beast had slipped into the Ifalong.

Then it was on her, claws scrabbling at her clothing, baring her flesh while its mouth passed briefly over her face, pausing at her lips before dropping to her throat, worrying, tearing . . .

✻

"She's going to blow!"

The Girl froze for an instant, seeing in the Bale Wolf the sum total of every nightmare she had ever had. Then she jumped to her feet. Manuel was there, fighting with something she couldn't see . . . Then she saw it, shadowy and revolting, clawing at his throat for a second before sidling into some dimension where it avoided Manuel's desperate kick.

She ran for the toilet at the rear of the carriage, pushing past the struggling passengers. A Bale Wolf materialized before her, slashing at her groin in passing, before turning its attention to its original prey, Sir Charles. It winked out. Sir Charles's eyes widened as silently he fought the monster that he alone could see, and the clothes began to fall from him in shreds.

"You, most of all." The voice was a snarl among the screaming, and she couldn't tell where it came from. She reached the toilet, flung the door open and fell inside.

But the Bale Wolf was in there with her.

It jigged up and down on the washbasin, watching her trying to unlock the door again. Her fingers were like putty. It slashed at her breast and its claws ripped the flesh cleanly down the rib. She doubled up, vomiting. Instantly it was on her back, biting at her neck while its legs wrapped around her waist and its bony fingers dug into her shoulders until, losing her footing on the blood-slippery floor, she fell . . .

"She's going to blow!"

Then Silver, taking in the situation, flung his crutch like a javelin. As it passed through the torso of a Bale Wolf, the creature uttered a screech of triumph and disappeared. Blood suddenly gouted from Silver's throat.

The Girl stared in bewilderment and horror. Everybody seemed to be thrashing about. What was happening? Manuel looked right through her, and she flinched as he aimed a punch just above her right shoulder. She passed Zozula as she edged to the rear door. The old man seemed to have gone crazy, windmilling his arms, yelling.

A voice spoke in her ear. "You, most of all, Girl. You, with your soft fatness, all cozy there in your womb of safety. You, so gentle and pretty and inventive and good, with no fears, never knowing danger or anger or pain . . ."

"I know those things," said the Girl, reaching the door and jerking it open.

"You know nothing," said the voice. "But you will. You will."

The Girl slammed the door and stood in the dim vestibule between carriages. What was going on?

And the voice continued. "We can never show you what it's like to be rejected as unclean, as we were. But we can show you fear, and pain. A person ought to learn those things, before she dies . . ."

The voice was soft and the hands were obscenely gentle, too, stroking and prodding her body as if it were meat.

"Go away!"

"This is the best way . . . slowly. Pain is so much worse when the fear precedes it. I'm going to hurt you soon. I'm going to hurt you a little at first, then more, and more . . . Until your mind snaps inside that pretty head of yours. Until you go mad. You will soon look forward to going mad, my pretty fat baby."

The door crashed open and Blondie Tranter ran through, beating with her hands about her head as though to drive off invisible birds. "Oh, God! Oh, *God!*" She slid to the floor and rolled over and died with the horror frozen in her eyes.

"Too fast," said the voice.

"Where *are* you? Manuel! Help me, Manuel!" She still couldn't see the Bale Wolf who held her—but through the open vestibule door she now saw a score of darting, tearing beasts in the carriage, flitting among the passengers, flickering into being, slashing, flickering out. They were merciless. They had no pity. There were the Bale Wolves.

"Now . . ." said the voice.

Before she died, she saw Manuel toppling, and the thing on his back was eating him as he fell . . .

*

"She's going to blow!"

The diabolical creature hopped toward the Girl, scratching at its flank and chattering wordlessly. She slipped into the aisle and pushed past Bambi, who murmured, "It'll all turn out right in the end," while the blood poured from her brown shoulders.

The Bale Wolf dodged after the Girl. Pandemonium broke out among the passengers. She made for the Locomotive, backing, watching the creature that flitted from place to place with incredible rapidity. Silver's crutch clattered past her and she grabbed it, and held it before her. The Bale Wolf jumped, an agile leap that took it to the ceiling and back.

She swung the crutch at where its knees had been. Then she ran for the door.

A tall, black-cowled figure barred her way. "There's no way out here," he said.

The Bale Wolf was upon her, salivating. Drool trickled down the hair of its jaws as it seized her arm.

Then suddenly it was gone.

AFTERMATH

●●

*T*he roar was like a thousand volcanoes. The Girl was apart from it all, detached, floating in Space and watching it all happen—but not a part of it. Not affected. Manuel, Zozula and Mentor were there, too; she sensed that.

Flames and smoke swept through the vestibule and into the carriage. The Girl saw something that she was to carry with her for the rest of her life, etched into her memory—an image of death. The fireman, standing in the full blast from the Locomotive, raised his arms so that his cloak hung from them like condor's wings, and he stood there while the flames boomed past him—and the cloak did not burn; it didn't even flutter.

The fiery breath affected the other passengers, however. Belief faded.

The Bale Wolves disappeared.

The carriage began to dissolve. The Train was breaking up. The passengers were still there, screaming as they tumbled in the blast of the furnace, but the Train was evaporating and leaving its cargo stranded in the Greataway.

The Girl, still detached, found time to wonder how the Rainbow was handling all this. Sir Charles fell past her with flailing arms. The others were falling, too, receding into the blackness of Space, which opened up all around and consumed the false fabric of the Train. Only Silver was still there, standing beside the fireman. The blast had left him untouched, too.

But he was fading. He looked at himself, then clutched his arm. A growing horror showed on his broad face. "By the Powers . . . !" And then his voice was gone, and his hat, and his sea-cloak. Now he was a shadow, and the steam was blowing through him as he struggled with the final, unbelievable irony.

Long John Silver was only a composite smallwish.

That threatening figure, which had dominated the Skytrain for all its existence, was no more real than the phantom Train itself. He wept as he faded. He cursed, he invoked gods and devils from all of human history —to no avail. He was gone, and only the fireman was left, gaunt and eternal. The mists faded, and the Locomotive took its place in the legends of Mankind, in the Song of Earth.

"I'll see you again," called the fireman—only the second time the Girl had heard him speak, and again it sent a sick shiver through her.

Manuel was there, and Zozula and Mentor. Together they and the Girl hung in limbo while the Rainbow adjusted and the Greataway adjusted, and finally, on balance, they found themselves back on Earth.

"Silver wasn't real," said Manuel.

"He should have known," said Zozula.

"The Bale Wolves . . ." said Manuel. "I fought eight of them, one after another. I died every time. They weren't human. What . . . what were they?"

They sat on a grassy hillside at sunset, and the ocean glittered crimson below them. "They are man's most ancient fear," said Zozula. "They're the werewolves, I think. They've existed in legend as long as memory, and it seems they exist in fact as well, ever since they were created on the People Planet. They're not Dream creatures in any sense of the word. They're real, and they're out there." He looked up at the night sky and the stars and he shivered. "Up there on the Nameless Planet, with all the powers of evil."

"We can't fight them," said Mentor. He lay face down, embracing the earth.

"We must," said Manuel.

"You don't have to, Manuel," said the Girl. "I'll be all right."

"We're not just thinking of you, Girl," said Zozula severely. "We have Domesful of neotenites depending on us."

"I know." But she also knew what Manuel had meant, and now she took his hand.

Mentor suddenly sprang to his feet and his tear-wet face shone crimson in the sunset. "You people can do what you like," he cried, "but I'm not setting foot on that Train again! Never, as long as I live." He clutched

Zozula in an extravagant gesture. "Take me back to the People Planet! I was wrong to leave. I want to go back to Selena!"

"You coward!" shouted Zozula in great embarrassment, pushing him away so violently that he fell on his back. "You've been quick enough to complain about Selena during the past few days. Why should she want you back up there?"

"She loves me," said Mentor.

"What?" Zozula's embarrassment changed to rage. "You have the gall to accuse a Cuidador of loving *you*, a vat-clone?"

"She does. She said she does."

"Liar!" Zozula launched a kick at Mentor's ribs but Mentor rolled quickly aside and Zozula, too, fell on his back. Almost insane with fury, he scrambled over to Mentor and seized him by the throat. They began to roll down the hillside, grappling and screeching.

Manuel said awkwardly to the Girl, "I don't like this. It's undignified. Zozula should know better."

The Girl expelled her tension in a little shout of laughter. "They're worse than Bale Wolves." She watched as Zozula climbed to his feet, dragging his clone-son after him, and began to climb the hillside toward them.

"How did we escape from the Train, Girl?" asked Manuel. "I'm sure everyone else got Total Death."

"I don't know. Maybe it was the Outer Think, as Zozula said. Perhaps I . . . and maybe you . . . oh, I don't know. The main thing is, we're here."

"But we have to try again."

Zozula arrived panting, pulling Mentor by the scruff of his neck. "And this yellow-bellied son of a caiman is coming with us," he said, "just as soon as we've thought of a way to beat those Wolves."

How did they escape from the Train? Some later historians gave credit to the Girl's mynde, assisted by Manuel—which implied the definite existence of romantic love between the young couple. Others give little credence to this, pointing out the theoretical impossibility of a Wild Human forming such an attachment for a neotenite, and put forward the idea that the escape was due to the direct intervention of Starquin.

The minstrels chose the former viewpoint of course:

The Wolves devoured the passengers, the Train
  was blown apart.
But Manuel and Elizabeth conjoined with mynde
  and heart.

RETURN TO DREAM EARTH

Selena had been summoned from the People Planet and Caradoc from Dream Earth, and the council of war was being held in the Rainbow Room.

"We were beaten," said Zozula, having described their encounter with the Bale Wolves. "The brutes were too good for us. They were always one move ahead. How can you capture a creature that can anticipate everything you do? There was a big-game hunter on the Train, and I'll swear I saw one Wolf jump out of the way of the bullets before the hunter even pulled the trigger."

"We've done all we can," said Mentor. "Nobody could have done more."

"I didn't say that," said Zozula quickly. "We have to come up with a new approach. A frontal attack will never defeat a Bale Wolf. We know that now."

Mentor said, "We can't even reach the Bale Wolves now. The Train blew up. That's the end of it."

The huge image of Caradoc spoke. "The Train's still there. It will always be there. And it will always blow up. It exists on infinite parallel happentracks, so no matter how many times it is destroyed, it will still always exist."

Selena said, after an unhappy scrutiny of Mentor, "We don't have much time. Another four neotenites have died. They weren't diseased in any way; they just stopped living, like the others."

"Well, *I* don't know what we can do," snapped Zozula, irritated at the way problems were piling up. "Don't you have any suggestions, Caradoc? You have all the resources of the Rainbow at your disposal."

"Only a warning. If you decide to ride the Skytrain again, be very careful how far you go. I've been researching the past, and I've found traces of a malignant power out there—the old people used to call them Hate Bombs. I don't know what the effect of these Bombs is, or even how they work. But it seems they're powerful enough to prevent several hundred Earth colonies from getting through to us."

"Earth colonies . . ." murmured Zozula. "I'd wondered about that. I assumed they never contacted us because they'd lost the power of the Outer Think."

"No. They can't pass the Hate Bombs. You have an empire out there, Zozula, if you could only reach it."

"True Humans . . ." said Selena.

"The majority of humans out there will have adapted to their own worlds," Caradoc pointed out. "If you saw them, you'd probably think they were Wild Humans. It only needs a small change in environment to change a human."

Manuel laughed, earning a sharp look from Zozula.

"If we could remove the Hate Bombs, we could make contact," said Selena.

"After we capture our Bale Wolf," said Manuel.

But Zozula had been thinking. "Not so fast. Let's consider this carefully. Let's be perfectly sure we *want* to let these people in, before we start making plans."

"Of course we want them in," Manuel said. "Why not? Just think of what they could teach us . . . The different worlds they've seen. The Greataway. The aliens." His eyes were shining, his expression faraway. "Just think how good it would be for Earth, and for the Wild Humans. We could relearn all the things we've forgotten. We could learn how to operate all our machines. We could even learn how to build them. All those questions we're asking ourselves about the things we see around us —those people will have the answers. It'll be the start of a new age!"

Selena was watching Zozula. "An age that will have no need of Cuidadors," she murmured.

There was a sudden silence.

When Zozula spoke, he sounded far too abrupt. "Anyway, it's all academic. If Caradoc doesn't know how to tackle the Bale Wolves, that means the Rainbow doesn't know. And if the Rainbow doesn't know, nobody does."

The Girl spoke for the first time. "Somebody might."

"Who?"

She flushed. "Well, I don't mean somebody might know more than the Rainbow. I mean . . . I mean it depends on what question you ask, and how you ask it. And *who* you ask."

"I know what you mean," said Caradoc. "I can ask the Rainbow questions about human history and get straight answers. But if I ask a Dream Person the same question, I can't always understand what he tells me. Dream People exist on a different plane from me, with a different reality. There's a whole dimension of facts that they alone have access to." He smiled at Eloise. "Eloise exists in my mind as a smallwish, yet I don't know what she's thinking. And I know she *does* think."

"Of course I think," said Eloise. "And I think you try too hard, Caradoc." She grinned at him mischievously.

"Or did I smallwish her to say that?" asked Caradoc. "In the end, there are some things I'd rather not ask about."

The Girl said, "I must go back into Dream Earth, Zozula. I'll be able to find some of the answers that are beyond Caradoc's reach."

✳

The pain was gone. After weeks of sore feet, aching chest, breathlessness, nausea, incontinence and headaches, the Girl felt good again. She ran her hands over her body and found it slim. She bent down and touched her toes. The sun was warm and music came from a nearby inn. She jumped, and her calves and thighs felt strong, and she stayed off the ground for a long time. She laughed and jumped again for the sheer joy and freedom of it, and when she landed she felt her breasts jiggle firmly, and it was very healthy and feminine to have them back. It had rained recently and the earth smelled good, and she smelled good, and she ran to a puddle to get a look at herself.

A beautiful creature looked up at her from the water.

Her hair was short and thick and richly dark where it had been thin, straggly and mousy. Her eyes were warm brown and her face was round without being plump. It was a cute face, a mischievous, gamine face. Delighted, she skipped across the country lane and touched the trees and smelled their resin. It was all so *real,* not the least bit phoney, as she'd remembered it. Her body was tingling with some obscure need, and after a while she identified it: Just another of those good things that go with a good body—she wanted to make love.

It was a pity Manuel wasn't here.

But there were plenty of people at the inn. She heard laughter above the music. People were having a good time in there. Upstairs were bedrooms with brightly flowered curtains, and there would be soft beds with crisp white sheets.

Dream Earth was *fun*.

Manuel should share this with her. Or if not actually Manuel, then someone very much like him. Someone so much like him that she'd never know the difference.

"I wish . . ."

And she stopped herself. Some residue of purpose stayed with her, and the smallwish remained unuttered. It would only have been that: just a smallwish, like Eloise. And she had plenty of psy, loads of it. Really, just one smallwish wouldn't have made too much difference, would it?

"Oh, hell," she said aloud. Then she ran into the inn before she could change her mind.

Everybody looked familiar. That was one of the good things about Dream Earth—it was like meeting old friends again. Marilyn was there, and Burt and John and Captain Sylvia. They talked about the same things in the same idiom. It was as though she'd never been away. As usual, there was the sprinkling of strangers to make things interesting. At a table in the corner a group of Pirates sat, plotting in low tones. And there were a number of swarthy folk; something in the cast of their faces reminded her of Manuel. Obviously, a new fashion had come into favor in her absence. A giant anteater wandered among the tables, thick tail waving, slender snout prodding at morsels on the floor. She guessed that some influence from the real world had touched Dream Earth: There were reminders of Pu'este here—or maybe she'd never noticed them before.

"I'm going Latin just as soon as I have the psy," a blonde Sandra said, confirming the Girl's impressions.

There was a place at the Sandra's table and the Girl sat there. They looked at her in some surprise—a Mog, a Raccoona and a Pan, as well as the Sandra, who asked, "Who are you?"

"I'm Myself, I think," said the Girl.

"You haven't done too badly." The Pan watched her admiringly with his faun eyes.

The Girl said, "I have to get to the Oracle."

"Then use some psy, darling."

"I don't want to. I may need all I have."

"Well, *I'm* certainly not going to smallwish you there." The Sandra was now regarding the Girl with active dislike.

"I just thought . . . Maybe you knew somebody who'd consulted the Oracle recently, and you could give me directions . . ."

They roared with laughter. "Who in hell wants to consult the Oracle?" shouted the Mog, in between gulps of beer. "Who in hell cares?"

The Raccoona said quietly, "Only intellectual freaks consult the Oracle, darling. Do we look like intellectual freaks?"

And it was happening again, that thing that happened all too often on Dream Earth, the thing that had in the past caused the Girl to be Herself, to try to escape from the endless round of pleasure. Things closed in. The table seemed smaller and the laughter louder, and Pan's face looked so close it was distorted, a huge beak of a nose almost obscuring the slanting eyes. Sandra's hair blotted out the room, and Raccoona's hands lay on the table like bear paws. The dream was turning into a nightmare.

The Girl stood.

Pan said, "Hey, stay!"

She blinked to try to rid her eyes of them, remembered she *could* smallwish herself away, whirled around and ran out of the door.

The sky was leaden and the tall clean pines had changed into spreading oaks with grasping branches and the road was slippery. She slid and fell on her back, feeling the cold wetness through her clothes. As she lay there, a bolt of lightning darted from above and exploded a tree into instant flame—and behind the tree was an unspeakable thing, advancing toward her. She couldn't move, and the thing was as tall as the trees, lurching forward on many clawed legs with viscid digestive juices dribbling from its jaws . . .

And behind her, guffaws of cruel laughter.

She told herself she had a job to do, and if necessary she had to do it the Dream Earth way.

She said to the sky, clearly and simply, "I wish to consult the Oracle."

✳

The drawbridge was lowered, the portcullis was raised and she walked into a fantastic courtyard of unicorns and bluebirds and sacred carp. Music played and eunuchs bowed and beautiful people in diaphanous robes strolled to and fro.

The fountain rose to the clouds.

And within the fountain hovered the face of a beautiful woman. Water played through the face and around it as the woman watched the Girl gravely, the eyes sparkling, the lips looking as though they'd just been kissed. The Oracle said in a voice as musical as a harp, "You've been here before, haven't you? You know what to do. Place your hand in the waters and ask your question."

"I have so many questions this time."

"Then you'll need a lot of psy."

"Most of my questions are about the Ifalong."

The beautiful Oracle smiled. "That's not unusual. People usually want to know about the Ifalong. Nobody cares about the past, and I think that's a pity. The past is a great deal more *real* than the Ifalong, and I think people around here could do with a dose of reality now and then. And the past is easier for me to describe because I don't have to evaluate happentracks—so it costs less of your psy. Are you sure you don't want to know about the past?"

The Girl laughed. "Just one thing, then. How did I get this nice body? I didn't Bigwish it. And it's too pretty to be Myself. And it seems to be unique in Dream Earth, although . . ." She frowned thoughtfully. "My face is familiar. I'm sure I've seen it somewhere before. Please tell me where."

The Oracle closed her eyes. "It's very likely that you caught sight of an oil painting of that face, in the living quarters of the Cuidador Selena on the People Planet."

"You're right!" the Girl cried, excited. "Manuel loved that face, I'm sure he did! I wish he could see me now!"

"Is that a smallwish?"

"No," she said hastily. "It was just a figure of speech. Will I be able to keep this face and body when I go back to Real Earth?"

"Is that a question?"

"No, I can't spare the psy. I'll hope for the best. Just tell me how I got like this." Her face looked up at her from the fountain's pool, lively, lovable.

This time the Oracle's eyes remained closed for a very long time as she searched the memories of the Rainbow. Eventually she said, "I don't know."

"What do you mean, you don't know? I thought you knew everything."

"I only know what the Rainbow knows."

"But Zozula told me the Rainbow sees everything and knows everything."

"Zozula has a vested interest, my dear. Clearly it is impossible for the Rainbow to know the thoughts of humans, for instance. And—" she paused for an instant, "—the Rainbow cannot know the purpose of superior beings. It is a machine built by humans—and to a certain extent, built *of* humans. It has limitations."

The Girl was puzzled. "Well, I hardly think my face was a gift from some alien god."

And the Oracle replied, "I can hardly think of any other explanation, my dear."

It was frightening and unlikely, and the Girl didn't want to think about it. "Let's talk about the Ifalong," she said hastily.

"If you like."

"You must know there are monsters in the Greataway called Bale Wolves," said the Girl slowly, working out the least expensive way of getting the information she wanted. "And you already know that we—Zozula, Manuel and I—have tried to capture a Bale Wolf for use on the People Planet."

"That costs you no psy."

"Well, then . . . You know we failed, and I can tell you we want to try again. Now. The happentracks of the Ifalong are infinite, right?"

"That is correct, my dear." The Oracle was smiling.

"Yes, well . . . There must exist a happentrack in which we succeeded. Somewhere in the future, on some happentrack, we will capture a Bale Wolf and bring it back, right?"

"Right."

"You mean we will?" cried the Girl excitedly. "We will?"

"On remote happentracks. Such is the nature of the Ifalong."

"Well, then." The Girl took a deep breath. "My question is: How will we do it?"

The Oracle closed her eyes. This time she was silent for so long that the Girl began to fear the effort had sent her into a coma. But the Rainbow was working, probing unlikely happentracks, considering and rejecting alternatives, darting along critical paths with the speed of light.

The Oracle said, hours later, "You will overcome your fear."

The Girl jerked awake; she'd been dozing. "I'll what?"

"You will overcome your fear and enlist the help of the only creature in the Rainbow who has the power to defeat the Bale Wolves. Together you will rejoin the Celestial Steam Locomotive and fight the Bale Wolves for a second time, and this time succeed in your quest."

"That sounds pretty good to me."

"It is an extremely remote possibility," the Oracle warned her.

"Why?"

"Because on the majority of happentracks you will not be able to overcome your fear. In your mind, the creature whose help you must enlist is very terrible."

"What can be so terrible?" Deliberately, the Girl recalled her adventures with Manuel and Zozula, and before that, on Dream Earth, with the creatures she'd met there. "The Basilisk? The Tyrannosaurus Wrecks? The May Bees? I'm not frightened of them anymore. They're pathetic, really. Just jokes. And on Real Earth? There's nothing. Just people and animals."

"And within your own mind?" asked the Oracle.

"Nothing."

"Then on this happentrack you will not succeed in your quest."

"I'm not frightened of anything, I tell you!"

"Nor will you succeed on *this* happentrack."

"He scares me so much I can't bear to think of him!" The Girl burst into tears. "He's the most evil monster in the Universe, and when he touches me I lose control of myself, like a baby, and my legs won't work, and neither will my mind. I can't fight him. I can't go near him—I can't even think of him!"

"And yet on *this* happentrack you will succeed," said the Oracle.

Outside the Oracle's castle was a quiet river, lined with willow trees, where a few people rowed in traditional clinker-built boats and kingfishers watched the water with beady eyes. The Girl found a bridge and stood at the top of the arch with her arms on the railings and her chin cupped in her hands, watching the leaves drift by. It was a very peaceful scene, created by thoughtful people who'd had sufficient interest in the world around them to consult the Oracle. Once their question was answered, they had needed a place to ponder the meanings, and so the river had come into being—and the ancient timber landing stage and the jolly boatman who rented out the boats. The scene had a lot of depth, a lot of clarity, a lot of circumstantial detail. It reminded the Girl of Real Earth.

She was exhausted and out of psy, but she needed no smallwish to get out of here. Zozula was watching through the scanner and would recall

her when he figured the time was right. That would probably be soon—
and meanwhile she had to come to terms with herself . . .

In that way the Girl faced her destiny. Of course she was scared; she
was undertaking the most terrifying quest known to Man. Even the Song
of Earth concedes that she was frightened:

> She trembled on the bridge that spans the River
> Fountainthought,
> And vowed she would not rest until the Devil Wolf
> was caught.

Her body flinched at the memory of the tearing wounds that had been
inflicted on her, again and again, during the battle. Her mind balked at
contact with that stinking *evil* that surrounded the Bale Wolves, so that
everyone else seemed to be drawn into it and dirtied by it. She drew some
consolation from the fact that Manuel and Zozula would be there with
her.

But what really lent her courage was the fact that *she was going to do
it.* It was written in the Ifalong. Nobody else would; she knew that and
the Oracle knew it, too. Whether she wanted it or not, a Bale Wolf would
be captured and brought to Earth, and she would be responsible. She, the
Girl.

Why her?

Because she was the only person on Earth who knew how.

And the realization of *how* it would be done scared her even more than
the doing of it. For a moment she clung to the thought of the Bale
Wolves, because her fear of them was less than her fear of that indescribably evil creature who would help her destroy them. Then, slowly, gradually, she allowed herself to start thinking of Blind Pew and how she must
face him once again.

THE TRIAD ENLISTS HELP

The Girl told Zozula and Manuel everything—except the moments of temptation, and they probably guessed those. Again they undertook the outlandish journey: first through the Do-Portal at the far end of the Rainbow Room, where they answered the questions of the elephantine Reasoner and were admitted to Dream Earth. Then aboard the fiery Locomotive, with its dreadful crew and with its passengers still laughing, screaming, drinking and fighting—and looking forward to meeting the Bale Wolves. Then, quickly, the disembarkation at the Land of Lost Dreams, where the Rainbow stored all the smallwishes that had outlived their usefulness in Dream Earth . . .

The terror of the Girl.

The slow walk through the barren, jagged land with Zozula, Mentor and Manuel some distance behind, lest their quarry should be scared off by the sound of many footsteps.

The pause at every Stygian cave entrance, the strange beasts, the eerie sounds. The attack of the May Bees, and the defeating of them. And finally, the grotesque figure standing there, quite unexpectedly in the sunlight around a corner of rock, standing there and addressing a point of space somewhere in front of his nose.

"Avast there, me hearty! Now who will aid a poor man whose eyes were carried away by cannonball while in service of King George—God bless His Majesty!"

"I'll help you," said the Girl, trembling.

Judging the distance with uncanny accuracy, Pew lunged forward and threw a skinny arm around her, drawing her close. "And that ye will, me beauty . . ." He stiffened, hands running over her face as though it were a keyboard. "Ye be no stranger, girl!"

"No, I—"

"By the powers!" exclaimed Pew in sudden hoarse rage. "If it isn't the treacherous whelp who deserted the ship! I've been a-looking for ye, lass . . ." He held her at arm's length, and took up the stick, which leaned against the rock face.

In the distance, Manuel and Zozula began to run forward.

"Let me go!" The Girl struggled, terrified and nauseated. "I want to help you!"

"And help me ye will, girl." He raised the stick. "Just as soon as I've trimmed yer sails a little."

Zozula had dropped behind, but Manuel, running as only a Wild Human can, hurled himself at the blind man on the instant the stick began to descend. Pew, too intent on the Girl to hear his approach, uttered a croak of surprise. They spun around and fell to the ground. The Girl staggered away, shuddering, feeling dirtied by the contact. Nightmare happentracks sped through her mind.

Manuel aimed a roundhouse blow at Pew's thin face. Long before the punch reached him, Pew squirmed aside, and Manuel's fist slammed into the dirt. The youth yelled in pain and rage, grappling with his adversary and trying to get into position for another punch. With uncanny anticipation, Pew avoided him every time. Together they were rolling about on the dusty ground, wrestling and kicking, when Zozula arrived, panting.

"I'm going to kill you . . ." grunted Manuel, beside himself with rage and frustration. And then he realized how to do it. It was no good trying to hit Pew; the man could anticipate every move.

But he couldn't do anything about a slow, inevitable death.

And Pew guessed what was in Manuel's mind. He screamed—a shrill birdlike screech that quickly faded into the desert air.

Keeping hold of the blind man's clothing, Manuel worked his hands upward while Pew thrashed from side to side like a gaffed fish. Soon Manuel's hands pinned Pew's shoulders to the ground, then he moved higher and his fingers dug into the creased skin of Pew's throat. Then he began to squeeze.

"So you'd hit the Girl, would you . . . ?" Manuel's senses were obscured by a red haze of rage, and he hardly noticed Zozula pounding on his back.

"Let him go, Manuel! We need him alive!"

"Mercy . . ." whispered Pew.

"Die, blind man."

"Manuel! Get off him!"

The combined efforts of the Girl and Zozula dragged Manuel's hands away. Pew twisted free, then rolled onto his face, coughing and gagging. Manuel looked up, the madness fading from his eyes, to be replaced by a kind of puzzled wonder. What had got into him? He looked at Pew, and what had been a monstrous thing of evil was now an unclean old man throwing up into the dirt.

"I . . . I'm sorry," said Manuel to the Girl.

She smiled shakily. "I didn't know you had it in you, Manuel."

"Did you see the way he dodged those punches?" Zozula stirred Pew with his toe as though he were a dead animal. "I see what you mean, Girl. He can anticipate danger. Maybe he can't always do anything about it, but at least he recognizes when it's coming. He's just the man we need."

Pew sat up slowly, massaging his neck. "I'll thank ye to respect a poor blind man's infirmities . . ." he said indistinctly.

"You're coming with us, Pew," said Zozula.

"Aye . . . That's as may be. Where are ye bound, may I ask?"

Zozula said, "We're going aboard the Celestial Steam Locomotive. I think an acquaintance of yours drives it."

Pew started violently. "The Locomotive, is it! By my Lady, why didn't ye tell me in the first place, sir?"

And, chuckling to himself, he climbed to his feet, picked up his stick and began to tap his way along with them as they walked north.

The Girl walked a little apart from the others and after a while began to lag behind. Mentor dropped back with her and, in due course, said, "He's an unpleasant character, isn't he? Just as well he isn't real."

Getting no reply from the Girl, he glanced at her. He was surprised to see the pallor of her face and the dull, dead horror in her eyes above the tear-stained cheeks. Awkwardly, he said, "Here, give me your arm. You must be tired."

THE SECOND BATTLE WITH THE BALE WOLVES

*M*anuel looked about himself in some bewilderment. Things had changed in a subtle fashion, in that way they do when you doze off for a minute without realizing it.

The passengers were exclaiming in surprise, staring out of the window as the stars flashed by. Zozula, Mentor and the Girl watched too, and something nudged the back of Manuel's memory, some recollection of a series of events that seemed to be fading from his mind as fast as he tried to catch them.

Then Long John Silver appeared with a smile of false joviality, but as he swung his way past Manuel, the youth could see the lines of his jaw— the tenseness, the clenched teeth that turned the smile into a grimace. Silver paused at the door for a moment, then turned and faced them all, smiling still.

Then he caught sight of Zozula, who smiled back. His own smile faded as his gaze traveled to Manuel and the Girl, and finally to Mentor. "Belay there," he said softly. "Is this a stowaway?" And he made a great lunge with leg and crutch, and stood before Mentor. "What foreign shores d'ye hail from?" he inquired.

"I . . ." Mentor looked at Zozula, puzzled. This was a different happentrack. Silver didn't remember him, it seemed.

"Brothers ye be, I'll be bound," said Silver, his sharp glance snapping from one to the other. "And yet not brothers. Well now . . . How be ye fixed for psy, Mister Stowaway?" He smiled coldly. "We have a little test for newcomers, to see if they can afford the fare. D'ye see a parrot on my shoulder, eh?"

Zozula said tiredly, "He wants you to smallwish a parrot there, Mentor. Humor the fool, will you?"

"I . . . I don't know how."

"Oh, for heaven's sake. Like this." Irritably, Zozula blinked and wished.

Silver uttered a squeal of dismay.

A huge vulture sat on his shoulder, scrawny of neck and evil of eye, shuffling untidy black feathers. Silver swung at it with his crutch and it gave an ungainly hop, landing on his head. It hung its neck, peering into Silver's face upside down. The passengers roared with laughter and Sir Charles discharged his twelve-bore with a deafening report, prompting the vulture to excrete onto Silver. The driver reached up, seized the bird by the neck and dashed it to the floor.

"Mayhap ye find that comical," he snarled. "And mayhap I'll show ye something more comical still." He smiled with an effort, his face working its way toward joviality by stages. "Come with me, and ye may drive the Locomotive, shipmates. Just the four o' ye—'tis a rare honor I offer ye, to be sure."

"We're fine where we are, thanks," said Zozula.

" 'Tis nothing to be afeard of. By the Powers!" Silver appealed to the passengers at large, "We have a craven shipmate here. Who'd a-thought it?"

Zozula stood. "Come on," he said to the others. "He can't hurt us."

Mentor hung back. "I'm not sure . . ."

Irritably, Zozula jerked him to his feet, and together they followed Silver forward. Manuel and the Girl trailed behind, with some misgivings.

The Triad had seen the Locomotive's cab before, but Mentor had not, and the sight was almost too much for him. He uttered a small cry of shock and jerked aside as the cowled fireman's shovel swung past his face and crashed against the firebox sill, scattering coals across the roaring furnace within. Mentor stared into the flames, which seemed to draw him forward. Roaring with laughter, Silver reached for a dangling chain and dragged at it, and a banshee wail echoed through the cab like a lonely yell of terror.

Then Silver glanced at the pressure gauge and his expression changed. "By thunder!" he shouted at the fireman. "Ye've gone and done it this

time, ye soft-headed lubber. Cease yer shoveling, for pity's sake, or it'll be
Davey Jones's locker for the whole ship!"

The fireman swung back, cloak swirling, and his shovel screeched
against the footplate as he scooped up another load of coal.

"Avast there!" yelled Silver. He jerked at the regulator, opening it
fully, so that the beat of the exhaust quickened to a manic throbbing and
the cab vibrated in sympathy. "Avast there, afore ye blow us all to Kingdom Come! The boiler can't take any more!"

As the stoker swung toward the firebox opening, Silver let go of the
regulator and seized the shaft of the shovel, and a grim struggle ensued.
Sweat rolled down Silver's broad face as he was forced slowly backward
until he was brought up against the very lip of the furnace and the hot sill
pressed against the back of his one leg. "Belay there," he groaned. His
gaze, darting about the cab, settled on the Triad. "I . . . I've brought
some shipmates," he gasped. "Mayhap ye'd be pleased to meet them."

At this, the fireman let go of the shovel and Silver stumbled forward,
off balance, to collapse to the footplate floor. From this position he raised
a hand, summoned a smile, and shouted, "Mates! I'd like you to meet the
best friend a man ever had, the best worker ever to set foot in an engine
room—the fireman of the Celestial Steam Locomotive!"

The fireman stood motionless. The shovel lay on the footplate.

"We may as well play this thing through," said Zozula tolerantly, and
he stepped forward, extending a hand.

"Y'see?" said Silver. "He's stopped work—that he has! 'Tis the only
time he ever does. Likes meetin' folk, he does." There was huge relief on
his slab face.

The fireman's hand emerged from under his cloak. It reached steadily
toward Zozula's—pale, bony, long-fingered.

Zozula said, chuckling, "I'm very pleased to—"

"Stop!"

It was Mentor, and his voice was high with fright.

"Eh?" Zozula's hand stopped, a centimeter from the fireman's.

"For God's sake don't shake his hand!"

"Why not? I don't see what harm—"

And Mentor flung himself at Zozula, toppling him backward onto a
heap of coal. Zozula swore, beginning to fight back. Beneath his cloak,
the fireman's skeletal shoulders shrugged, and he picked up his shovel.

"Just keep still for a moment while I explain, damn you!" panted
Mentor.

"You'd better make it good." The coal was digging into Zozula's back and the ignominy of his position infuriated him. Again he tried to throw Mentor off, but his clone-son hung on grimly.

"Listen to me!" gasped Mentor. "He's Death, don't you understand? That fireman is Death himself. If you shook hands with him, that would be the end of you."

"Death? Don't be ridiculous. He's just a smallwish. He can't harm real people."

"So why are the neotenites in the Dome dying?"

"They've got some disease."

"This fireman is the only disease that matters, Zozula. I heard about him the last time we were on the Train, before you arrived. That woman Tranter told me. She said people disappear when Silver introduces them to the fireman. And she was right—look! He doesn't have a face! He's Total Death—this is what it's all about. He snuffs out people's minds here in Dream Earth, so their bodies die back on Real Earth."

The fireman paused in his shoveling and turned their way. And Zozula saw the empty cowl make a sharp movement, as though the phantom head were nodding. Suddenly he shivered. Then his fear turned to quick anger. He disengaged himself from Mentor and stood, facing a cowed Silver.

"Is this true?"

"Aye," muttered the driver. " 'Tis the truth, for sure. But 'tis the only way I can stop the devil shoveling."

Zozula said, "Whatever you and this fireman are up to, Silver, it's killing people on Real Earth. You've got yourself mixed up in something you don't understand, and you've got to stop it."

"It'll take more'n me to stop this devil!" protested the driver. A low laugh came from beneath the fireman's hood.

"If you don't stop him, Silver, there will be nobody left in Dream Earth. Do you know what that will mean? No more passengers. And if there are no passengers, then there will be no Long John Silver. You're just a smallwish, man! Can you understand that?"

"Me a smallwish? Come now, shipmate."

"Take my word for it. You must keep the passengers away from the fireman."

Manuel, who had been struck speechless by events, spoke at last. "Let's get out of here."

" 'Tis the lives of a few against the lives of every passenger on the Train," said Silver, pleading.

The Girl was already limping through the tender's narrow corridor.

"Don't maroon me, shipmates!" cried Silver. "Don't leave me alone with this devil!"

As Zozula, Manuel and Mentor turned to leave, Silver crowded after them, pawing at their backs. Sobbing, he whispered to Mentor, "D'ye think I've forgotten ye, lad? Oh, no—old Barbecue never forgets. We had a deal, didn't we? And haven't I kept my side of the bargain? Have I allowed anyone to lay a finger on ye?"

"No. I suppose not."

"Most certainly not. I'm an honorable man—ye may lay to it. But as for *ye* . . ." His mood changing swiftly, he seized Mentor by the shoulder, his huge hand like a vice, "Ye've tricked me, lad! Once when ye stood by and allowed yon pirates to desert the ship, and nary a word o' warning to me. And now—this. I tell ye, lad. Only a fool tricks Long John Silver!"

"Get away from me!" Mentor half turned, shoving.

"Ye'll pay yer dues, shipmate."

A hand gripped Mentor's and, furious, he tugged at it, intending to jerk its owner to the ground. But the hand held firm, and it dawned on Mentor that it was unnaturally cold and hard, almost fleshless . . . He turned round.

The fireman stood there.

As they reassembled in the carriage Manuel was a little surprised at the speed with which Silver had recovered his equanimity. The driver came swinging jovially into the carriage after Mentor—who looked pale and scared—and immediately addressed the passengers in a bellowing shout: "The sun is over the yardarm, messmates! 'Tis time to splice the mainbrace!"

But for once there was no answering roar of enthusiasm. The passengers sat silently, with expressions of embarrassment and distaste. Bambi's gaze flickered toward a corner of the carriage, and for once even she could see no redeeming feature in the situation. Her face showed disgust. Silver followed her gaze.

Blind Pew stood there.

Silver backed away, one hand to his mouth, eyes wide with terror. He reached the swaying wall and could retreat no farther. Pew, smiling coldly and still silent, took two slow strides toward him and laid his stick across the flip-up seat; then he felt for him.

He ran his fingers over Silver's face quickly and comprehensively.

Then he smiled and nodded, and the smile was gone again, and his face was like seamed marble. He picked up his stick and sat on the flip-up seat, adjusting his cloak about him. Under the green eyeshade, his eyes resembled pale stones on a wintry beach, cold and moist and heartless as he faced the passengers.

Silver tried to run for the Locomotive, but Pew slid his stick across the doorway without changing expression.

Manuel shivered. It might have been the effect of the appalling Pew sitting there like a judge, or perhaps the temperature had dropped. People began to recover from the shock of Pew's materialization and the clink of glasses against bottles could be heard, and the murmur of the card games resuming.

What happened next was so unexpected that Manuel thought he'd imagined it.

An eye appeared at the window.

And yet he hadn't been looking at the window. In point of fact, he'd been watching Pew and thinking how he'd like to get his fingers around that scrawny neck again. It was some seconds since he'd last actually looked at the window—and he'd noticed it was foggy out there, but there had been no eye.

He heard Zozula say, "It wasn't there."

The Girl screamed. There was a startled babble of comment.

"AH HAH!"

A hideous creature appeared on the luggage rack right above Manuel's head. It squatted on thin, muscular shanks and peered down at him through the slats so that its face appeared from between its thighs—a face like a baboon, like a swamp, like rotting meat, like a nightmare. Fluid dripped from between the slats and Manuel jerked away; the varnish dissolved from the woodwork, leaving a grey, slimy stain.

Thick-armed and agile, the brute swung down and reached for Manuel almost casually, as an ape reaches for fruit. Then, quick as a flash, the creature hopped aside. Manuel flung himself back in his seat and kicked out with all his strength at emptiness. The Bale Wolf dropped into his lap.

Beside him, the Girl was struggling from her seat, while nearby Zozula swung aimless punches. Manuel caught the gleam of something red in the Girl's hand, something heavy that she swung and then lost. The Bale Wolf bobbed up and down in his lap, knocking the wind out of him. Manuel was dead—and he knew he was dead. The beast was playing with him. Mercifully, he seemed to have stepped outside himself and for the last few seconds of his life was an observer, watching the death of the passengers and the Girl and Zozula, and Manuel. Manuel, noticed Manuel, had a Bale Wolf in his lap and it was shortly going to tear his throat out. Elsewhere, he noticed, Silver was slashing with his crutch to no effect, and Sir Charles seemed to be choking.

And nearby, noticed Manuel, a Bale Wolf squatted beside the Girl, who lay on her back on the floor. She made pathetic sweeping gestures with her fat arms, weakly trying to fend the creature off. The Bale Wolf held a little knife—just a short thing, but long enough to reach the Girl's heart. The Bale Wolf played with it, teasing her. It touched her stomach with it, cutting the cloth of her dress and laying bare the flesh. Then it jerked the knife back. The Girl swatted at the place where the knife had been.

Manuel fought his way toward her.

"He-he-he-he!" His Bale Wolf uttered a high-pitched giggle and tripped him. Lying down, Manuel saw the Girl's Bale Wolf snarl, all fooling done, and raise the knife high.

"No!" Manuel shouted. "Leave her!"

And just for a moment the Bale Wolf paused and glanced at him. Manuel saw a rush of movement; then the Bale Wolf drove the knife downward with all its force. He saw no more, because his Bale Wolf had jumped onto his head and was reaching for his throat. He rolled onto his back and the creature rolled with him, keeping its hold. As consciousness began to leave him and he slipped into a well of despair, he saw Zozula go down fighting and Sir Charles fall like a tree. He saw Blondie Tranter bleeding and screaming while a Bale Wolf teased her with its claws, and he saw Bambi smiling, patting on the head a creature that was preparing to disembowel her.

And he saw Blind Pew stand and swing his stick, and lay a Bale Wolf cold at the exact moment it materialized.

It lay twitching on the floor. Pew stepped over it and advanced down the aisle, a gaunt black figure using his stick like a flail with no regard for friend or foe.

But he left a trail of broken Bale Wolves in his wake. They dodged between happentracks, seeking to catch him unawares, but he knew they were coming, and with his uncanny precognition, he swung his stick time and again, clubbing them senseless at the instant of materialization. One by one they fell, to lie bleeding, twitching and whimpering, too dazed to skip into an adjacent happentrack, too bemused to avoid the crushing seaboots of Pew as he stamped and swung his way down the carriage.

There came a great howl, echoing the length of the Train, and the remaining Bale Wolves left the passengers, who collapsed where they stood, crying with pain and fear and disbelief, and relief. The Bale Wolves turned and stared at Pew. The howl became a jabbering snarl as they attacked in a body, bounding over the seat backs like a monkey troop and getting in one another's way as they crowded Pew, tearing and slashing as they backed him against the wall.

Yet Pew stayed on his feet. He'd produced a knife, a sharp sailor's knife, now that the stick had proved too cumbersome for close quarters, and with this he hacked and stabbed and out-thought every move of the Bale Wolves until they backed off, snarling in a semicircle, bleeding and watching him with their fierce little eyes.

Pew said into the sudden quiet, "So it's a standoff, me beauties. I'm a poor blind man and I can't see to kill ye—not unless ye attack. Then it's a different kettle o' fish, ye may lay to that. It's a strange sense o' danger I have. So what's it to be, me beauties? Do ye leave us to continue the voyage in peace—or do ye die?"

And one by one, the Bale Wolves disappeared.

All except one, who lay in the aisle half under Zozula's seat, a victim of one of Pew's more vicious blows. The beast stirred, and his outline began to shimmer . . .

Zozula seized the fire extinguisher that lay nearby and crashed it down on the Bale Wolf's head.

Its outline firmed up.

Manuel shouted, "We've got one! We've got one!" Then his excitement evaporated.

The Girl lay beneath Mentor, and from Mentor's back there protruded a short knife. He was not moving, and Manuel knew he was dead. He rolled the body aside to reach the Girl. She lay with her head turned away. A sudden terror seized Manuel as he knelt beside her. She was very still. Her shoulder was bare, the clothing torn away. In the flesh was a jagged wound, semi-circular, from which blood seeped slowly. The skin around the wound was black and ugly-looking. She was breathing—very faintly, but definitely breathing.

"We must get her to the Dome," said Zozula. His eyes kept straying to his clone-son, his expression unfathomable.

"How?"

"It's just a question of belief," said Zozula.

Meanwhile, Silver was levering himself to his feet with his crutch. The rest of the passengers, shaken, some weeping, many injured, were sorting themselves out. It seemed that Mentor's death was the only one. "Let's go home," said someone.

Silver crashed his crutch against the wall to gain attention. "Shipmates!" he roared. "I promised ye adventure, and by the Powers, we're having it. 'Twas a royal victory, eh? 'Tis no time to be talkin' o' quitting. We beat the Bale Wolves and we beat them fair and square. Now we continue the voyage!"

"We want to go home!" the cry came from several passengers.

"Avast there!" Silver launched into a tirade against cowardice, mutiny and desertion, thumped his crutch against the floor for emphasis, while Pew listened with head cocked, and the passengers muttered.

Manuel said to Zozula, "Hasn't he had enough?"

"He can't quit. If the passengers leave the Train, Silver will cease to exist. I think he believes what I told him, deep down."

"What about us? The Girl always got off this Train before. If you think we can wish ourselves off, you'd better start wishing quickly, Zozula. The Girl's very sick!" The sharpness of Manuel's tone recalled Zozula to the problem and he concentrated, closing his eyes.

People were climbing from their seats, advancing on Silver in open mutiny now, and the driver's voice became shrill as he harangued them, backing toward the door. Zozula opened his eyes again. It was beginning to look as though the whole Train would be returning to the Dome with no conscious effort on his part. Silver tripped and fell, and his one leg waved in undignified fashion as he tried to scramble up again. "We're going back, by God!" shouted Sir Charles, jabbing the driver with a shooting stick. "Get a grip on yourself, man. Turn us around!"

"Silence!"

Pew stood above Silver like a giant. The shouting died away.

The blind man looked taller, monstrous in his black cloak. With his green eyeshade and beaklike nose, he resembled some great hooded bird of prey barely held in check. His opaque gaze roved among the passengers, and they flinched before it as though he could see into their very souls. Silver looked up at him from the floor, clutched his ankles in supplication, then began to crawl up his body, whimpering. Pew dashed him aside with one blow of his stick and then addressed the passengers.

"There'll be no turning back," he said, so softly that they strained forward to hear, eagerly, wanting to get it right, not wishing to offend him. Then, hearing, they nodded at him and at each other; yes, there would be no turning back. Who could ever think of turning back?

Manuel found that his knuckles were white with tension and his hands were stiff when he uncurled them. "Get us out of here, Zozula," he said quietly, scared the frightful Pew might hear.

"I can't. I've tried. I can't make it work!" And now, at last, there was fear in Zozula's eyes. He had lost control. Pew was stronger than him. What had gone wrong? Only hours ago Pew had been their prisoner, a mere figment of the imaginations of the Dream People, who were in turn nebulous electrical charges in the Rainbow, which was supposedly controlled by him, Zozula. Sick at heart, he sat still, bewildered, beaten, mourning Mentor, his clone-son.

Manuel turned to the injured Girl and took her hand in his, and just for a moment her eyes opened and she looked at him. Softly he said to her, "Don't worry about a thing, Girl. I'll make sure you're all right. Just lie there quietly, and we'll have you back home in no time . . ."

He used no conscious effort or belief.

He looked at the Girl, and something seemed to flow between them. He couldn't describe it, afterward (although later humans had a name for it). It was similar to the way he felt when he did his mind-paintings—particularly when he did the painting of Belinda—but it was not the same. It was somehow stronger, and it did not come from him alone. It had something to do with the Girl's being there, too, but that was still not the full answer. It had to do with something inside him, a living entity that was part of him, yet separate, perhaps like a soul.

The Skytrain faded from around the Triad, and they found themselves on a hillside overlooking the ocean, and it was morning, the sun rising out of the easterly bank of crimson clouds.

IN LORD SHOUT'S ROOM

*B*efore the Mole had become Caradoc, he had lived for some weeks in a remote area of the Dome, having been brought there by his father, Lord Shout. Lord Shout was a Wild Human who had found the blank curved walls of the Dome depressing after the boundless space of Outside, so he had instructed members of his tribe to climb the catwalk on the Dome's outer surface and clean the muck of aeons away until the windows of his room were clear again and he could see the distant hills where his village lay. This had been somewhat shocking to Zozula, who had not realized that the Dome's surface was intended to be transparent. It was also a little terrifying, because the clear windows were as high as the clouds, and on a clear day surveyed a dizzying expanse of Earth.

Now Selena stood in Lord Shout's room.

She trembled as she looked at the great Outside, so open, so clear, so limitless compared to the only Outside she had ever known: the low clouds and tiny confines of the People Planet's lone island. But she was a Cuidador, and outside this window was the future; she and other Cuidadors must get used to it.

Hearing a sound, she turned.

Zozula stood there. Her heart leaped with joy, but she managed to conceal it. "I hear your journey was a success," she said.

"We captured a Bale Wolf—Brutus has it now. But the Girl was seriously hurt. And . . . and we lost Mentor, I'm afraid."

"So I heard." She turned away.

"He died like a hero. I was a fool—he had much more courage than I gave him credit for. The Girl told me he saved her life. He threw himself in the way of a Bale Wolf's knife and took the blow that was meant for her. He was a brave man, after all."

"Of course he was. He was your clone-son." Her voice was muffled.

"He gave a bad impression, at first."

"That was my fault. I raised him badly. I spoiled him."

"I . . . I was ashamed of him, Selena. I kept thinking he was what I might have been. What I *am*, underneath. A coward who wakes up screaming at night."

"We all do that, Zo."

Standing beside her, looking at the vastness of Outside, he caught sight of a tear on her cheek. Awkwardly, he put an arm around her. "There was nothing we could do to save him. It all happened so quickly. He liked the Girl, I think."

"Don't we all?" she muttered.

"Listen, Selena . . . I'm very sorry. I . . . I realize you were fond of him. I'm not a fool, you know."

She swung round to face him, and her eyes were glittering. "Oh, yes you are!"

He backed away, astonished at her violence. "My dear . . ."

"Haven't you got the sense to work out *why* I raised Mentor, *why* I kept him in my quarters as an adult? Are you completely stupid, Zozula?"

"Well, I thought you explained all that. Research, and so on . . ." He flushed. "If you're trying to tell me you were lovers, well, it's really no concern of mine. What you do up there is your own affair."

"Yes, we were lovers."

"I don't want to hear about it." Now he too was getting annoyed.

"Well, you're going to, whether you like it or not. I've spent fifty years of unhappiness with Mentor, you know that? Fifty years of wondering why I did such a thing. Wondering if the caracals would tell people. Wondering if they already had and if the entire Station was laughing behind my back. Wondering if word would get back here, to the Cuidadors. Fifty years of guilt, Zozula. Watching Mentor growing up to look like *you*, and to walk and talk like *you*, and yet not to *be* you. Fifty years of watching him develop into a spoiled brat, of living with a poor substitute while you and Eulalie were living together, content with each other and hardly aware of the Dome around you."

There was a long silence. In the end, Zozula said helplessly, "I loved

Eulalie very much. Now she's dead, I don't know how to handle it . . . and I don't know how to handle people, either. I feel alone suddenly, and I feel as though the rest of the Cuidadors are my enemies, attacking me with their sympathy. Does that sound strange? I lived with Eulalie for centuries, and I never knew how much I depended on her. All that time, she was protecting me from the way I feel now, and I never realized it. *This* is why I've thrown myself into this quest of ours. It's not through a sense of duty—not really. It's because I can't face life without Eulalie, and because I find the company of Manuel and the Girl less . . . less embarrassing than the company of the Cuidadors. And because I suddenly hate this Dome. Does that explain anything?"

"Not really." But Selena's tone had softened.

"I'm just an arrogant old fool who's been caught out, Lena. That's the truth of it."

"I know."

"It's too soon for me to start thinking of the future."

"I know."

Tentatively, he said, "There's still plenty of time."

Meanwhile, the nurses, using ancient technology under the direction of Caradoc, worked on the Girl. She was still alive, but her breath was shallow and her pulse weak. The venom of the Bale Wolf was being carried through her system, although the wound itself had begun to heal.

Brutus took samples of venom from the Bale Wolf and fed them into the Rainbow. The creature lay on its back in a cage, breathing slowly and powerfully, drugged into insensibility. It had to be kept that way, unconscious, because no cage could have held it if it recovered its senses and its powers.

The Rainbow analyzed the samples. The answer came back: The Bale Wolf's venom contained a virulent agent with an effect similar to cancer, capable of changing the very structure of body cells, and quickly.

A nurse injected adrenalin into the Girl, simply to keep her alive. She was wasting away. Her substance seemed to be dissolving into the force fields in which she was suspended.

Zozula and Selena arrived and stood looking at the Girl for a long time. Brutus blinked and scratched, wondering how to tell them his news.

Eventually he spoke in a rush. "I added a sample of the Bale Wolf's venom to a True Human gene culture, but I had to destroy it. For a while

it grew fast and I thought there was an embryo developing. But then
. . ." He gulped. "It wasn't anything like a human embryo. It was a
crawling thing, and it began to move about too soon. I recycled it
quickly."

"How about tissue samples?" asked Selena.

"I tried that, too. The result was the same."

Zozula was regarding the Girl. "She's become so thin, so quickly. She
won't last much longer." His eyes were unnaturally bright when he
turned back to Brutus. "We've failed. Everything was for nothing. I don't
understand it . . ." A vision of an old woman came to him, and the way
she had described Time and the quest of the Triad. "Maybe it's just that
we're on the wrong happentrack," he said. "But I was so *sure*. I suppose
it was simply my arrogance again. I was assuming everything we did was
important, when in fact it had no significance at all. And now I've killed
the Girl."

"You did everything you could, Zo." said Selena. "You had to try to
cure the neotenites. And at least you know now why they're dying."

"But I can't do anything about it. The fireman on the Celestial Steam
Locomotive is Death himself. He's inevitable, and we can't fight him.
Like the Locomotive itself, he'll always exist. And that stupid smallwish
Silver will always introduce people to him. Nobody is truly immortal,
because even if their bodies receive the best of care, there comes the time
when their minds decide to call it quits."

"I suppose so." Selena took Zozula's hand. "Thank God you didn't get
scratched, Zo. And at least Manuel isn't here to see the Girl die. What
happened to him, anyway?"

"I sent him home." Zozula's tone was short.

"Why? Wouldn't he have wanted to stay with the Girl?"

"He did, but I wouldn't let him. Don't you understand? All of this is
my fault. I couldn't stand his watching the Girl die. He was very fond of
her, you know. He was beginning to blame me, and he was right."

Selena regarded the Girl. "I wouldn't have believed a person could
change so quickly. That venom is pure poison—she's no heavier than me,
now. In an hour or two she'll be little more than a skeleton. Even her face
has changed."

"And she's grown eyelashes," said Zozula. "Her hair is much thicker,
too."

"If you forget the way she ought to look," said Selena slowly, "she's
really quite attractive. What a pity she can't stay just like this."

"I think she might!" Brutus suddenly swung round to face them, and there was a blazing light in his eyes. "The Bale Wolf's venom would have killed you, Zozula—my tests proved that. You're a True Human. But the Girl isn't; she lacks something. What she lacks is what the Bale Wolves took away with them, all those thousands of years ago. And now . . . I think this Bale Wolf has given it back to her, in its venom. Look at her!"

The Girl was breathing easily now, slim and pretty.

"She's going to be all right," said Brutus.

✳

Selena and Zozula returned to Lord Shout's room. It seemed to be an appropriate place to consider the future, up here where the land was spread before them.

After a while Zozula said, "We're close to the time when our duty is done. I should be feeling pleased about this. So why don't I, Selena? Why do I feel scared?"

She laid a hand on his sleeve. "We've lived a long time. It isn't easy to face change. And you're wrong about our duty being done. We'll be spending the rest of our lives organizing the release of the New People. We can't just turn them loose to starve. We have to build a new society Outside. We and our children. Our True Human children."

"Except that they won't be True Humans for long," said Zozula. "Ironic, isn't it? In generations to come, they'll evolve and adapt. They'll develop big lungs to cope with the thin air, and there will be other changes. They'll turn into Wild Humans."

"And there's another factor."

"Oh? What's that?"

"You remember what the saybaby told us about the Macrobes and the Everlings?"

"Yes. The Everlings were a failed experiment, weren't they?"

"That's right. Now Brutus has found out they weren't the only experiment that took place in those days. Listen to this."

Holding tight to the memory potto, she told Zozula a story. It is a story that, in later years, assumed the quality of a legend, and is sometimes heard in the Song of Earth under the title of "The Giant of Buenos." The final version, polished by the minstrels, goes like this:

Once there was a tiny creature called a Macrobe that lived within a larger creature, called an Everling. It was the Macrobe's sworn duty to spread his kind throughout the Galaxy, and this he had done in many ways, but now he was trapped in the Everling because this creature could not reproduce.

Then the great god Starquin, scanning the Ifalong, found that this Macrobe was important in the scheme of things and must be taken back to Earth, because it would soon be needed there. So one night, while the Everling was asleep, Starquin sent a bat to suck his blood. When the bat had finished, it flew to a Rock, where an old woman caught it and, by mysterious means, dispatched it to Earth. And the Macrobe went, too, having passed into the bat with the Everling's blood.

Now, the bat was a dull, stupid creature, but the Macrobe was very clever—and moreover, the Macrobe had a very strong sense of self-preservation. Arriving on Earth, it caused the bat to seek out the most powerful creature around. This creature was a huge Wild Human who for years had terrorized a village of Earth known as Buenos. And this giant, annoyed by the bat fluttering around his head, caught it in his great paw and ate it. Now the Macrobe had a very powerful host.

The giant then went out on one of his periodic rampages. He strode into the village of Buenos and kicked down several huts. Then, as was his custom, he demanded a ransom.

"Otherwise," he roared, "I will lay waste the entire region!" And, within the giant, the Macrobe was sad because it seemed to the little parasite that the giant was asking for trouble.

As it happened, the Macrobe need not have worried, because the villagers were under the influence of the Kikihuahua Examples. They used no metal or fire, they didn't kill anything and they were generally peaceable. The Macrobe, however, did not know this.

Now the giant seized Asesina, the beautiful daughter of the village chief and bore her to his cave. She lay there unresisting all that night, and he possessed her many times.

In the morning a deputation from Buenos approached the cave entrance, and the chief called timidly for the release of his daughter. "She has served you well," he cried, "and the ransom is now as good as paid." But at the first rustlings within the cave he backed off, and behind him his companions fled. "Mind you," he called quickly, "I am a reasonable man and am willing to negotiate."

But it was his daughter, Asesina, who appeared. Her clothes hung in tatters and she was drenched in blood.

"My darling!" called the chief. "What has he done to you?"

"It's what I've done to him," replied Asesina, brandishing a huge knife. "I've killed the bastard. And now," she added, as smoke billowed from the cave. "I've set fire to his body."

"But what about the Kikihuahua Examples?" cried her father.

"They were not relevant to the situation, Father. This came to me as a vision when I was lying beneath the weight of the giant. It seemed that I was possessed with an entirely new outlook, wherein the Examples had no place. My own safety became paramount, so as soon as I was able, I took the giant's knife and drove it into his heart."

"I cannot condone what you have done," said her father. "But it's good to have you back."

Life in the village of Buenos continued as before, except that Asesina had changed. She became stronger and fiercely loving and more than a little violent. The young men sought her out and loved her back; such loving had not been known for centuries in the slow pace of the village. Asesina's children grew up strong and loving, too. Even on his deathbed, however, her father lamented the change that had come over Asesina since that night with the giant.

"I can't think what got into her," he said.

This was substantially the story that Selena told Zozula, although the Rainbow's version was less colorful, more factual.

"It's interesting . . ." said Zozula. "So there used to be Macrobes out there." He gazed at the panorama. Wisps of smoke rose from the village, where the Wild Humans were preparing for their annual festival.

"There still are," said Selena. "I had the saybaby check out the local population. We may not be the only people who use the Inner Think, for instance. There are all kinds of things happening Outside that we know nothing about."

"We have a lot of learning to do, and it's ironic to think that the Wild Humans will be our teachers, after all I've said about them in the past. But I'll get used to the idea."

"The Macrobes will spread again, through us and the neotenites—the New People, that is. That will help."

"I still find the idea of Macrobes a little unsettling, Lena. I always thought the Inner Think was just a knack."

She smiled. "The Macrobes can only make things better. They've learned from their mistakes, too. By the way, the saybaby identified two people in Pu'este who have the Macrobes in their genes. One of them is an old priest; but he's of no consequence."

"And the other?"

"Manuel."

HORSE DAY

•••

*T*he Cuidadors showed Manuel out of the Dome, kindly but firmly. The quest was over. The Bale Wolf had been caught and the rest was up to the scientists. Zozula shook his hand and said he'd drop by in a couple of days and let him know how the Girl was, but that meanwhile there was no point in his hanging around.

Grieving for the Girl and angry at his dismissal, Manuel returned to Pu'este. By now it was midafternoon and the sun was hot overhead. He looked in at his shack and found everything in order, but the place didn't seem to be his home anymore. His depression deepening, he climbed the bank and took the road inland. Wise Ana was not at home. Her little shop was closed, the wares all stacked inside, out of the sun. Barra the herdsman, strolling by with a baby vicuna in his arms, said he hadn't seen Ana for days. Manuel walked on to the village.

He met a scene of frenzied activity. Women sat before their cottages working busily with thread and bright raffia. Men brought armfuls of straw, stirred vats of dye and built a great mountain of combustibles in the middle of the hut circle. Children ran about, squealing with excitement, getting in the way and earning the sharp disapproval of their elders. Only old Insel was unaffected, lying flat on his back as usual, cloudgazing and muttering prophesies.

Chine bustled up. "You, Manuel. Go over to the north slope and bring in the animals. Quickly, now."

It was a poor task for Manuel, Space rider and conqueror of the Bale

Wolves, so he ignored the old chief, instead wandering away among the huts.

Today was Horse Day. Tonight would be a time of feasting and celebration, culminating in the huge bonfire, the great Dance when the Horse would vanquish the Snake, the ceremonial Pouring-on-of-Waters and the blessing from Dad Ose.

After his initial annoyance—Manuel hated Horse Day, with its aftermath of drinking and sex and outbursts of violence—he decided that maybe it was no bad thing. He needed some activity to take his mind off the Girl and the Dome and his empty feeling that somehow things had ended before they'd begun. So he helped the women spin their flossy balls of cottonweed that would represent horse clouds in the coming pageant. The young men glanced at him in scorn as they passed by; Manuel had become even more weird during his traveling.

Later, as darkness fell, the village became quieter. People retired to their cottages to dress up. On the far side of the meadows the dancers prepared the Horse and the Snake, their shadowy, secretive movements revealed in flashes of light from their lanterns. Manuel wondered whether to go and see how they were getting along, then decided instead to see if Wise Ana had returned.

Her shop was still closed, however. Standing in the darkness, he toyed with the idea of walking to the Dome, but decided against it. He went home instead and turned on his Simulator and began to fashion a mindpainting from his memories of Polysitia: the grass, the heaving shoreline, the whales.

In his introspective mood he did well, and the shapes that swirled within the box were subtle and evocative—and presently, without his consciously willing it, a face began to form in the background. At first he thought it was Belinda coming through again, and he almost switched the machine off because he could not bear to relive the terrible moment of her death—and that was his most prominent memory of Belinda now. Somehow the tenderness had faded, leaving violence and a flying body, twisted and broken, disappearing into the ocean and lost forever. He didn't want to go through that again. But something stopped his hand as he reached for the knob.

This face wasn't Belinda.

It is not always possible to *recognize* a face in a Simulator. Sometimes there is only an impression, a feeling and a movement and a few touches of light and color that somehow suggest a person. Now Manuel looked at the mind-painting and wondered who the person could be. Two things were certain: She was nice, and she was pretty. He rather thought she had dark hair and an elfin appearance, with mischievous brown eyes, like that oil painting in Selena's quarters. She was fun, and she cheered him up.

He added a few touches, then switched off the Simulator and made his way back to the village, feeling much better.

A girl danced toward him, covered with puffy white cottonballs that glowed pink in the firelight. She danced with a swaying movement that was meant to be seductive, and under the cottonballs she was naked. Manuel watched her and smiled. A certain side of a girl's character could be gauged by the number of cottonballs she wore. This girl showed more skin than cotton, and what few balls she wore were not placed to conceal anything much except her face.

"Dance with me, Manuel!"

So he took her in his arms and they danced to the insistent beat of the maracas, drums and flutes of the Pu'este orchestra, while all around them the other dancers circled, some in costume, some, like Manuel, normally dressed. As the girl rubbed her face against Manuel's shoulder, some of the cottonballs fell away and she looked up at him, laughing.

"It's Ellie, isn't it?" he said resignedly.

"Who else!" She laughed, tossing her hair. "Are you still listening to the sea, Manuel? Or have your travels taught you that there are other things in life?"

"There is a lot more in life," he agreed, feeling old and very wise.

"Good. Then come to my hut, Manuel—just for a moment." In rubbing against him she had contrived to shed more cottonballs, and now she stepped back so he could get the effect of firelight on her tanned body. "Come on."

And probably he would have, but somehow the face of the girl in the Simulator arose in his mind's eye, and he knew that it wouldn't work. "Not right now," he said, and wondered at himself. A flurry of activity on the other side of the fire gave him the excuse he needed. "They're starting the Dance."

Everybody sat down in a big circle around the fire and uttered hisses and catcalls as the Snake came weaving its way through the audience and into the bright firelight. The Snake was big this year, at least twenty meters long and supported by ten pairs of legs, gaudily colored, made of stitched cloth and furs, with a fringe of scarlet alpaca wool and a great fearsome head of painted clay on a wooden frame that swung this way and that and provoked screams of terrified delight from the children. For a long time the Snake cavorted and the crowd bestowed their good-natured derision upon it, guessing at the identities of the legs. The band pounded away indefatigably, and Ellie squeezed Manuel's hand.

Then the Horse arrived amid cheers. The Horse, the savior of Mankind, would do battle with the Snake and drive it from the skies. More kuta was passed round and the audience drank and settled back to watch the ceremonial tournament. The Horse, like the Snake, was sustained by pounding pairs of legs, but only four rather than ten. Its color was comparatively drab and its face wore a kindly grin. In truth it was a dull animal compared with the Snake, but such has been the comparison between good and evil down the ages.

The combatants fenced for an opening. The Snake moved sinuously, its occupants weaving from side to side as they ran with bent knees—making the whole effect one of menacing stealth. The Horse people, however, stayed in a disciplined row and ran upright with high knees, so that the animal appeared to prance along with jerky dignity. The audience, feeling the effects of the kuta, urged the battle to its climax.

The opponents were no doubt anxious to conclude the matter, too. On the priest's rostrum (from which Dad Ose would pronounce the blessing after the Pouring-on-of-Waters) stood their prize—a great jug of potent fluid known as "nid," a distillate of various herbs and fermented sugars prepared exclusively for Horse Day celebrations and infinitely more powerful than the beery kuta.

Battle was joined. The Horse, head nodding, lurched against the Snake, which sidled away, abashed. The Horse reared up and its head rose high in the crimson light of the fire so that it looked like Vengeance itself, and its smile seemed to become a stern frown of Retribution. Sensing the drama, the audience quieted down. The Horse tottered, overbalanced, and its head crashed down across the back of its adversary. Cries of pain emanated from the Snake.

The Horse charged again and the Snake cringed back, and for a moment it looked as though the fight was virtually over, that the traditional conclusion was near. Then the audience noticed a deviation from the accepted ritual of combat. The tail of the Snake had swung round and, with shouts of rage, was attacking the rear of the Horse.

The Horse wheeled, swaying and grinning, losing discipline and folding in the middle as it attempted to beat off this cowardly onslaught. Now the Snake completely surrounded the Horse, and the two animals were becoming lost in a tangle of struggling figures. The battle lost its formal aspect. The crowd howled with delight. The animals were trodden into the ground as the teams cast off their trappings and fought with bare fists, a jumble of thrashing silhouettes in the dancing flames.

The battle was soon over. Outnumbered, the Horse team took to their heels and fled into the darkness, leaving the field of victory to the Snake. After a moment's pause, during which they might have been expected to reflect on the enormity of what they had done, the Snake team, showing no remorse, raised the limp carcass of the Horse and flung it onto the fire. Flames roared into the night sky.

The forces of Evil had triumphed.

Fat Chine, knuckles pressed to his mouth in superstitious horror, murmured, "Oh, my bones . . . Oh, my bones . . ."

It was a confusing moment, and the audience was not sure how to take it. However, every such moment has its man, and Dad Ose clapped his hands sharply and strode to his rostrum.

Afterward, talk in the village centered around whether Dad Ose had really known what was happening around him. He had lived a very long time, and he had presided over countless Horse Day celebrations. To him, the whole thing must have become mechanical. It is conceivable that he hadn't noticed that the outcome of the battle was in any way surprising. The good fight was over, the flesh of one of the animals had been ceremonially cast into the flames and it was time for the Pouring-on-of-Waters. The purpose of this rite was to produce billowing clouds of steam from the holy Waters, symbolizing a generation of new horse clouds following the death of the Snake. It was a fine and cleansing act.

So Dad Ose, an impressive figure in his flowing robes, took the gourd and, uttering the sacred words, flung it over the glowing remains of the Horse.

A huge ball of fire materialized out of the embers and sprang directly at him.

The audience screamed in awe, suspecting Divine Judgment. Dad Ose rolled in the dirt, beating at his flaming robes. For some time nobody went to his aid, fearing that they, too, might incur wrath from Above. Then Manuel, tearing himself loose from Ellie, got some rugs around the priest and extinguished the flames. For a moment people watched him nervously, until a fresh outburst caught their attention.

The Snake team, gathered around the rostrum for their celebratory cup, found that the pitcher contained only holy Waters. Dad Ose had thrown the nid on the fire.

✳

Dark night, and the world still existed. Starquin had not destroyed it because of the sacrilegious doings in the village, and reassuring horse clouds now curtained the stars. Manuel walked home. Behind him, the villagers drank kuta, fought and made love, and, thought Manuel, they would all be feeling the worse for it in the morning.

And what were his own regrets? Why did he feel so sad?

Maybe he should have had sex with Ellie. Maybe he shouldn't have left her sitting there unhappy and deserted because all the other young people had paired off. But he couldn't help the way he was, could he? Ellie knew he was different; she knew that sex alone was unsatisfactory to him. Or maybe, she still couldn't conceive what he'd tried to explain to her.

The road was very dark, lined with black trees and sighing, sleeping animals. Sounds of celebration still carried to him, and turning around, he could see the glow of the fire and the sparks rising against the black hillside. Farther away a single light burned high; that would be from Dad Ose's church, where the priest was licking his wounds. Manuel walked on, and now he saw a glow ahead.

Wise Ana was back home.

Suddenly his depression was gone, and he quickened his footsteps. Ana would welcome him; she always did. She would offer him one of her strange drinks, and then they would sit together by the fire and talk—and maybe, in due course, fall comfortably asleep . . .

Manuel still couldn't quite face the idea of sleeping in his own shack, alone.

He reached Ana's cave. The light streamed from a crack in the heavy cloths that covered her doorway. He was about to push them aside and enter, when he heard voices and paused. Ana had company. Disappointed, he wondered what to do. Maybe she wouldn't want to see him. She was an odd person in many ways, and he never had quite understood the nature of her dealings with people, or why strangers came from distant lands to see her, or where she went when she traveled . . .

"Come in, Manuel. Don't hang around out there in the dark!"

And that was another funny thing—that sixth sense of hers. Manuel entered. Ana leaned on her counter in her accustomed pose, in conversation with a girl, who turned round as he crossed the room. He nodded to her briefly, resenting her presence; then he stared. She was a pretty girl, with dark hair and a snub nose, and a smile that went straight to his heart. She was different: Slender like Belinda but definitely not a Polysitian, and her eyes were brown and bright. But that was not the only reason he stared until she laughed aloud.

She was the girl whose portrait hung in Selena's quarters.

For a moment nobody said anything. Then Manuel asked, wonderingly, "Do I know you from somewhere?"

Ana answered for the girl. "This is Elizabeth, Manuel. She likes to be called Beth, for short."

Manuel looked at Elizabeth.

Ana said, "It's Horse Night—you don't want an old woman like me around. Why don't you two go for a walk along the shore and get acquainted. The air's like wine—maybe the ceremony worked, for a change. Me, I'm going to go visit a relative, and I won't be back for a couple of days. So you're quite welcome to use my home while I'm gone. I know your own place is kind of unwelcoming just now, Manuel. You'll find plenty of food here, and drink—oh, and don't let Beth stay out too long. It's going to take her a few weeks to get used to our changeable atmosphere. If she gets tired, use the Life Cave in the back there."

And with that, Ana, one of the great figures of history, and certainly not an old woman by any standards other than those of humans, pushed through the drapes at her doorway and walked into the night and out of the story of the Triad.

"Will you show me your land, Manuel?" asked Elizabeth, as though she were a foreigner.

"Of course." Manuel took her hand and they went outside. Ana was nowhere in sight. A hazy moon glimmered through the horse clouds, giving enough light to walk by. They took the road to the beach. Manuel felt very comfortable with Elizabeth, as if he'd known her for a long time. "I've met you before, haven't I?" he said.

"Have you?" The whiteness of her smile was visible. "Do you think I'm pretty, Manuel?"

"Yes. And different. You've come from a long way off."

They talked of animals and people, ideas and philosophy. They walked along the beach, looked in at Manuel's shack, climbed onto the cliff and followed the guanaco trails in the moonlight. In the end they talked of love.

Manuel said, "This is how I want it to be. This is how I always thought it would be—but it never was. Except once, but that's all over now because she's dead. Now it's like that again, and I can hardly believe it."

His arm was around her waist and he squeezed her as they watched the moon on the water. "I'm scared you'll go. I want to be here, with you, forever—do you know what I mean? It doesn't sound stupid to you, does it?"

"It sounds good, Manuel."

"Perhaps none of this is real—perhaps I'm back in one of those other worlds and in a moment Zozula will come and I'll be on the Train again . . ." His eyes searched her face. "A terrible thing happened to me recently, when I had to fight some monsters. I remembered seeing them first, *then* I actually saw them afterward. It happened the wrong way around. The memory came before the event. Now it's happened again, and it's not terrible at all. I remember loving you—and now suddenly here you are, and I love you. How can that happen?"

Elizabeth said mischievously, "Maybe I'm your dream girl. Maybe you've always imagined someone as perfect as me, and now here I am. What are you going to do about it, Manuel?"

But Manuel was not amused. A fear was growing in him, a fear that fate was playing with him again, that—for all he knew—Elizabeth was no different from the village girls, with their fleeting attachments and their inability to form emotional bonds, their inability to . . . *love*. This girl, he wanted to keep. This girl, he loved. Did she feel the same?

Haltingly he said, "There's a thing people used to do—I learned about it a long time ago, and I don't think anyone knows about it but me. But it seems that in the old days people liked each other more than just for sex —I mean, there was another feeling . . . they called it *love*. Anyway, when they loved, when they were so sure of themselves and of the other person, then they had a priest *marry* them, which means—"

"I know what that means," said Elizabeth. "Where I come from, people do it." *But they only do it for fun, for kicks, to live out a role that has caught their fancy for a while,* she thought. *This isn't what Manuel means.* Suddenly she realized she was hundreds of years older than Manuel and she'd experienced everything a human can dream up. She looked at Manuel, his young face so serious in the moonlight, and she felt unworthy of his love, even though she wanted to return it and knew she did return it. But in a way she was playing with him, and this wasn't fair.

So she said, "You can't separate love from sex."

"I think I can."

"That's only because you're different and you've been unlucky. I knew another person who was unlucky in a different way, and because of it she had to try to separate love from sex, too, and it didn't work for her, either." *Now,* she thought, *you throw it away forever, you fool.* "You knew her, too. You called her the Girl. She wasn't the kind of creature you'd have sex with. Did you love *her,* Manuel? Did you?"

And he said, "Yes."

Then she had to tell him, of course. And instead of the shock and bewilderment she expected from him, he accepted her words as though they confirmed his own beliefs. And he visibly relaxed, as if what she had said simplified matters. In the end, she was the bewildered one, but Manuel, laughing and kissing her, pulled her down to the grass and made love to her in a way she'd never have believed possible. And when at last they were finished and they lay holding each other as though they couldn't get close enough, she had no doubts at all. Manuel was right. It was all quite simple.

Manuel Talks with God Again

••

*D*ad Ose spoke to his Macrobes. He didn't know they were in there, of course, and he would have been horrified if he had. He thought his human body was complete in itself and had needed no assistance—other than mental power alone—to live its 496 years.

I live, and I always will live. Every cell of my body is regenerating at this very moment . . . How could God treat him so badly? How could he allow such humiliation to occur to his servant? In his mind's eye Dad Ose saw himself rolling in the dirt, flapping at his blazing clothing until Manuel—of all people!—ran forward to save him . . . "Forget it, Forget it!" he found himself shouting aloud. He must concentrate. He sent his mind down into the palms of his hands where the burns were . . . Like stigmata; he was being made to suffer for his belief, he was being cruci-fied . . .

"Ahhhh!" He shouted in an extreme of embarrassment, trying to shout down the memory of the children sniggering as he had stumbled away with blackened and shredding robes. The shout echoed around the cool stone of the church and he flushed, realizing he had made that stupid noise himself. It had happened and it was over and it was unimportant— he was too wise a man to allow such a little setback to unbalance him. *Dying is meaningless. There is no reason for it. I will eliminate that Clock that tells my body to age.* Those kids with the dirty faces, laughing at him. *I will eliminate, eliminate the Clock.* Manuel and that girl, Ellie. *First the feet, flow with the bloodstream and regenerate the cells. The ankles, soothe the tired ankles and nourish the flesh, the bone—"*

"Hello, Dad Ose!"

What? What? Dear God, it *couldn't* be! Yet he stood there, that wretched mysterious boy, the sun warming his dark hair as he paused in the doorway holding the hand of some trollop—a different one this time.

"Sorry, Dad Ose . . . I didn't know you were sleeping."

"I was *praying*, God damn it!" snapped Dad Ose inexcusably, then collected himself. "Come in, my children. What can I do for you today?"

"I want to speak to God."

"What!" This was an insult. Dad Ose bounded to his feet and strode down the aisle. His palms itched. He would smash those two kids' heads together, knock some respect into them . . . They stood there with the sun around them like a halo, holding hands. There was something serene about them, something . . . holy. He stopped, and swallowed.

Manuel repeated, in some surprise, "I want to speak to God, like I did before. I find it's easier here, somehow. Your church is quiet and old, and he comes through better."

Dad Ose felt as though he were in some kind of suspended animation, and he found himself saying, "Manuel, I've lived in this church for over four hundred years, and in all that time God's never spoken to me."

"That's probably because you don't address him by the proper name," said Manuel with disarming simplicity.

"Oh? And what's his proper name?"

"Starquin. I'm surprised you didn't know that. Starquin the Five-in-One."

"The Five-in-One, is it? Let me see now: One, the Father, two, the Son—"

"No, Dad. Length, Width, Thickness, Duration and Psychic Entity."

So straightforward was Manuel's manner that Dad Ose found his own anger rude. And that girl, beside Manuel, seemed to radiate a quiet goodness. They were sincere, these two. So instead of throwing them out, he said, "My God is the only true God, Manuel. He has endured since the beginning of time, and always will. Yours is a false God."

Probably at this moment Manuel realized something of the conflict within the priest, because he chose his words very carefully. "I really think we're talking about the same person, Dad, although Starquin has only been on Earth for 250,890,147 years and he will be leaving soon. But what I have to say to him is very important, and I only found this out last night, when Beth and I were in bed. Do you mind? I'll talk aloud, so you'll see I don't say anything that you might disagree with."

"Oh, go ahead, then," said Dad Ose helplessly.

Manuel sat in a pew, drawing Beth down beside him, and rested his head in his hands, closing his eyes. Then, slowly at first, but gaining confidence, he spoke.

"Dear Starquin. I have done everything you asked me to, and I'm sorry if I misunderstood what you really wanted. I made friends with the man at the Dome, who turned out to be Zozula, and not such a bad kind of man at all. I was kind to people and to animals and even plants and machines, except when I thought their will was against yours, and it all seemed to work out well, and I really think that human beings will be a lot better off for what we've done.

"I've seen some terrifying things and I've seen a lot of people die, but I know now that these things are necessary, because if everything goes the way we want it, then life is very dull—and anyway, these bad things are just as necessary to your plan as the good things. So I can see that it's right that Selena is treating people with Bale Wolf venom, and I thank you for including this in your plan, because it's given me Beth, whom I wouldn't have had otherwise.

"Starquin—maybe I'm too proud. I've always thought I could understand what it was all about. Even when Belinda died, I told myself it was your will and there must be a reason. And yesterday I thought I saw that reason. The people in the Domes had to be saved and I had been chosen to do it, and my reward was to be Beth. That's what I thought. But now, after last night, I don't understand anymore.

"You tell me we have to go away. You tell me we have to make ourselves ready to face another test, and that we must go back to the Dome.

"Well, Starquin," and here Manuel's voice became stubborn, "I don't want to. I've had enough, and I want to settle down at home. I'm through with excitement for a while, and facing death isn't my idea of fun anymore. Haven't I done enough?"

There was silence in the church. For a while Manuel stayed there, shoulders hunched and face buried in his hands, as though flinching from the possibility of Almighty anger. Dad Ose stood and Beth sat motionless, watching.

Then gradually the sounds from outside began to intrude, the bird song and sighing of wind. Somewhere an animal snorted. The wind stirred a tree outside the window, and the shadows moved over the pews and the stone floor. Manuel looked up. There was still a residue of fear in his eyes. Beth squeezed his hand. A warm breeze fanned through the stonework, stirring the dust.

Dad Ose spoke.

He was going to say something fairly gentle to this misguided youth, something about the sin of pride and its inevitable fall, something wise and kindly and avuncular.

Instead, the words that came were not his own.

He said, "I will not command you, Manuel, because I can read the Ifalong well enough to know you will do my wishes of your own accord. You and Beth will come to no harm. Since this is the last time I will speak to anyone on your planet, I will thank you now for all your help. Goodbye." Dad Ose closed his mouth.

There was a long silence. A cock crowed.

Manuel said, "Come on, Beth. We'd better get along to the Dome."

Dad Ose watched them go, watched them walking hand in hand down the dusty road to the village and the Dome, and his mouth had dropped open again.

Starquin had spoken through him.

The astonishment and terror gradually abated, then grew into something else—an enormous flush of pride: He, too, had been chosen as Starquin's instrument.

He looked around his church, seeing the trappings that served religion as he taught it, and as he had learned it in the North, hundreds of years ago. He had taught a good religion, carefully weighing the various messiahs who had emerged down the ages and using the best of the teachings of each, always bearing in mind that the important thing was the Supreme Being. Someone up there cared.

So, what was in a name?

And, if Someone up there was moving out, what did that matter? At least he, Dad Ose, was now completely convinced of his existence, and could devote the rest of his life to preparing Mankind for his inevitable return . . .

Lighthearted, and feeling younger and more secure in his belief than he could remember, he made his way briskly to the village. People down there would be feeling the need of spiritual comfort, this morning.

DAEDALUS AND ICARUS

••

*H*ow could a steam locomotive fly? Well, it couldn't, of course, but that didn't stop a lot of people thinking that it could. It was just another legend, a distortion of what had happened millions of years ago.

Maybe they were closer to the truth in Ionia, an ancient land where the men once more herded goats and the women once more tended the hearth. Ionia had seen its share of changes—a fleeting moment in history when the valleys and hillsides disappeared under the press of concrete and steel and people—but later, time slowed again, and the storytellers told slow tales around the evening fires.

They told the story of Daedalus the inventor and his son Icarus.

It seemed that Daedalus seriously offended Starquin in some bygone era. Starquin had watched the land grow beautiful, millennia upon millennia. He had seen the plants thrive and the animals flourish and evolve, and he'd seen Mankind arrive to share his enjoyment. Through the eyes of the Dedos, he'd often come close, so close that he could observe individual men and their doings—and, if absolutely necessary, he could influence them, although it was against his Rule.

But Starquin failed to observe Daedalus. By the time Starquin found out what Daedalus had done, it was too late. Too many humans were affected on too many happentracks.

Daedalus had invented the steam locomotive and fathered the Industrial Revolution.

It happened in the flicker of an eternal eyelid, and Earth was suddenly spoiled for Starquin. Steel rails glittered unnaturally in the sunlight, and the gentle wind was obstructed by tall buildings. Propellers churned the quietness of the sea, and smoke dirtied the clouds. And humans were everywhere, no longer interesting and unique, but threatening to overwhelm other creatures by their very numbers—and, ultimately, to force the progress of Earth into their own pattern instead of Starquin's.

It happened in the flicker of an eternal eyelid—and just as quickly, it was certain to go away. Unlike the dinosaurs, however, it would leave a mess. Earth would be depleted of its possessions, and wreckage would litter the land. The wreckage would rot and disappear, but the possessions would not be replaced; indeed, many of them were lost in the Greataway. Starquin could do nothing except exact punishment.

So he plucked Daedalus out of one happentrack and he set him down in another, at a later period when he might witness the results of his invention. And he set his son down with him. This son was Daedalus's only surviving relative, and very dear to him. His name was Icarus.

Starquin imprisoned Daedalus and Icarus in a huge compound with high walls. And he filled the compound with the results of Daedalus's work—a great litter of wrecked steam locomotives. And he left the two of them there to rot.

But Daedalus had not, on *this* happentrack, invented the locomotive. Starquin had plucked him out of time too carelessly. Daedalus gazed at the giant shapes with curiosity and interest, and he began to tinker with things. Far from being desolated by his predicament, he became fascinated and delighted. Only Icarus, staring at the tops of the high walls and wondering what was outside, was unable to share his father's joy.

"This place is a prison, Father. I want to get out—I can't stand the confinement." Icarus was a free spirit, and in due course would—but that is another story.

Daedalus was a workman and an inventor, and a man of narrow but intense vision, unlike Icarus, who was a dreamer.

"There's a lifetime's work here, Son. These great machines—I'd dreamed of such, but I'd never seen them." He instinctively understood the purpose of the great boilers, and he filled them with water and lit fires in the fireboxes and watched the pressure rise. His eyes followed the plumes of steam into the sky while he listened to his son's lamenting.

"I will die if I am trapped in here any longer, Father."

While Daedalus worked on, his son wasted away, until gradually the work and the discovering began to lose its appeal and his son's sickness began to obsess him. He wondered if there were some way in which his inventive powers could be turned into avenues of escape. He watched the steam rise into the calm air.

He had a fair idea of the purpose of the locomotives. He had even succeeded in repairing two and had driven one a short distance along a length of twisted track. They were apparently a means of transport. But it seemed a lot of trouble, building huge machines like these for a simple purpose that could be accomplished by a horse—and what was more, a horse was not confined to tracks. So there must be something else.

It was winter before he realized what the locomotives were really for, and by this time Icarus's cheeks were sunken and his face flushed. He lay in one of the locomotives, his breath coming fast, and Daedalus knew he had to get him out of the compound soon.

It was the steam that gave Daedalus the clue he sought. The steam rose into the sky. The purpose of the boiler was to create steam by boiling water, and confined within that huge boiler must be an immense amount of steam, possessing prodigious lift. Only the weight of the locomotive itself kept it from flying away into the sky. So how to get it off the ground? The secret was in the wheels, and at last he realized their true purpose.

So he labored in the snow, while Icarus coughed on the locomotive footplate in the heat of the fire, and eventually he laid a straight track toward the high walls and curved the track upward at the end so that a locomotive, rushing along it, would be launched into the air. That was the impetus he needed; that was what the wheels were for—to help get the locomotive airborne.

Then, because he wanted to take no chance of overloading, he built another, similar track and fired up his second locomotive for Icarus.

Finally, he discussed his plan with his son. To his surprise, Icarus was overjoyed, thinking little of the danger—but questioning his father again and again on the capabilities of the locomotives.

"I don't know, Icarus." Why were his son's eyes so bright? Why was he standing, when a few minutes before he'd seemed too weak to rise? "The impetus of the wheels will throw the locomotive into the air, and the steam will lift it over the wall. More than that I can't tell you."

"Flying . . . We'll be flying, like birds. Do you realize that, Father? Doesn't the thought move you?"

"Machinery moves me. So, we may fly a short distance. My main intent is to get you out of here. I thought that was what you wanted, too."

"Yes . . . But flying . . ."

The locomotives stood side by side. Icarus, flushed and bright-eyed, stood at one regulator, his father at the other.

"Now . . ." said Daedalus.

Simultaneously they pulled on the regulators, and in unison, the two locomotives rolled down the tracks, gathering speed. The compound echoed with exhaust beats as smoke was hurled into the sky. Rail-joints rattled under the wheels. Daedalus saw the intense expression on his son's face and wondered. Icarus glanced across at him and grinned a fierce grin of joyous anticipation. Side by side, the two locomotives roared toward the wall.

The beat of exhaust deepened as they hurled themselves at the grade and began to climb. The man and the boy held the regulators wide open, urging every last gram of power out of their bellowing mounts. The rails fell away beneath them.

They rose into the air.

Daedalus held his breath as his locomotive leveled out, skimming the top of the wall with a scant meter to spare. He looked ahead and saw a fair land stretching into the distance, wooded hillsides and lakes with winding rivers glistening in the sunlight—quite unlike his native Ionia, but beautiful, and a fine place for Icarus and him to settle down in. He saw a cluster of friendly cottages, and he eased off the regulator and opened the cylinder cocks, blowing off steam. The locomotive began a gentle descent. He motioned Icarus to follow him.

But Icarus still clung to his regulator, and the smoke roared from the chimney, drawing the furnace into an inferno and building ever higher pressure in the boiler. He was laughing, eyes blazing, and faintly his father heard the words, "Flying, I'm flying! Into Space, into Space . . ."

Daedalus landed, descended from the cab, looked up and wept.

Icarus flew on, ever higher, until his father could see him no longer. He rose until the clouds were beneath him, and where they parted he could see a green land below, rivers and villages and coastline, like a colored map. That land didn't interest him, because Space lay before him. His lifelong dream was about to come true. Tugging at the regulator, he rose . . .

He rose until he reached the limits of Earth's atmosphere, then the furnace began to falter and flicker, because there was no oxygen to feed it. The boiler pressure dropped. Frantically he shoveled in more coal, but it served only to dampen the fire further.

The locomotive fell.

Icarus screamed. The locomotive fell back into the atmosphere, but the fire was out, the steam pressure low. Icarus fell, down, down, through the clouds until he smashed into the summit of a great mountain, creating a crater a kilometer wide, and only then did the furnace reignite, but it was too late.

Icarus was dead.

The boiler exploded with a mighty roar, and fire and steam gushed from the summit of the mountain, which men called Stromboli. From time to time Stromboli still explodes and throws steam and molten stuff into the sky—and men say "Icarus has fallen on another happentrack." And since there are happentracks without limit, Icarus will always fall and Stromboli will always erupt.

And Daedalus?

Years later, when he was an old man alone in his cottage, his only possessions a few goats, Starquin appeared to him in the form of a Dedo.

"Why did you do it?" asked Daedalus. "Why did you take Icarus? I was the guilty one. I spoiled the Earth." Over the years he'd had dreams of the future, and he'd seen what he'd done on other happentracks.

The beautiful woman looked at him. There was no pity in her eyes, no humanity—because at that moment she was totally possessed by Starquin, the Logical One.

She said, "It is the way of a man to invent only one thing in his lifetime. You invented the steam engine—nothing more. But Icarus—had he lived, he would have discovered the Greataway. Mankind is not ready for that, Daedalus. Not yet."

So saying, she disappeared, leaving Daedalus alone.

THE HATE BOMBS

•••

Countless years after Icarus, Mankind *did* discover the Greataway, and the age of Invisible Spaceships began. The Invisible Spaceships—as fast as thought and as clean as the new moon, powered by the Outer Think. They were much more practical than Icarus's locomotive—or even the Celestial Steam Locomotive, which came later and which was not a true Invisible Spaceship—because only insubstantial Dream People could ride it.

The secret of the Outer Think was lost after the war with the Red Planet, so the minstrels say. This is not strictly true, because Selena's vulpids, among others, used a limited version of mind travel. But it makes a good story and gives the minstrels the opportunity to credit the rediscovery of the Outer Think to Manuel and Elizabeth, the Great Lovers.

On that morning, after Starquin had spoken through the mouth of the priest, Manuel and Elizabeth made their way to a pool where axolotls lived, in the shadow of the Dome. Here they held hands.

They materialized on the Skytrain for the last time. Blind Pew was in charge now, tapping his way up and down the aisle, a figure of infinite menace. The fun had gone out of the voyage, and the passengers were scared and silent. The Bale Wolves had been defeated on this particular happentrack and, so far as the passengers could see, further travel was pointless.

"I want to go home," Bambi said plaintively.

Pew said, "Hist—there's stowaways aboard! By the powers, I'll rummage them out and keelhaul the dogs!"

"It's only us," said Manuel. "So shut up and sit down, Pew!"

Pew's stick made an audible hiss as it swung toward Manuel, and it would surely have killed him if it had not, at the moment of impact, suddenly faded and passed right through him, leaving him unharmed.

"By God!" exclaimed Sir Charles. "The young whippersnapper has the measure of Pew!"

"Pew's only a smallwish," said Beth. "He's in your power if you have the courage to face him down."

Silver suddenly bobbed up, hobbling from the direction of the Locomotive. "Don't be doing anything hasty, now, shipmates! Save your psy. Reckless wishing could send us all to Davy Jones!"

Bambi sat very still, staring at Pew. She said, "If we're very careful, we can wish away little things on this Train without hurting the composite. I think this horrible blind man is only a little thing that has become blown up in our minds. A tiny man my father once made, he said . . ." She was beginning to talk quietly to herself, a frequent habit of hers. Her gaze drifted to the window, where a supernova glittered countless light-years away. "Makes no difference where you are, anything your heart desires will come to you . . ." And her voice became inaudible, but she turned and looked at Pew again.

And suddenly Pew was naked.

He stood there bereft of his shapeless black hat and green eyeshade, and his great swirling stinking cloak was gone, and his shirt and pants, and even his cracked seaboots. He stood there a blind old man, face pointing this way and that in sightless bewilderment, his hands cupped over his groin. He was skinny and wrinkled and defenseless and totally pathetic.

He was a solid smallwish and it would have taken more than Bambi's psy to remove him entirely, but she had hit upon a way to whittle him down.

With a croak of despair he bolted for the Locomotive, bony shanks pumping.

"Well now, me hearties," boomed Silver, visibly gaining in stature. "Now here's a pretty kettle o' fish. Not that I have any time for the likes o' Pew, but we must have discipline." Nevertheless he found it hard to conceal his glee, and after a short oration on the value of teamwork, he shouted, "The Song, shipmates, let me hear the Song!"

And at that moment, the Celestial Steam Locomotive ran into a Hate Bomb.

*

Manuel and Beth were lost in their little world of love at the time, holding hands and planning their future in Pu'este, when a group of images passed through their minds.

First they saw Silver swinging toward them, a smile on his broad face, while from his free hand feathers fell, and a trickle of blood as he crushed the parrot in a clenched fist.

Next came Pew, fully clothed but for his eyeshade, and his eyes were like moons in his pointed face, dull moons that roved about before fixing a blind gaze upon them. Then one eye winked, a slow, grotesque hooding of the orb.

Thirdly the fireman came, and he had no face at all. The cowl of his black cloak contained a head that was featureless but not smooth, composed of ridges and furrows in independent movement, as though a carpet of maggots were devouring a side of meat.

And for the fourth image, Manuel and Beth each saw something different.

Manuel saw Beth, and yet it was not the Beth he knew. This new girl looked like Beth and she was smiling, but it was a smile of false invitation like a prostitute's, and she thrust her hips forward as she swayed toward him, and her dress fell off one shoulder so that the breast was exposed— not only to him, but to a vast number of eyes that suddenly materialized around them. Then this new Beth spoke, and she said, "Come to me, honey!" and as he stood, hypnotized, she produced a glittering little knife from the pocket at her waist and held it before her, so that he could not help but impale himself as he was drawn irresistibly forward . . .

Beth saw Manuel smile tenderly at her. He said, "Kiss me, my love," and as she did so, her tongue probing toward his, he suddenly bit down . . .

. . . and they found themselves fighting, somewhere there was a knife, and around them the passengers were fighting, also. Not only were they possessed with hatred for each other, but there was a dreadful fear in them, too, so that they fought with desperate and murderous intent; and the knife was a millimeter from flesh . . .

"I love you, Beth," said Manuel, trying not to struggle.

The knife was against his throat now, and her crazed eyes stared into his.

"I love you, Beth," said Manuel.

Her eyes widened with the first uncertainty, but it was too late, and the maddened brain gave the signal to the muscles, and the knife slid forward.

"I love you, Beth," said Manuel, keeping still.

And suddenly the roar of hatred faded, the sulfurous air became sweet and the passengers quieted down, looking at one another in puzzlement, wondering what they were fighting about—and why, a second ago, they'd had every intention of fighting to the last man.

Beth stared incredulously at the knife in her hand, then dropped it to the floor, and the final image—of a sad-faced, dark man who had wanted to rule the world—faded from her mind in a rush of loving psy as she caught hold of Manuel and hugged him, and felt his arms around her, too.

And thus was the first Hate Bomb defused. After that it became easier. The Hate Bombs had served their purpose; they had saved Humanity. It was a pity that Humanity had in the meantime mislaid that special quality of love that would have allowed the Bombs to be nullified earlier—but now Manuel and Beth removed them one by one.

LA BRUJA

●●

> *Sensed in a dream within life's clangorous street,*
> *Herself haste-free, a girl beside a monolith.*
> *Endless traffic stirred her black-winged cloak—*
> *Not yet her body; she stood impassive as the Rock*
>   *itself.*
> *Step alive! I took her arm. Her strange calm*
>   *caused me distress.*
> *Her eyes unveiled, she touched my hand to stone.*
>   *I saw . . .*
> *Immensity undreamed, and human haste was*
>   *meaningless.*
>   —*Street Witch,* by Edward Luckstream,
>   52599C–52703C

*A*na drew the purple drapes aside and stepped into the pavilion of Shenshi. The ancient Dedo leaned against her Rock, watching her daughter expressionlessly.

"The time has come," she said.

"That's good," said Ana.

"It is not an occasion for satisfaction. It is not an occasion for anything except the knowledge that my Duty is done and my Purpose fulfilled. Satisfaction is a human emotion, Ana."

"Please let me experience it just a little longer, Mother. What a pretty girl Elizabeth is! She's just perfect for Manuel."

"Naturally. I took a great deal of care over her appearance."

"But I thought it was just chance. I thought the Bale Wolf's venom cured the Girl and turned her into Elizabeth."

"All humans must have a good dose of evil in them, otherwise they're

not truly human. The venom of the Bale Wolf will cure every neotenite
on Earth."

"But Elizabeth's *face.*"

"I experimented for many thousands of years, using an Everling artist
who is a blood relative of Manuel, although the artist never knew what
was happening. Finally, I tested Manuel with a portrait, and he reacted
favorably. Elizabeth was Manuel's perfect woman. As the Girl, she loved
him already. So the two of them, with powerful emotional ties, were
capable of removing the Hate Bombs. Nobody else could have done it. It
was all carefully calculated."

"Well, whatever the reason, they have each other now." Ana smiled.
"I've so enjoyed this last century. This is a wonderful way to finish it
off."

"You've enjoyed it because I allowed you human emotions for a while.
It was necessary to the Purpose that you should appear to be a normal
human. You played your part successfully and manipulated the humans
to our ends. That is as it should be. However . . ." Shenshi permitted
herself a wintry smile—purely to make herself understood to Ana—and
continued, "You may have a few minutes more, until I die."

"You're going to die so soon?" Horrified, Ana hurried to Shenshi's
side. She took her mother's hand, feeling something crackle there, but
hardly noticing it. "Why? Don't leave me now, Mother. Not after all
we've done."

"I am old and frail. The Joy will be too much for me."

"The Joy?"

"The Departure of Starquin."

"Oh, I see . . ." Ana stood beside Shenshi for a while, regarding the
Rock with some awe. Then she became aware of the paper her mother
was holding. "What's this?"

"It's nothing. Just a poem a human wrote once."

Ana read it. After a while she said, "It's quite nice, I suppose. At least
. . ." Her eyes widened. "Mother! He knew your name!"

"You're not the only one the human poets wrote about, Ana. I spent
my years among them, too, you know. When my mother was alive I was
allowed emotions and human contact, just as I've allowed you." She
pointed. "There's a sandy cliff to the south. Millennia ago a group of
gentle humans lived there. They didn't fight, and maybe I thought humans would always be like that. I became more friendly with them than I
should have, and they took me into their houses and treated me as one of

them. There was little Traveling then, because humans had not yet discovered the Greataway.

"One man in particular—his name was Mijel. He made me feel things that I don't believe our kind has ever felt. He was kind and gentle, and he held me in his arms often—as I sometimes hold you, only the feelings were different. They were feelings of Earth, not the Greataway. Mijel gave me these feelings, and he wrote me a poem—then, like all humans, he died.

"I used to go and look at his village, but I couldn't bring myself to talk to the people anymore. Many of the generations went by, and they forgot that once I'd been their friend and they began to regard me as a witch again. Then the ice came, and the earthquakes, and the village was wiped away. And the people were gone." She fell silent, staring at the Rock as though trying to read the past in its translucent depths.

"But you kept the poem," said Ana, looking at it. Then she said, "Did you show him the Rock? What's this about a monolith?"

Shenshi said, "I, too, was foolish in my day. But there was no danger. A city stood on this spot, and the Rock was very well disguised. He might have caught some glimmering of it in another happentrack, but that's all. He was a very perceptive human. What a waste, that their lives should be so short."

"And ours so long." Ana regarded her mother with compassion. "What does it feel like, dying?"

"It feels as though Time is coming alive. All the past is dead, because one millennium is much like the next—just a desert of years with a few memories, like oases. But now . . . I catch hold of each day when the sun rises. I take it in my hands and my heart, and I try to hold it for as long as possible. But suddenly it's a living thing, and it slips through my fingers and it's gone and it's night again, and I lie there in the dark and I mourn for that day gone as if it were a lover."

"How did this first start happening?"

"It came inside my head, so slowly I didn't notice at first, because my body was still strong. At first there was just a quick alarm, as when a capybara thinks he hears the jaguar. Then it was gone and I forgot it. Just that once, it had seemed a little harder to send the Traveler on his way. Then it happened again and the jaguar was closer; I could smell him —or could I? It might have been the scent of an old den, abandoned and safe. But I remembered what my own mother had told me, and I knew I'd had the first sign—so I gave birth to you, my daughter. Travelers came and went, and my mind was hunted now, the strength of the Essence draining away, just as the legs of the giant rodent weaken—because no animal can escape the jaguar, who is death incarnate. So I ran, hunted, doing my Duty as I must, because I was born to it, as you are born to it, and only one of our kind has ever done anything different, and we carry her shame with us forever. Now my mind runs no more. It is collapsed, waiting, panting. And it hears a rustling in the jungle nearby, very close."

The daughter shivered because the cold breezes of night were trickling down the hills, and because she was reminded that Starquin, the Five-in-One, is the epitome of logic and would not have created a being that lived on after its purpose was fulfilled.

Impulsively, she said, "You think of death the way a human does. And you kept the poem all this time. I love you, Mother."

The Rock glowed.

The facets lit up, one by one, covering a quadrant close to Shenshi's head. She stepped back, the glow lighting her face and smoothing the lines until she looked quite young again. Then she placed the palms of her hands against the facet that shone the brightest. She stood as still as the Rock itself while she accepted the Traveler into her being. Her face filled with a joy that was not a human joy. It transcended all lower emotions, and Ana felt humble as she watched and wondered, and willed her mother to live through this last minute.

Shenshi divined Starquin's intent, and she touched the facet he required and sped him on his way with her Essence. Now her expression was one of great pride, her eyes fixed on the Rock, her Duty done. Ana, sensing it was over, moved forward and took her mother in her arms, mourning at how light she was, how brittle. She took Shenshi away from the Rock and laid her on the bed. Shenshi lay stiff, consumed, no more sentient than stone, but with that expression of pride still on her face. She was nothing now, merely Earthly material already beginning to decay, but Ana held her and cried. Starquin had gone and life had gone, and now Shenshi was no more than any little old human lady, lying dead, all glory flown.

✳

Starquin departed. His going was not attended by any noticeable phenomenon.

Centuries later the inhabitants of the Red Planet discovered that the route to Earth was clear again, and they came screaming through the Greataway with their Weapon. They unleashed it on Humanity.

Humanity never knew it happened.

By this time the Macrobes had spread throughout the genes of Mankind. Everybody could practice the Inner Think. The Red Planet's weapon was harmless. And the Outer Think? That was in the genes, too, although the source has never been isolated. Some say it is an accidental gift from Starquin, passed on to Humanity by a certain legendary Dedo. But that is another story for another century.

And as for the present story, Manuel and Elizabeth returned to Pu'este and lived their lives among the animals and Wild Humans, just like anyone else. They never spoke of their travels or of the momentous things they had done—except to two people: an old man and a woman who would outlive them all. The four of them used to get together every year or so and talk about old times and drink kuta.

The death of Manuel and Elizabeth is not recorded. One day after a difficult night of snake clouds, both were missing from the shack on the beach. They were never found. There is a story that a sapa scarf said to have belonged to Elizabeth was found near the Dome, beside a pool where axolotls lived. The snake clouds, whistling down from the mountains, had uncovered some kind of smooth rock nearby, and the scarf was wedged against it.

HERE ENDS THAT PART OF
THE SONG OF EARTH KNOWN TO MEN AS
THE OUTER THINK

IN TIME OUR TALE WILL CONTINUE.